CRIMEWAVE 4 : MOOD INDIGO

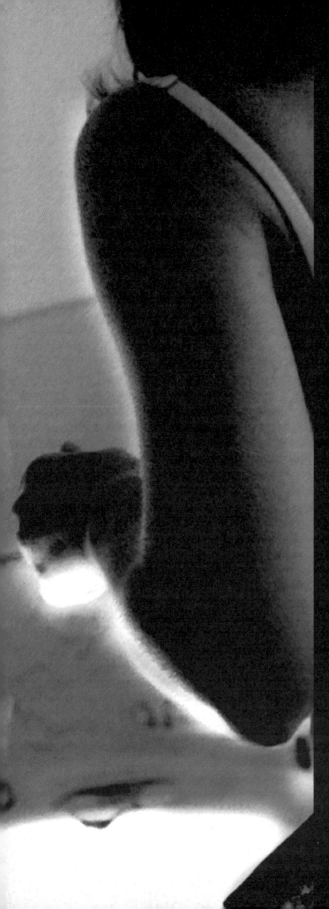

Editor
Andy Cox

Publisher
TTA Press, 5 Martins Lane, Witcham,
Ely, Cambs CB6 2LB, England
telephone: 01353 777931
email: ttapress@aol.com
website: www.tta-press.freewire.co.uk

Four-Issue Subscriptions
UK £22 • Europe £26 • RoW £30 • USA $44

Submissions
Unsolicited submissions of short stories
welcome. Please study several issues of
Crimewave before submitting and always
enclose a brief covering letter and a self-
addressed stamped envelope. Overseas
submissions should be disposable and
accompanied by two IRCs or simply an
email address (this option is for overseas
submissions only). We are unable to reply
otherwise. Send only one story at a time,
double spaced on A4 paper with good
margins all round and preferably mailed
flat or folded no more than once. Do not
send submissions by recorded delivery.
There is no length restriction placed on
the stories published in Crimewave, but
we don't accept reprints or simultaneous
submissions. Letters and queries are very
welcome via email but unsolicited story
submissions are not – they will simply be
deleted. Naturally, no responsibility can
be accepted for loss or damage to unsolicited material, howsoever caused

Advertising
Please contact the publisher for details

Distribution
Please contact the publisher for details

ISSN
1463 1350

ISBN
0 9526947 4 3

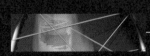

SEAN DOOLITTLE

THE GRIFT
OF THE MAGI

Sean Doolittle is a US writer whose
short fiction has appeared in a variety
of publications ranging from the ever-
sleazy Cavalier magazine to the late Karl
Edward Wagner's lamented annual anthology The Year's Best Horror Stories.
His first novel, Dirt – a Los Angeles crime
noir set in and around the funeral in-
dustry – is forthcoming from UglyTown
Productions. Sean lives in the middle of
the American midwest with his wife
Jessica, no kids, and no felony convic-
tions as of yet.

I. TRAVELERS

–i–

There was only one night of the year when three guys like Luther Vines, Scaz Gerstenfeld, or Denny Hoyle could walk into the home of a man like Cedric Zaganos, take his money, and not get found a couple days later reeking up a dumpster somewhere.

On the subject of taking money from a man like Cedric Zaganos, it didn't much matter who you were. The point was that only on one magical night out of 365 were such miracles allowed. This was the kind of night that reminded you what you could make out of life. A night filled with opportunity and brimming with possibilities.

The best part was, it just so happened to be Denny Hoyle's favorite night of the year anyway.

"I'm serious," Scaz said from the passenger seat, for maybe the tenth time in two miles. "I think I'm gonna pass out."

"You're just jealous," said Denny, from the back. "Account of you don't smell classy like me and Luthe do."

"Cat piss," Scaz said. "Cat piss is a classy smell. Formaldehyde. Bong water! Bong water is classy. You sorry bastards just plain reek."

"Don't either."

Scaz just turned in the seat to gawk at him, one side of his face shaded red and green in the lights from Luther's fancy stereo. Denny pulled a little glass bottle from his coat pocket and feinted with it, finger poised, while Scaz recoiled and bobbed his head in an evasive manner.

"Get that shit away from me, man, I'm not even kidding."

"Aww, come on," Denny told him. "Little dab."

Earlier in the day, a few hours before they had to go pick up Scaz at his place, Denny and Luther had ducked inside a department store at the mall to use the john. On their way through the cosmetics aisle, there was this swishy young guy — bleached swoop of hair flopped over one eye, some corny hat rigged with mistletoe on his head — who had stepped out and spritzed them each with a shot from a little tester bottle of cologne. *Happy*, he'd said.

Denny Hoyle hadn't understood; he'd just shrugged and told the guy, *good for you, sport*.

No, the guy told him, smiling. *Happy! It's the name of the fragrance.*

It didn't make Luther happy, that much was basically obvious. But then, Denny Hoyle had never known Luther Vines to be the happy type as a general rule.

Personally, Denny didn't think the stuff actually smelled half bad. So while Luthe was calmly twisting the sales guy's thumbs out of their sockets, Denny Hoyle took a quick spin around the counter, stuffing all the little tester bottles he could find into his coat pockets. Figuring he could maybe give out the extras as presents when they got to Cedric's place.

"You gotta put a little *on*," Denny explained to Scaz Gerstenfeld now. "Let it blend with your natural hormones and shit. Hold still."

"You spray me, I'm kicking your ass," Scaz said. "Seriously. You want your ass kicked? Go ahead and spray me with that shit."

Behind the wheel, Luther Vines said: "Kick me both your motherfuckin' asses in about two seconds."

There was a quiet moment.

"He's the one doing it," said Scaz.

Denny faked at him one last time with the tester bottle, grinning while Scaz flinched again.

But when he saw Luther's eyes on him in the rearview, Denny Hoyle decided to do the wise thing. He dropped the bottle back into his coat pocket and settled back in the seat.

It was the weather. That was the main problem. They were making shitty time in the storm, and Luthe was in one of his moods. Denny had tried telling the guy they should leave earlier in the day. They'd been talking about this all week on the radio, he'd said. But Luther wouldn't listen, as usual. And right on schedule, the sleet had started coming down late this afternoon.

By the time Denny and Luther had gotten to Scaz's place on the North side, the sleet had turned to snow, fat heavy wet stuff that piled up fast. By the time they'd gotten out of town, the sun had gone down, the temperature had dipped, and the snow was turning coarse like sand. Then the wind revved up.

Now, it was pretty much a big white howl on all sides. Luther's low-slung Buick wasn't much for it to begin with, and the cheap-ass tires he had weren't helping matters. At this rate, even Denny could see they'd be lucky to roll in by midnight.

Meanwhile, Luther's attitude was getting darker by the creeping slippery mile.

"This sucks," Scaz said.

Luther Vines didn't say a word. He just gripped the wheel and glared out the windshield, where the headlights reflected off the wall of swirling white ahead.

Denny tried to inject a little optimism into the situation. "Shit, it's only eight. We're cool."

"Please," said Scaz. "It's eight *now*. And we've gone, what, like three miles in a half hour? It'll be New Year's before we get there."

"Be Spring before they find you assholes, you don't shut the fuck up," Luther advised.

"Come on, guys," said Denny Hoyle. "It's Christmastime."

But even Denny had to admit that his heart really wasn't in it. Scaz had a point, and honestly, it was kind of too bad. Tonight came but once a year. Be a shame to miss it on account of a little snow.

Every year, on Christmas Eve, the big man hosted a big company poker tournament at his big house on the big acreage upstate. Say what you wanted about Cedric Zaganos; underneath, he was a decent guy to work for in Denny's book.

By long tradition, the game was open to all members of the organization who could scrape together a reasonable ante stake. From management to part-time runners, from made Lieutenants to contract guys in three states. Bought cops, borrowed consultants, some years even your odd public official or two. On Christmas Eve at Mr Z's, all came together as fellows — to share the free food and the free booze and the free girls Cedric brought in from uptown. The whole lot of them gathered elbow to elbow around the same tables. They chilled out and had a few quarts of cheer. They played some cards together.

He'd only been working for Zaganos for a little while now — but from everything Denny had ever heard, it sounded like a really nice time. For those twelve hours or so, nobody was above anybody else. Nobody better or worse. All comers basically made equal by the spirit of the season, Mr Z's hospitality, and the luck of the draw.

Maybe, Denny Hoyle would think later, it all worked out for the best anyway.

Looking back, maybe on this particular night luck hadn't exactly been on their side to begin with.

"Um," he heard Scaz say. "Hey. Vines."

Denny would remember noticing that Scaz's voice seemed even more uptight than usual. But before he could pay much attention, Scaz Gerstenfeld let loose a yelp of serious concern.

"Vines!"

About that time, Luther Vines said, "Bitch."

He stood on the brakes and cranked the wheel.

Then they were sliding.

–ii–

It seemed to take a long time.

When it was over, Denny Hoyle grabbed the seat and hoisted himself up off the floormats and checked himself over. Everything important seemed like it was still attached.

But from up front, he heard a low moan. It sounded like it came from Scaz.

Cautiously, Denny said: "Luthe?"

Nothing.

Denny situated himself and called to Luther again.

"Heard you the first time."

"Shit," Denny said. "What happened?"

Luther said nothing. He just rolled his big shoulders and popped his neck and looked around.

All Denny Hoyle could see out the windows was white. And also tree branches. It was freezing and windy in the car.

He reached over the seat and poked Luther in the shoulder. "Luthe. You okay?"

From the passenger side, Scaz lifted his head, moaning again.

"What happened?" said Denny, to anyone. He felt like a sack of pudding. There was wetness on his coat; he freaked for a quick second, thinking it might be blood. Then he checked and realized, with relief and some disappointment, that it was just his Happy stash. Some of the bottles had broken in his pocket. He was marinating in the stuff.

"My fucking arm is broken," Scaz whispered.

Denny peeked over the seat. Luther flipped on the dome light.

And they both looked at Scaz, who was slumped against an evergreen branch, which poked in through the shattered passenger-side window. Scaz looked pale as the drift piled against the windshield, which, Denny quickly calculated, they'd plowed into nose-first.

In the dim yellow light cast by the dome overhead, he could see part of Scaz's right forearm where the sleeve of his black leather coat had bunched up. There was a big purple hump, lumpy and wrong-looking, right above the wrist. Looking at it, Denny Hoyle felt his stomach do a queasy roll. Scaz closed his eyes and rested his head against the seat again.

"Nice driving, Vines," he wheezed.

Luther muttered, "Break the other one for you, you want."

"Luthe," said Denny, for the third time. "What happened, huh?"

"Camel," Scaz whispered.

"Sorry, partner," Denny told him, thinking the guy was asking for a smoke. "I'm out."

Scaz shook his head weakly. "In the road."

"Huh?"

"A goddamn camel, you deaf asshole." Scaz grimaced and squeezed his eyes tight. "Two humps. Captain Reflexes here almost plowed into the damn thing."

"The hell you talking about?" Denny reached over and felt Scaz's cheek. "You got knocked out or something, man."

"Get off me," Scaz mumbled. "It was a camel."

"Fuck it was," said Luther.

"You saw it as well as I did, Vines."

Denny didn't know what to say. "Maybe it was a deer."

"It was a camel."

"Cow maybe."

Luther offered nothing. He was already getting out of the car.

The new blast of frigid air gave Denny the chatters. He took a look at Scaz, slumped there against the crumpled door — his eyes closed, glass in his hair, his face all scuffed and bruised from the tree branch. Cradling his busted arm close to his chest.

"Can you hang?" Denny asked him.

Scaz didn't answer.

Not knowing what else to do, Denny crawled over the seat. He restarted the engine, killed the dome light, cranked up the heater, and piled out after Luther into the dark bitter night.

They were banked off the left shoulder of the highway, the Buick angled sideways against a stout fir tree. All around, the wind had swept the snow into razor-backed drifts. Denny and Luther stood up to mid-shin in the stuff. Luther, wearing nothing but his light Nike warmups over his usual tank top and gold chains, surveyed the situation with a stormy expression.

Denny pranced in place, blowing warm air into his hands and rubbing his bare palms together.

"Whatcha think?"

Luther said nothing.

Denny looked at the car. "I can try pushing, you want."

"Camel my ass," Luther muttered.

Denny Hoyle didn't know what else to say. He could barely hear Luther over the wind. It was freezing. It was dark. They had to be miles from anything. It was Christmas Eve, and standing here alongside the empty drift-covered highway, Denny was forced to acknowledge that Scaz was right. This was a bummer.

As a matter of fact, under the circumstances, Denny was forced to acknowledge the possibility that they might be seriously screwed.

He was just about to ask Luther if he had any ideas when they both saw a dim yellow glow over the last hill behind them in the road. In a minute, there came a low sound beneath the wind. Then twin golden beams, piercing the storm.

Denny looked at Luther and felt his heart leap. Maybe they weren't completely short on luck after all.

"Luthe!" he cried. "Check it out."

Luther just looked at him in that certain fashion he used sometimes.

Denny Hoyle didn't need to be told. He turned fast, slipped, stumbled, and went down in a cold powdery puff of snow.

But he scrambled to his feet and moved on, fast as he could trudge. Heading for where he thought the center line of the highway must have been, waving his arms above his head all the way.

–iii–

"A doctor," the yuppie shouted, pulling his lambswool collar tight around his chin. He squinted against the whirling snow. "My brother-in-law is a doctor. They're just a few miles from here. We were on our way there."

The yuppie's name was Tillman. He had a $500 coat, $100 gloves, a $50 salon haircut and one of those four-wheel-drive SUV's.

Over the wind, Denny shouted back: "You don't mind, you sure?"

"Come on," Tillman called. "Let's get your friend in the car where it's warm."

Luther just stood with his hands shoved inside the waistband of his warmups. "So you got this four-wheel-drive over there, and you don't got no pull chain?"

Tillman shrugged apologetically and cinched his collar tighter. "Sorry." He jerked his head back, toward the 4x4, which was idling alongside the highway behind them. "You guys need a hand bringing him over?"

Denny declined and clapped Tillman thankfully on the shoulder. He slipped Luther a scolding look, which Luther Vines ignored. Then he plodded alone through the snow back to the Buick and helped Scaz out through the driver's side.

Back at the Land Cruiser, Tillman held open a side door and manfully directing his brood to make room. Inside, Denny saw Tillman's pretty young brunette wife turned in the front passenger seat, an expression of generous concern on her face. A pretty teenage daughter scowled, gave up her position, worked her way around an arm rest, shoved herself into the far end of the back seat, and stared out the dark-smoked window toward the treed Buick. Meanwhile, her kid brother, who looked about nine as far as Denny could tell, stopped playing his GameBoy long enough to look at Scaz's crooked wrist with awe.

After they got Scaz boosted in and situated, Denny hustled around the backside of the Cruiser. Luther Vines was already coming through the snow toward the SUV, toting a bright red bucket in each hand.

"Want some help?" Denny asked him.

Luther just gave him that look again.

So Denny hurried to the open trunk of the Buick, grabbed two buckets of his own, and headed back to the 4x4.

It took them less than three minutes to transfer all twelve buckets from the trunk of the Buick to the backspace of the Land Cruiser. Tillman stood patiently in the cold wind, watching them curiously, holding the tail door open with his body, his coat closed with both hands. He watched. He watched, but he didn't say a word.

When the three of them finally piled into the Cruiser, pounding the cold from their fingers and stomping numbness from their toes, Richard Tillman finally looked over his shoulder and asked, "So are you guys volunteers or something?"

"Something," Luther Vines told him, in a tone that caused Tillman to glance at his wife, grin uneasily into the rearview mirror, and drop the 4x4 into gear.

–iv–

"Swear on a stack of bibles, fellas. We saw it on the news before we left town. Didn't we, Cath?"

Denny Hole couldn't believe what he was hearing. He glanced over, wondering what Luther was thinking. If the cranky tilt of his bald black head was any indication, Luther Vines didn't seem to think Tillman's story was quite as interesting as Denny did.

But according to Tillman, some church out in the 'burbs was supposed to be having a Christmas Eve service tonight, complete with a live-animal Nativity scene for the kids. Only problem was, the whole pageant had gotten called off two hours before showtime, since one of the chapel custodians accidentally left the gate to the animal pen unlatched, and every last critter in the manger had escaped into the brewing storm.

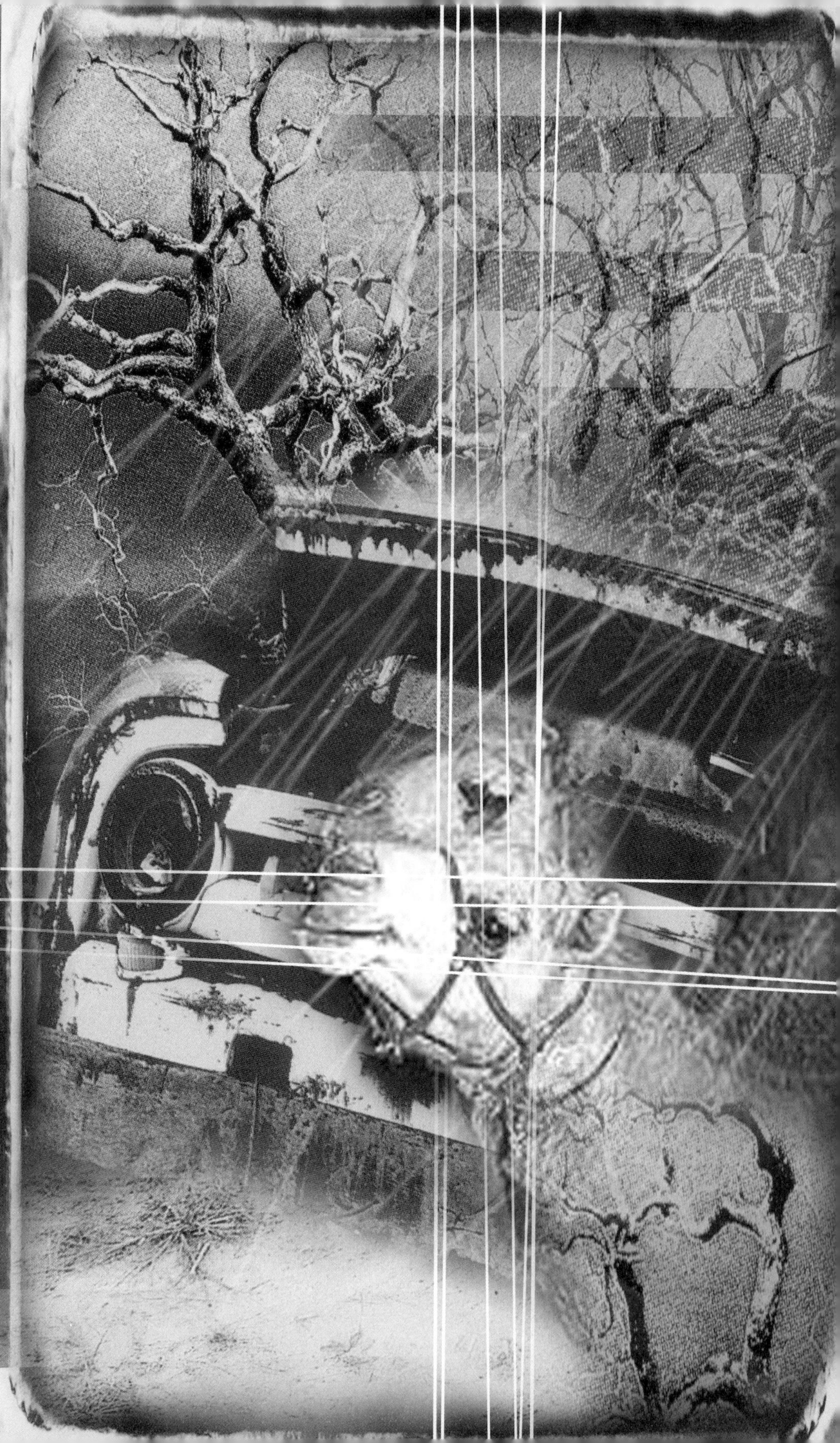

"I'll be darned," Denny said, mindful of the fact there were kids in the car and adjusting his language accordingly. "How'd they figure a whole live camel got all the way outta town nobody seeing it?"

Tillman laughed. "No ideas here. You guys are going to have one heck of a story to tell, that's all I know."

Tillman didn't seem to notice Luther's dark demeanor. Behind the wheel, the yupster was doing a good job working the treacherous roads, while his wife and daughter watched out their respective windows, and the kid stabbed at his video game with his thumbs.

They were Richard, Catherine, Chelsea, and Joshua: the Tillman family. Denny liked them right away. Except for Chelsea the teenager, who came off just a little bit on the hateful side, they seemed like a pleasant bunch of folks. The first thing Catherine did was find a bottle of aspirins in her purse, which she gave to Scaz, who just popped the lid and poured a bunch into his mouth, like Tic Tacs. And not one of them commented on Denny's overpowering Happy smell, which by now was making Denny Hoyle's own eyes water.

In the middle seat it was Luther on one side, Scaz slumped on the other, Josh and his GameBoy wedged in the middle. Denny held down the back with Chelsea, who hadn't said a word since the three of them had joined on. In fact, she'd wedged herself so far into the corner away from Denny, she might as well have been clinging to the outside of the SUV.

"Your name is *Scaz*?" Joshua asked.

"Josh," Catherine Tillman said.

"It's like a nickname, kid," Denny explained. He'd been handling the introductions, out of politeness, before deciding to cut it short based on the hard glare coming at him from Luther's way. "Account of he's from Scarsdale."

"From where?"

"It's in New York."

Joshua Tillman processed this information. In a minute he turned himself all the way around in the seat. He perched up on his knees, hung his arms over the back, and said, "What's his regular name?"

Denny Hoyle was trying to think up some fake names for the three of them when he realized something. He looked at Luther, who appeared to have stopped paying attention. Denny sat. In a minute, he reached over the seat and nudged Scaz gently on the shoulder.

"Hey, man," he said. "What *is* your first name, anyways?"

Scaz only wheezed in reply. He was starting to sound like a city bus making stops every other block. Up front, Richard Tillman glanced at his wife again, who did not glance back. Josh accidentally giggled and pinched his lips shut.

"You can just call him Scaz," Denny said. "That's what he likes."

Josh turned to Luther, taking in the warmups and the gold chains and rings Luther wore. He seemed like he was about to ask something. That was when Luther gave the kid a look that made Denny Hoyle fearful for Josh Tillman's growth schedule. The kid clammed up for a few minutes.

And they all just rode for awhile. Forward progress was noticeably improved in the warm smooth-riding Land Cruiser, where you could feel yourself sitting up higher. Denny Hoyle liked the feel of the drifts giving way beneath them, churned under by the big knobby 4-by tires.

And these Tillmans. They seemed like quite a clan. Denny learned that Catherine's sister had just had a baby the day before, so the whole crew was heading there to spend the holiday, see the new kid, and help her sister out around the place. Denny told her congratulations on being a new auntie. Catherine smiled pleasantly and told him thank you.

All things considered, Denny Hoyle was having an okay time. He knew it was stupid, but he couldn't help himself; it was kind of nice to be heading somewhere with a nice family like this on a Christmas Eve. Sure, it was basically a charity thing, but still: it had a coziness. There was some Christmas music on the CD player, which was turned down low.

While they rode, Denny tried starting a conversation with Chelsea Tillman, just to be polite — maybe help her feel less uncomfortable, him being a total stranger, not to mention Happy-smelling, and her stuck with him back here. But it was nothing doing. Chelsea Tillman just stared out her window like he'd never been born. Denny decided maybe it would be just as well if he let her alone, and soon he was getting the nickel tour of Josh Tillman's GameBoy.

"Wanna play?" the boy asked him. "I can set it for two people."

"Nah, I ain't no good at them things. You do it to it, partner. I'll just watch."

And off went Joshua Tillman, all thumbs, careful not to bump Luther Vines in the seat next to him, at the same time holding the game out so Denny could see. Soon he was hunching over the small screen like a jeweller. The machine emitted a bunch of goofy sounds and Josh went at the buttons like crazy with his thumbs. Denny tried to figure out the game by looking at the screen, but it didn't make a bit of sense to him. He couldn't understand how the kid even knew what the hell he was supposed to be doing.

"You're pretty good at that thing," Denny told him. "I guess you prolly play all the time, huh?"

"I just got it today. It's my early present."

Denny said, "You're early present?"

"Uh-huh."

"What's early present?"

"It's the present we get early."

"You kidding me?"

"Huh-uh," Josh said.

"Whatcha mean *early*." Denny was having fun now, ribbing the kid a little. "What early? Santa don't even come till tonight later."

Josh Tillman barked out laughter without taking his focus from the game in his hands. "You don't believe in Santa."

"You ain't even gonna tell me you don't."

Josh laughed some more.

"Ah, kid, you're breaking my heart." Denny grinned in the dark, slipping Chelsea a wink. She wasn't even looking at him. "So, what, you just open up your presents whenever you feel like it, or how's this work exactly?"

"We get to pick one for early present. Then we open the others on Christmas. And our stockings."

"Sounds like a sweet racket," Denny said.

"Huh?"

"Never mind."

The GameBoy expelled one last dying warble, signifying, Denny gathered, the end of the game. Josh Tillman turned it off and looked at Denny.

"Do you know what you're getting for Christmas?"

"In a car wreck, I guess."

Josh looked over at Scaz with true empathy. "Being sick on Christmas sucks. I had chicken pox last year."

Denny Hoyle was shocked to hear Scaz Gerstenfeld actually respond.

"I'm Jewish, kid," Scaz told him. "We don't have Christmas."

"You don't have Christmas?"

"Hannukah."

"Huh?"

"Hannukah, kid. That's our deal."

Josh just looked at him.

"What, you never heard of Hannukah before?"

Josh glanced back at his older sister, who continued staring out her window at the dark night and the glowing white drifts and the driving sleet all around. He leaned over the seat and whispered something in her direction, but she ignored him. Josh looked back at Scaz and shrugged politely.

Scaz grimaced and shifted his arm gingerly. The movement caused him to suck in a sharp breath. Behind the wheel, Richard Tillman glanced nervously at his wife, who once again paid him no acknowledgement.

"What's Hannukah like?" Josh asked him.

"I don't know how to explain it, kid," Scaz said. "Kind of like Christmas times eight."

GameBoy quiet in his lap, Josh absorbed this concept with obvious wonderment. Scaz drew shallow, ragged breaths.

"Jesus was Jewish. I learned that in Sunday school."

"Capital J, my friend."

"My Sunday school teacher said Jesus was King of the Jews."

"Don't get me started."

"So how come we don't get Hannukah?"

Scaz closed his eyes. "It's complicated, kid, look...I'm kind of in excruciating pain right now."

"Yeah," muttered Chelsea Tillman at last. She spoke to her brother without turning her gaze from the window. "So shut up already."

"Chels," said Richard Tillman in a fatherly tone.

But Josh was totally intrigued. He turned to Luther, who was glowering at the floorboards with his big arms crossed. "Do you get Christmas?"

Luther glared at the kid. "I'm fuckin' Jewish too."

Josh laughed delightedly. In the rearview mirror, Richard's Tillman's eyes grew wide. Catherine turned in the passenger seat and said, in a quiet voice, "Josh."

"He said the F-word!" Joshua told her, beaming.

"I heard. Let's stop talking for awhile, sweetie, okay? Your dad's trying to watch the road."

Luther snorted.

"You're a black person," Josh told him.

"No shit."

"Black people can be Jewish?"

"No," said Scaz, in a thin voice.

If Denny hadn't known better, he'd have thought that Luther looked almost like he was starting to enjoy himself.

And Josh Tillman was definitely enthralled. "Are you really Jewish?"

"Way to find out," Luther said, winking at Catherine.

Under the circumstances, Denny Hoyle thought that Catherine Tillman did an impressive job of ignoring Luther Vines — who could be, when he really wanted to, among the stone-cold scariest dudes Denny had personally ever met.

"Come on, Josh," was all she said. In the rearview, Richard appeared to be experiencing gas pain.

Of Luther, Josh requested: "Say something Jewish."

"Assalam alaikum," Luther said.

Josh bounced in the seat and clapped his hands happily.

Scaz Gerstenfeld mumbled something, but Denny Hoyle couldn't hear what he said.

Up front, Catherine shifted uncomfortably in her seat. Beside her, Richard Tillman manned the wheel in a tense but steadfast manner, steering them onward toward shelter.

II. Bambino

–i–

It was after nine o'clock by the time Tillman turned off the main highway, crept one last unplowed quarter mile, and finally nosed the Cruiser out of the storm. They rolled up a long paved driveway lined with tall pine trees on both sides.

Observing from his window, Denny Hoyle couldn't help but be impressed by their destination.

Some house, was what he was thinking, as he surveyed the rambling multi-level nestled back in an open wooded lot. The house glowed with yellow light from within. Outside, the whole place was festooned with white lights made to look like icicles. There was a snowy gabled roof, two brick chimneys trailing wisps of smoke, and a three-car garage.

Under normal circumstances, the sight of a place like this generally made Denny Hoyle start to wonder about the dog situation as he began thinking in terms of window alarms.

But for some reason, approaching this impressive homestead with the Tillman family gave Denny a taste of a whole different perspective. He had a warm and invited feeling. So what if the invitation happened to be mostly by default? Denny felt within himself a strange sense of peacefulness. Toward the house they rolled.

Joe and Marly Jurgens met them at the door. With smiles and a festive urgency they motioned the Tillmans inside, bringing them out of the cold and into the warm. Denny heard Catherine Tillman say, "Where is he? Take me to my nephew!" There were hugs, kisses, laughs, and Merry Christmases.

And then came Luther, Denny, and Scaz.

Joe Jurgens brought them in and closed the door with a curious expression and the sound of jingle bells.

Denny Hoyle had to give the man credit. Here was this guy who had no idea what was going on; all he knew was that it was freezing outside. But he greeted each of them with a pleasant nod and brought them in like they were any regular guests. Denny saw the guy and his wife exchange quick glances, but that was all.

Richard Tillman explained the situation while Catherine and the kiddies unbundled in the entryway. Luther stood there in his warmups; Denny and Scaz left their coats on.

"Shut up," said Jurgens. He was a tall man with an athletic build and fur-lined moccasins on his feet. "A camel! I don't believe it."

"Well, whatever it was, I'm afraid we've got an injury," Tillman said gravely.

Marly Jurgens had already noted Scaz Gerstenfeld's strained pallor; she was helping him inside the main room, to a white couch that was slightly larger than a schoolbus. The couch was angled to face a huge crackling fireplace. Nearby, in a corner where the ceiling angled high, stood probably the most picture-perfect Christmas tree Denny Hoyle had ever seen outside of TV.

Chelsea Tillman had disappeared inside the house. Josh was already bivouacked in front of a big screen television in yet another corner of the living room: shoes off, coat still on.

Joe Jurgens looked at each of his three stranger-guests in turn.

"Some night," he said, in a tone that was half laughing, half suggesting what a good thing it was somebody had happened along when they did. Denny noticed that Jurgens ran a quick, apprehensive eye over Luther and his choice of blizzard attire.

"Man says you a doctor," Luther Vines said.

Now Joe Jurgens glanced at his brother-in-law. "Well," he said, "I guess that's true."

"You a doctor or ain't you?"

"I am. I am indeed a doctor."

Luther Vines narrowed his eyes. "Kind of doctor?"

"I'm a urologist," Jurgens said simply. He looked to Tillman again, as if to ask, *what did you want me to say?* "Listen, I'll go find the phone. Why don't you guys come on inside and make yourselves at home? Get the cold out of your bones."

Jurgens left them in the entryway. Denny watched Richard Tillman follow, talking to his brother-in-law in quiet tones. Both men glanced back once toward the entryway.

Denny stood there nervously, suddenly feeling out of place and stupid. He tried to think what it was a urologist did, exactly.

When Jurgens and Tillman were finally out of sight, Denny took a step toward Luther, dipped his head, and hissed, "Can'tcha even *try?*"

Somewhere in a nearby room, Denny heard the thin, warbling sound of an infant crying. Soon the tones of motherly cooing reached them, as Caroline Tillman appeared with a bundle of blankets in her arms. She was beaming, talking sweetly to the squalling bundle. Her sister Marly stood grinning at her side. Scaz watched the whole thing blearily from the couch nearby.

"Aww," Denny said. "Luthe, check it out. They got a little baby."

Luther Vines just looked at him with an expression Denny Hoyle couldn't quite read. He seemed to be wondering about Denny exactly what Denny Hoyle wondered himself sometimes about Luther Vines: *How does a guy like you get by?*

"Guys," Marly Jurgens was saying, motioning at them from the living room. "Come on in and say hi to Creighton."

Beside him, Denny heard Luther snort.

Denny gave him a disapproving eye. Marly Jurgens motioned again, smiling inclusively. Denny debated for a second. Finally he shrugged.

"Fine," he whispered to Luther. "Be that way then, ya Scrooge-ass bastard."

Denny grinned politely at Marly Jurgens, took off his sport hikers, left them in a puddle of melt in the entryway, and went in to check out the tyke and maybe warm up a little next to the fire.

–ii–

"It's the storm," Joe Jurgens explained. "I'm afraid it's got us pretty much shut down out here."

They were gathered where Scaz was sprawled, all of them around the sofa in the living room. Jurgens was holding a small sleek cordless phone receiver in his hand. Looked like a 900 megahertz long-range job to Denny. Sony. Denny noticed basically out of habit. Nice piece of electronics, that's all.

Nearby, Marly and Catherine were changing the baby on a blanket spread out on the carpet, listening to the talk while they wiped and powdered.

"Listen, here's the situation the way I see it," Jurgens said. "The nearest hospital is about fifteen miles. We can try getting you guys there tonight in one of the four-wheel drives if you want. Or we can ride out this weather, I'll look after your friend here the best I can for tonight, and we can start out by daylight first thing in the morning." He looked at Scaz. "Skip, is it?"

"Scaz," Scaz said. He had his eyes closed.

"Ah. Sorry." Jurgens appraised them. "The way it's still coming down out there, I'm thinking it might be smartest to wait — but it's your call, Mr Scaz. You're the hurt one."

Before Scaz could answer, Luther Vines motioned at Jurgens. "Use that phone?"

"Sure thing." Jurgens handed it over.

Luther took it and headed off, in what Denny Hoyle assumed, based on his experience with home interiors, was the direction of the kitchen.

Jurgens watched him go. He looked briefly at Tillman. Then he looked at Denny.

"Sorry about this," Denny said. "Sure is nice of you to help us out."

"Not a problem," said Jurgens.

From the floor, Marly called for her husband's attention. "Joe, look at what Cath and Richard brought for Creighton!"

She was grinning, holding up a piece of reddish clay pottery about the size of a football. Denny looked close and realized it was a pig.

"Hey, another piggy bank," Joe Jurgens said. "Just what the kid needs. Thanks, guys. Thanks a bunch."

Richard Tillman held up his hands. "Don't look at me. I wanted to get the kid into a mutual fund."

Marly Jurgens stuck out her tongue at both of them. For Denny's benefit she explained: "Creighton has a piggy bank collection. This makes number six. Oh, I love it!"

"It's from Abu Dhabi," said Catherine, pointing out a fingermark in the kiln-fired clay, which supposedly proved how the pig had been crafted by hand.

"It's so gorgeous," Marly said, appreciating the pig. "Thank you so much!"

Denny stood smiling to himself, watching while the two women chatted and their husbands poked fun.

And in a minute or two, Luther Vines returned. He handed Jurgens back his phone without saying a word. Then he turned to Tillman and said, "Yo. Look here a minute."

All at once, Denny Hoyle got a bad feeling. It started in the pit of his stomach and sort of tingled out from there. While Catherine and Marly fussed over Creighton and his new piggy bank with the latent prints on it — Joe Jurgens asking Scaz if he could take a look at that arm — Denny watched Richard Tillman confer with Luther in a darkened archway a few feet away.

With a sinking sensation, he watched Luther pull up the front of his warmup jacket. Richard Tillman looked down, saw what was there, and when he looked up his eyes were wide and round. In a second, Denny watched him hand over his car keys to Luther.

A beat or two later, Tillman — pale and tight-lipped — had returned to the living room. Luther Vines waited by the front door, keys to Tillman's Land Cruiser in his hand.

Denny Hoyle heard Catherine Tillman say, "Richard?"

Richard shook his head quickly, lips still pressed together like bloodless worms.

To Denny, Luther said, "You comin'?"

Denny just looked at him. Then he looked over his shoulder. Richard and Catherine Tillman appeared to be arguing. Joe Jurgens had picked the baby up off the floor and was talking to his wife, who was staring at Denny with a terrified expression. Even Josh had stopped watching the big television. He was looking over curiously.

Denny looked back at Luther and said, "Aww, Luthe. You ain't either."

"Said you comin' or what's the deal?"

Denny hustled over and spoke in a fast whisper. "You ain't even gonna steal these people's yup rover, you gotta be shittin' me. They're trying to help us out!"

"That's what they doin', kid. So let's haul ass already. Got me some card playin' to get to yet tonight."

"What about Scaz?"

"'Bout his punk ass?"

Denny couldn't believe his pal Luther Vines sometimes.

"Luthe, all due respect, I gotta tell you. I mean, we done some deeds, now. But this is some raw shit you're pullin' here."

"Yeah, it's a blue motherfuckin' Christmas all the way around, ain't it? Come on, we outta here."

Jingle bells sounded as Luther opened the front door and headed out. Denny just stood, letting the cold in, not knowing what to do.

It was a confusing moment.

Normally, he'd be right on Luthe's heels. Normally, Denny Hoyle might've figured folks like this were rich enough to take a hit now and then. Besides — it probably served 'em right for being so clueless in the first place, here in their big house at the end of their long driveway, with thirty grand worth of furniture in the living room and their four-wheel drives in the garage, collecting their piggy banks from Cuba or wherever the hell.

But for some reason, Denny Hoyle was having a dilemma.

He jammed his feet into his street hikers, left them untied, and tramped out the door after Luther, into the snow.

"Hey," he said. "You just hang on a minute."

Luther kept walking. Denny Hoyle hustled to catch up.

"One a them's mine, Luthe. I earned it."

At the Land Cruiser, Luther finally stopped. He turned and shook his head slowly at Denny, like he was the dumbest guy Luther had ever seen.

Denny just looked back.

"Whatever you gotta do, kid," Luther finally said, jerking his head toward the rear of the Cruiser. "Move it or lose it."

So while Luther slipped in behind the wheel and cranked the engine, Denny went around back and opened up the tailgate. He picked one of the heavier buckets and pulled it out, its thin metal handle icy in his bare palm. Then he shut the tailgate, latched the swing bar, and stepped out of the way just in time to avoid Luther backing over both his feet.

Listening to the snow crunch under the Land Cruiser's big tires, Denny watched Luther Vines back out through a frozen cloud of exhaust. Denny watched him haul the wheel, turn around, and roll off. He watched until the red tail lights reached the end of the long driveway, winked once, hung right, and disappeared.

When he got back inside the house with his cold red bucket, Scaz hadn't moved from his place on the couch. Josh Tillman was crying, and Catherine was trying to buck him up with a motherly hug. Richard Tillman looked like he'd swallowed something he wasn't sure he should have put in his mouth in the first place. Chelsea had emerged from wherever she'd originally ducked. Joe and Marly Jurgens stood together, baby Creighton in their arms.

"Folks, I really feel bad about this," Denny Hoyle said.

The ironic part, to Denny Hoyle's way of thinking, was that the Salvation Army buckets had started out being his idea.

It had come to Denny early this morning, while he and Luther had been heading downtown to get some pancakes and put their heads together on how they were going to scare up their stakes before tonight's game. (It hadn't been what Denny Hoyle would've called a growth year for either of them, earnings-wise. The plain, sad truth of it was they were strapped hard, the both of them, with no good prospects either one.)

But this morning, Denny had been truly inspired. They were cutting through the old warehouse district down near the riverfront when they drove by the Salvation's downtown branch. Which was where Denny saw the line of volunteers in the snowpacked parking lot, all standing around a guy with earmuffs and a clipboard. The whole crew was bundled up like Eskimos and looked like they were freezing their asses off anyway.

And Denny practically heard his idea as it was born, like a bell clanging faintly in his ear.

Cold as it was? And Christmas Eve? No way had everybody on that dude's clipboard showed up at 7:30AM to freeze their nads ringing bells all day.

Denny told Luther his idea. Luther thought it was the dumbest thing he'd ever heard.

"Sure," Denny had told him. "Okay. Tell you what, my bald-head amigo: watch and learn."

Then he had Luther park a few blocks down, so he could go get in line and try to figure out who he was supposed to pretend to be.

A half hour later, Denny faced Luther again from his assigned corner, outside a Gap store at the mall. His bucket was hanging on its stand. Over his regular clothes, Denny wore the gear he'd been issued: red vest, Santa hat, and handbell. He gave the bell a clang and grinned.

"How do I look," he'd asked Luther, feeling smug.

And Luther had said, "Like a fuckhead."

Denny had merely nodded. "You just pick me up at three, smart guy. Then we'll see."

When three o'clock finally rolled around, Luther pulled up right on time. Denny was beat as beat could be. Both arms ached from ringing the bell, and his eardrums were clanging. He couldn't feel any of his fingers and his feet felt like blocks of wood.

But he'd had a blast. He'd chatted with a few hot-looking college girls, and he got a kick out of watching the holiday shoppers all day. And most importantly of all: he'd raked in the cabbage like a maniac.

So when Luther ambled over, hands shoved down the front of his warmups, Denny had hefted his bucket and grinned.

"Gee, Luthe," he'd said. "This bucket's so heavy, I almost can't even hold it anymore. Where should I put it, huh? Huh, Luther? Smart guy?"

That was when Luther opened the trunk of the Buick and said, "How 'bout in there with them others?"

Denny had looked, but at first he hadn't believed what he saw.

Guy had a whole trunk full of red metal buckets. Wire handles and slotted lids, just like the one Denny had in his hand. It looked like a damn Salvation Army storage shed back there. All Denny could do was sigh.

"Cheater."

And Luther Vines had done something Denny Hoyle rarely heard him do. He laughed.

"You such a sorry motherfucker," was what he'd said. "Come on. I gotta take me a piss 'fore we go get the Scaz."

Now, standing in the entryway holding his bucket, facing the Tillmans and the Jurgenses, Denny Hoyle felt less like a guy with a bright idea and more like a low-down scumbag. On display.

When he'd walked back in the house, Joe Jurgens had quickly taken the cordless phone away from his ear. Calling the cops, Denny figured. By the look on the urologist's face, it didn't look like he'd had time to get through.

"*Mom.*"

"Chelsea, I said not now."

Denny found an out-of-the-way corner on his right, at one end of what looked like one of those old train station benches refinished to look nice. Denny put the bucket out of sight and faced them all again.

From where Denny was standing, it looked like a family Christmas photo. Except nobody was smiling. Catherine Tillman reached out beside her and tried to take her daughter's hand. But Chelsea yanked her arm away. Denny was trying to think what he should say when something hit him in the foot.

He looked down and saw that it was a wallet. Tillman's wallet. Guy had just reached out with his arm and looped it over, like he was throwing horseshoes. Now he stood there with his hands in the air, like the whole thing was some kind of stickup. When Denny looked up at him questioningly, Richard Tillman actually flinched.

Denny Hoyle didn't know how to respond.

"Um…" he said, and that was all he could think of.

He caught Catherine Tillman's gaze briefly, but she quickly dropped her eyes. Denny released a weary breath. He picked up the wallet and placed it on the antique bench.

Joe Jurgens was the first of any of them to make what amounted to a genuine move. He came forward. Behind him, his wife reached out with one arm and whispered his name fiercely, cradling baby Creighton in her other arm.

But Jurgens gently pulled away from her grasp and continued his approach. When he reached Denny he lowered his voice and said, "Look, may I talk to you? Down the hall?"

Feeling like a total shithead, Denny Hoyle shrugged and said, "Sure."

–iv–

"Wait. Just wait here."

Down the hall looked like a cigar bar converted into a home office. Denny found himself standing in a dim lamplighted room with high ceilings, built-in bookcases, and stout furniture with leather upholstery. There was a big desk with a computer on it. Jurgens disappeared behind the desk for several minutes.

Meanwhile, Denny stood with his back to a closed walnut pocket door, waiting for Jurgens to pop up with a .357 and start plugging him full of holes.

Now he didn't just feel guilty; Denny Hoyle felt like a chump besides.

It was just that he'd always been sure he'd wind up blowing his own pecker off sooner or later, toting a piece around the way Luther did. Not to mention the fact it turned a regular break-and-enter into an armed job in the eyes of the law. Those kinds of headaches Denny Hoyle figured he honestly did not need. Which was why he'd never really carried much heat to speak of.

Now, waiting here — Jurgens out of sight and him with his back to the door — Denny reconsidered the wisdom of walking light as a professional choice. If Cedric Zaganos ever got word that he'd got his ass blown off by a yupster urologist on Christmas Eve (or worse — sweet Jesus! — the news that he'd been taken hostage and held for the cops), the name of Denny Hoyle would be a company joke for months. Years. Crew guys'd be laughing about his chump ass decades on down the road.

But from behind the desk, there came the unmistakable sound of a floor safe being opened. And when Joe Jurgens reappeared, it wasn't with a gun, but with a handful of something that caught Denny by even greater surprise. Jurgens crossed the carpet and placed the contents of his load one by one on a low glass-topped coffee table nearby. They were velvet boxes of the kind Denny Hoyle had seen a hundred times before. Jurgens opened each before he set it down, like a salesperson arranging a spread. Inside: miscellaneous jewelry that made Denny Hoyle, even under present circumstances, take a considerate pause.

Then Jurgens went back behind the desk again. This time, when he returned, he was carrying stacks of bills. They were bundled twenties, Denny noted. Jurgens placed them next to the jewelry in four squared-away columns. Denny counted twelve bundles in all.

When he was finished, Jurgens straightened his back and said, "It's all yours. You have my word that the police will not be called. Just…please, don't hurt anybody."

Denny looked at the urologist for a minute. All at once, he felt sort of insulted. He truly didn't know why. Maybe just because it was Christmas and all. He looked at the loot. Looked at Jurgens.

"Guess you keep a lot of cash around, huh?"

Jurgens shrugged flatly. "Just take it. There's a DVD player wrapped up underneath the tree. And a new pair of earrings for Marly. You can have those, too. Take it all. I can get you a bag. Or a suitcase. Whatever you need."

They stood there and looked at each other for another minute or more. Jurgens stood with his hands at his sides. Literally offering up the family jewels.

Denny Hoyle didn't know whether to admire or pity the guy.

Part of him thought it was kind of moving, the way the man stepped up like he did. But another part of him thought: *you rich fuckers anyway*.

A situation like this guy thought he was in? Here he was, telling somebody what they could take. Explaining what they could have.

Deciding what was up for trade, like it was negotiable.

If it was Luther Vines this guy was dealing with, Denny was thinking, he'd find out better than that soon enough.

In a situation like this one could've been? Your stuff wasn't yours to offer. Not really.

Denny bent down and picked up one of the cash bundles. It was stiff new green; he could smell the ink when he riffled the edge with his thumb. Jurgens watched him.

He didn't jump when Denny tossed him the bundle. But he did look surprised.

"It ain't like that," Denny told him. "I never hurt a guy's family in my whole life."

Jurgens said nothing. He looked at the bundle of cash in his hand. He looked at Denny.

"You wanted to call the cops," Denny told him, "a guy couldn't even necessarily blame you. My opinion."

"Couldn't a guy." Jurgens watched him carefully. "And your friend in there?"

Denny shrugged. "Can't speak for him."

Jurgens finally seemed to be developing an understanding of their mutual predicament, such as it was. He stood quietly.

"You decided to let us hang out here long enough to ride out the weather first," Denny said, "you'd get my word we'd be gone soon as we could get that way."

"I thought you said you couldn't speak for your friend."

"Listen, you want the truth, friend is kind of overstating matters." Denny shrugged. "Don't even know the guy all that well, you get right down to it."

Without really paying attention to what he was doing, Jurgens placed the bundle of cash back on the coffee table. He straightened and said nothing. When he took his hand away, the bundle sat on the edge of the table, half on and half off the glass, looking like it could tumble to the carpet any second.

Denny didn't know what else to tell him.

"Mind if I use the pisser?"

Jurgens had turned. He was staring at something invisible near the floor.

"Down the hall," he finally said. His tone was distant. "First left."

Denny left him there, admiring the way the heavy oak door rumbled when he slid it open far enough to squeeze through.

–v–

"Urologist. That's like brain surgery, right?"

"It is for some people." This came from Catherine Tillman. "Depending on where your brain is located."

"That's great, Cath." Richard Tillman. "Perfect. We're doing this in front of the kids now?"

"Excuse me," said Scaz. He spoke from where he sat at the round oak table — leather jacket hung over the back of the chair, his arm stretched out in front of him. "Anybody mind if we focus on the patient here?"

They were all in the Jurgens kitchen area while Dr Joe looked at Scaz's arm. The kitchen had a breakfast bar and a little dining nook attached, and was about twice as big as Denny Hoyle's entire apartment.

"No," said Joe Jurgens distantly, answering Denny's question. He held Scaz's palm in one hand, gently probing his wrist with the other. "Urology isn't like brain surgery."

"Oh," said Denny Hoyle. He let it go for minute. But then his curiosity got the better of him. "What's urology mean again?"

"It means, if your friend here was struggling with erectile dysfunction, you'd definitely be in the right house."

"That's funny, doc," Scaz muttered. "Seriously hilarious."

Then he gasped.

"Sorry," Jurgens said. "Does that hurt?"

"Like a whore. Yeah, that too." All the color had drained from Scaz's face. "Look. Livingston. You sure you know what you're doing over there?"

"I think I've got the basic idea." He turned Scaz's wrist carefully. "I did a trauma rotation back in med school."

"And that was how long ago?"

"Fifteen years."

"Maybe I can wait."

"Mm. Be my guest. I'm sure some ER resident will be happy to re-break this for you tomorrow and set it properly."

Denny stood a foot or so away, peering down, watching Jurgens intently. It was kind of fascinating. He'd never really seen any medical practitioning up close this way. At least not any that wasn't on him.

"Okay," Jurgens said. "I'm going to try a little traction now. Are you ready?"

Scaz sighed, closed his eyes, set his jaw, and nodded.

Then he said, "Mother *cock*!"

Jurgens stopped was he was doing. Over at the breakfast bar, on Catherine's lap, Josh Tillman started to cry again. She held his head to her and talked to him. Richard Tillman looked off in another direction.

When Scaz opened his eyes, they were filled with water. Great beads of sweat had formed on his forehead and upper lip.

"Sorry," Jurgens said. "It's going to be a rough minute or two."

"Tell me you have some painkillers around here," Scaz said.

"Sorry again."

"Not even a Percocet? Anything?"

"The ibuprofen should help with the pain."

"Are you *kidding* me? Advils? I need morphine. Hell, doc, a Valium at least."

Scaz had closed his eyes, so he didn't see Jurgens glance briefly in his wife's direction at the mention of the Vals. Or the return look from Marly. Which was saying, if Denny interpreted correctly: *absolutely not*. Denny didn't comment.

Scaz finally opened his eyes and fished in one shirt pocket with his good hand. He pulled out a tight slender joint, wet it down, and left it pinched between his lips.

"Gimme a minute here, doc," he said, reaching behind him to dig a lighter from the pocket of his coat.

"Please don't light that thing in here," Marly Jurgens said.

Joe nodded at her in a soothing manner. "It's okay, honey."

Scaz fired up the jay and took a deep drag. He closed his eyes and held it in until he had to cough a little smoke out his nose. The acrid smell of pot now mingled with the sweet smell of cinnamon. Denny had noticed long fat sticks of it on the table, arranged with festive ribbon as a centerpiece.

"I said," Marly Jurgens repeated, her voice rising, "don't smoke that thing in here."

"*Marly*."

Everybody except Scaz jumped a little. Even Joe Jurgens seemed surprised at his own volume, the sharpness of his tone. His eyes softened when he looked at his wife. "It's okay."

They looked at each other for a long minute, while Scaz exhaled with an extended sighing sound.

Marly Jurgens's eyes welled up, but she blinked defiantly.

"Fine," she said tightly. "I'm taking our son into the living room before he gets stoned."

When she stood up, Catherine boosted Josh off of her lap and scooted over to comfort her.

From the counter where he leaned, Richard Tillman said, "I think we should all stay in the same room."

Without looking at him, Catherine said, "Nobody asked you, Richard."

Denny didn't realize he was speaking until the words were coming out of his mouth. "Hey," he said, making a motion with his arms. "Whattaya say let's all go into the other room there. Watch a little TV." He looked down at Josh. "How 'bout it, big guy?"

Josh wouldn't look up at him. He stuck to Catherine's leg like he was four instead of nine.

"I'd rather stay in here and try to get high," Chelsea muttered.

Very quietly, Richard Tillman said, "Move your ass, young lady. Right now."

"Go on, everybody," Joe Jurgens said. "Please. I need to concentrate. We'll be okay in here."

"Yeah," said Scaz, holding in a hit while he spoke. "Let the man work, people."

Denny tried to lighten the mood as much as he could. He smiled at Marly Jurgens as she passed him, but got only a hateful glare in return. Richard Tillman pretended he was administrating the situation. Meanwhile, he continued to flinch every time Denny Hoyle came within two feet of him.

Out in the living room, nobody said a word. Catherine and Marly took turns holding the baby. Denny stayed in there with them, hanging back out of the way. He stayed until he heard Scaz gasp, growl, and finally shout from the dining nook.

When he went back in, Scaz was slouched in the chair, panting, while Joe Jurgens wrapped his wrist and hand with an Ace bandage.

"Get her back in?" Denny asked.

"It's a bad break." Jurgens didn't look up from his work. "He'll still need X-rays."

Scaz took a little mini-hit and blew smoke toward the ceiling. His breathing was already starting to level out some.

"Okay," Jurgens told him.

Scaz looked at him. "That's it? We're done?"

"It's what I can do. The bandage should help with the swelling. And it'll keep your hand halfway splinted until you can get into a cast." Jurgens shrugged. "I wouldn't play racquetball."

Scaz grinned. His face was still pale and his eyes were red. He took one last hit, then reached across to drop what was left of his joint into the water glass next to his bandaged hand. The roach died with a quick sizzle. Scaz sat and rested for a moment or two.

Then he reached behind his back and pulled a big black .45 out of his jeans.

Jurgens looked at the gun. He looked at the floor. He looked at Denny with a tired expression.

And Denny looked from Jurgens to Scaz, feeling disgusted with himself for helping this asshole out of Luther's wrecked Buick earlier on.

"So I guess you're packing now," he said.

"Mostly just during the holidays." Scaz tipped the gun forward with his thumb on the hammer, drawing the hammer back two clicks. He wagged the barrel toward Jurgens. "So listen, doc. Before. You said 'four wheel drives'. As in plural."

Jurgens took another look at the gun and said, "As in."

Scaz grinned again. "I guess that means there's another one around here somewhere?"

Joe Jurgens stood where he was for a moment. He sighed. "I don't believe you people."

"Look, doc," Scaz said. "Think of it like this story I know. You ever heard this one? A woman is walking along and sees a snake frozen in the snow alongside her path. She picks it up and takes it home and warms it up near the stove. She feeds the snake and sits with it and nurses it back to normal again. She's feeling pretty good about herself by now. But the minute that snake feels like itself again, it bites her and pumps poison into her veins. And while this woman is feeling her throat close up on her, she asks the snake: 'Why did you do that, after all I've done for you?' And you know what the snake says?"

"I've heard the story."

"The snake says, 'Look, lady. You knew I was a snake when you brought me in.'"

Joe Jurgens didn't say anything for a minute. Neither did Denny Hoyle. Personally, Denny didn't know what the hell Scaz was talking about.

But Jurgens finally said, "There's a difference."

"Yeah? How so?"

"I didn't know whether you were a snake or not. But I helped you anyway."

Scaz seemed to think about this for a second or two.

"That's a good point," he finally said. "But you gotta figure, there's still a moral in here somewhere."

Joe Jurgens looked at Denny.

Denny looked back at him.

And without another word, Jurgens broke position and walked around the breakfast bar. He opened a cupboard and reached inside. He came out holding a single key on what looked like a spare ring. Jurgens brought the key over and placed on the table next to Scaz's arm. Which he'd just finished bandaging personally not five minutes ago.

"It's in the garage," he said. "I'll show you."

Scaz rose from the chair.

"Dude," Denny told him, "you got some balls on you. I'll give you that much."

"Congratulations," Scaz Gerstenfeld replied. "You finally figured out the difference between me and you."

–vi–

Last year, Denny Hoyle had spent Christmas in a bus station. The year before that? County lockup. The year before he'd gotten twelve stitches in his neck.

And every one of those was a damn sight holly jollier than this frozen turkey of a Christmas was turning out to be.

After Scaz took off in the yellow Honda CRV Joe Jurgens had bought Marly for their last anniversary, things in the Jurgens household just sort of kept on sliding downhill. In an upstairs room — behind a closed door, from the sound — Richard and Catherine Tillman screamed at each other for an hour, until Josh pooped his own pants and wouldn't come out from behind the Christmas tree.

Later, in another room, Marly Jurgens cried for so long that Joe had to get her that Valium after all. Denny could hear Joe talking to her over the baby monitor, which they'd forgotten in the living room. Joe talking. Marly crying. Then just quiet for awhile.

During another trip to the bathroom, Denny heard Richard and Joe in Joe's office. The sliding pocket door was closed most of the way; from inside the bathroom, Denny heard them talking through the joining wall.

He heard Richard Tillman say: "Hey, go ahead and tell me different, Joe. Nigger and a Jew. Am I wrong? Because you can go ahead and tell me if I am."

Chelsea Tillman had disappeared again, and Denny hadn't seen hide nor hair of her since.

Denny finally got so depressed that he didn't know if he could take it anymore. He seriously considered taking his chances on foot out there in the storm. By midnight, freezing to death was starting to sound kind of fun.

But by 2AM or so, the big house had fallen strangely quiet. Denny Hoyle went exploring, just to keep himself occupied.

He found Joe and Marly Jurgens asleep on the floor of the baby's room. Richard Tillman was in a basement rumpus room — passed out in a reclining chair with a half-drained bottle of Stoli at his hip, some kind of softcore cable flick playing quietly on a small color television.

In the living room, Catherine and Josh Tillman slept together, facing the back of the huge white couch like mismatched spoons. Josh was swimming in a pair of his Aunt Marly's sweatpants, which were rolled up and pinned. Catherine snored softly, her arm draped over his small shoulders. The big fireplace was down to glowing coals.

Looking at the two of them together, Catherine Tillman asleep with her boy, Denny was overcome with a powerful urge to bawl his goddamned brains out. He didn't know why.

He honestly didn't know what the hell was the matter with him these days.

All Denny Hoyle knew was that it was time to go. And that was just what Denny Hoyle planned to do. Outside, the storm had blown itself out a half hour ago. Just like that. One minute: ten-year blizzard. The next: a few flurries here and there. A few minutes after that, all was clear and calm.

The way Denny figured it, he was maybe three miles from Luther's car. Five, tops. Maybe by the time he got there, he'd be too cold and worn out to care it was Christmas Day.

He was on his way to the entryway where he'd left his shoes when he noticed the little clay piggy bank. It was still sitting where it had been left earlier tonight, out in the middle of the living room floor.

Denny didn't give it much thought. At least not until after he'd laced up his hikers, looked over the scrolled iron armrest of the antique bench where he sat, and realized the last thing he felt like in the whole wide world was schlepping that damned Salvation Army bucket all the way back to the car.

Denny thought about just leaving it.

He sat there and thought about other things.

Then, before he'd even thought about what he was doing, he'd prised the lid off his bucket of gambling money and gone back into the living room.

The pig was the kind that didn't have a plug in the bottom. It was one of those ones you had to break open to get the cash out.

And Denny found himself sitting with it, cross-legged on the living room carpet, his red Salvation Army bucket between his knees. Sitting there, in the dim light of the Jurgens Christmas tree, he fed coins through the slot in the pig's back.

Denny sat there thinking about all that had happened in the last few hours. For awhile he thought about baby Creighton, who couldn't have been much more than three days old. For awhile he thought about nothing in particular. The whole time, Denny fed coins one after another, until the sound of the falling money changed from a hollow rattle to a dull metallic click.

He was surprised to find it cleared his head a little, just to sit there and drop coins into that damned clay pig. It didn't take long before Denny Hoyle had lost himself in the task. He got so involved in what he was doing that he didn't even know when he acquired company.

All Denny knew was that at one point, about halfway through the bucket, he looked up and saw Chelsea Tillman watching him. She was sitting cross-legged on the carpet not two feet in front of him.

He jumped, then felt stupid. But he couldn't help it. It really startled the shit out of him.

"Oh," he said.

He tried a grin but it came out nervous. Chelsea Tillman looked at him. She had pretty brown eyes.

In a soft voice, she said, "What are you doing, anyway?"

Denny looked down at his project. He looked back up at her. He shrugged. "I dunno."

Chelsea didn't say anything. She looked at Denny's open bucket. She surveyed the scatter of bills he'd plucked from the coin pile, letting them collect on the carpet around his knees. After a minute she looked over her shoulder, toward where her mom and brother were sleeping on the couch.

Dropping coins, Denny followed her glance to the couch. "Pretty much sacked out over there I guess."

"Guess so."

They sat for a few minutes, neither of them saying much of anything. Denny dropped in a few coins. He wondered what had brought her out here now all of a sudden. He wondered where she'd been all night long. He didn't figure it was any of his business, so he didn't ask.

But after awhile, he looked up. He couldn't help it.

"Hey," he said. He kept his voice low instead of whispering. In his experience, a low voice was quieter than a whisper any day. "You mind if I ask you a question?"

"No."

"Your brother," he said. He nodded at the couch. "Ain't he a little old to be messin' in his undies?"

"He just started doing it." Chelsea looked at the pig while she talked. "Like a month ago. Last week I had to go pick him up from school."

"No kidding."

"Mom wants to take him to a psychologist. Dad doesn't believe in it."

Denny Hoyle thought about that. He dropped in a few more coins.

Just in the way of conversation, he said: "I guess your folks ain't getting along too good, huh?"

"They're getting a divorce." Chelsea shrugged without looking at him. "They think I don't know."

"Aww, hey," Denny said.

Chelsea said nothing.

Denny didn't know what else to say. They sat quietly for a minute.

"What they getting divorced about?"

"About the fact that my dad is fucking his office assistant."

Denny blinked at that. He looked quickly over to the sofa, where nobody stirred. Unconcsciously he dropped his voice down into whisper range. "You know, you prolly shouldn't talk like that."

"Why? That's what he's doing." For the first time all night, Chelsea looked him in the eye.

Denny looked back for a moment. Then he returned to his coin pile, knowing there wasn't much he could say to that. Matter of fact, he didn't even know why he'd said anything about her language in the first place. By the time he was Chelsea Tillman's age, he'd been boosting cars for about three years already.

He dropped in a few more coins.

"Sorry to hear," he told her.

"Yeah."

"You think your dad'll get married to this secretary gal?"

Chelsea went back to looking at the pig again. "Who cares? He's an asshole."

"Guess your mom probably thinks so, anyway."

"They're both assholes. All they do is scream at each other."

"Guess that'll happen." Denny dropped in a few coins. "They prolly don't mean nothing by it, though. I mean, they're your folks. They still love you and shit like that."

When Chelsea didn't say anything, Denny thought she was just being her regular quiet self again.

But when he looked, he saw that her eyes had filled up. She was biting down so hard on her bottom her lip Denny was afraid she'd draw blood. The tear puddles glinted in the light from the Christmas tree.

When she sensed him watching her, Chelsea batted angrily at her eyes and stared hard at the floor.

And all of a sudden, the whole thing made Denny Hoyle sad and uncomfortable. He felt like he ought to say something helpful. But who was he kidding? He was totally out of his element here.

"Hey," he finally said. He used his hands to separate what was left of his gambling change into two piles. Then he put his palms together like a snowblade and pushed one pile her way. "Help me stash this loot."

Chelsea wiped her face with the sleeve of her sweatshirt. She sniffed hard and sat there, looking at the floor some more.

After a minute, she lifted up her head and looked at the pile of change by her knee. She reached forward and picked out a quarter. Then she dropped it into the pig.

And for awhile they sat there alternating, dropping in coins one at a time. The bills they folded in half both ways. Denny followed what Chelsea was doing and used his thumbnails to make the creases sharp. They took turns slipping those in, too.

In no time they developed a system. Their change piles got smaller and smaller.

Pretty soon the pig was so heavy a person could've broken their toe on it, if they came through in the dark with bare feet and didn't notice it sitting there.

III. Wassail

Denny Hoyle slipped out of the Jurgens household just about fifteen minutes before dawn. Light was bleeding into the day.

And when the sun came over the horizon, it threw about a hundred shades of color into the sky. The whole world was white and sparkly. Every sound had a muted clarity. The air was cold enough to spike your lungs, but there wasn't so much as a whisper of a breeze.

It took Denny almost an hour to make it to the highway, trudging through crusted drifts up to his knees. He spent the last ten minutes of his trek listening to a growl in the distance.

By the time he made the main road, he was so pooped he thought he was seeing things.

But the big orange road department snow plow turned out to be real. Denny hustled to the intersection and ended up beating the rig by about two minutes.

So he waited along the shoulder while the plow eased to a halt with a heavy diesel rumble. The operator cut the engine back, rolled down the window, and stuck out his head. "Morning," he called down.

"Howdy," Denny said.

"Kind of a shitty day for a walk, ain't it?"

Denny jerked his thumb over his shoulder. "Went off about two miles back. Spent the night in the car."

"Well get your ass on up here, partner. Heater's on."

When Denny climbed up into the cab of the plow, the driver thrust out his hand and said, "Name's Grader."

He was a big burly sonofabitch with a grease-stained Carville coat and a Grizzly

Adams beard. Denny shook the man's big thick vicegrip of a hand.

"So Road's your first name, I guess?"

Grader sounded like an entire bowling alley when he laughed. "Road Grader. I get it. That's pretty funny. You'd be?"

"Pete Chelsea."

"Meetcha, Pete."

"Tell you what, it's damn good to meet you."

They bullshitted a bit while Denny slammed the door and got settled in the passenger springs. Grader asked where he was headed. Denny told him wherever he was plowing would do just fine.

Once the cab was sealed up nice and tight and warm again, Grader tilted his big shaggy head curiously. "Say."

"Yup."

"I'm not trying to sound gay or anything — but what's that you got on?"

At first Denny didn't know what the guy was talking about. Then he realized. In the most manful tone he could muster, he said: "Why, you like it?"

Grader shrugged his beefy shoulders. "Smells kinda classy."

And Denny Hoyle couldn't help but grin. He got such a kick out of it that he dug into the pocket of his coat and found the one single tester bottle of cologne that hadn't busted when Luthe wrecked the car. He held it up for Grader to see. Then he handed it over.

"Merry Christmas," he said.

Grader looked at the tester bottle in his hand. At first, it seemed like he didn't quite know what to make of it.

Denny told him to go on and take it, he was a traveling salesman for the company and had cases of the stuff at home.

Grader looked once at Denny. And then he laughed again.

"Well then Merry Christmas to you too, partner," he said, reaching down along the other side of his seat. When he brought his hand up, he was holding an open bottle of Jim Beam. He handed over.

Denny thought: *hello*. He took the bottle and had a good swig. It burned nice all the way down.

"Your health," he said, handing the bottle back.

"Yours too," said Grader, and had a healthy gulp of his own.

And after clearing his throat lustfully, he passed the bottle back for Denny to hold. With a deep basso shout that practically rattled the windshield wipers, Grader called: "Ramming speed!"

And off they crept, maybe two miles per hour, pushing the drifts apart on either side of the blade.

Not one time did Grader mention the donkey and the sheep, which followed along behind the big orange plow in the freshly-opened road. If he even noticed, he wasn't saying so.

For almost two miles, Denny Hoyle thought about bringing it up. But he decided not to say anything after all.

Instead, he settled in and did his part with the whiskey from the shotgun seat. From time to time, he checked his side view and smiled to himself, but he didn't say a word.

They passed Mr Beam between them.

On down the road they plowed.

Soon, Grader began to bellow out the verses to the Christmas tunes playing on the snow plow's crappy radio. Whenever Denny Hoyle knew the words, he joined along. ∎

SHELLEY COSTA

DOUBLE FAULT

Shelley Costa is Adjunct Professor of Creative Writing at the Cleveland Institute of Art, where she teaches fiction writing. Her work has appeared in Cleveland Magazine and The North American Review. She lives in Chagrin Falls, Ohio, and spends whatever time she can at a cottage on Lake Temagami in Ontario.

Paul Clague.

He can have two shots of Chivas without falling asleep. He can tell you why Kenny Lofton should have been Rookie of the Year in 1992. He can recall the names of the useless and the dates of the unnecessary. And he can give you serious assistance with your backhand. Altogether fine qualities in a husband. So I thought twelve weeks ago when I married him. So I still think. I watch him from the deck of Meridien, the lodge I've owned for ten years. The morning is cool. The coffee is hot. I like to burn my lip on the rim of the cup, the way I like letting the match burn down after I light the oil lamps. He looks up, shirtless, standing in the doorway to the boathouse with a greasy red rag in his hand. The hand that ripped the ball past McEnroe and Gerulaitis and even a young Becker. Only not often enough.

Call it whatever you like. *The predictable yearnings of early middle age*, is what my mother in Lake Forest, Illinois, said. *The pathetic ravings of the long unwed* is what my friend with the six children and a prolapsed uterus said. *Best damn move you ever made*, is how Paul put it, laughing, when we decided to get married.

He has had four Har-Tru tennis courts built behind the lodge. I watched the workmen paint the lines. To Paul they gave an instruction booklet called *Care of Your New Tennis Courts*. To me they gave the bill. *Well, he must have a good reason*, my mother says, with the senseless faith of women who wear their faded hair in loosening coils and find Theodore Dreiser current. It was also what she said when my father cashed in three IRAs and purchased an Airstream.

Paul was seeded 103 in men's tennis in 1982, known — so the clippings tell me — for his solid ground strokes and blistering volleys. Known, too, for his double faults under the pressure of competition. He lost, year after year, to the ones who went on to lose to the best. So, he taught. On Sanibel. On Hilton Head. On Kiawah, where we met at the pro shop. He was restringing a racquet and I was buying an overpriced fuchsia coverup to send to my mother, who powerwalks the Lake Michigan beaches in a sombrero and wraparound sunglasses, slathered with PABA-free sunblock rated SPF 30.

Well, he must have had a good reason, she said when my father emptied their savings account and drove off in the Airstream at four in the morning without her. She heard later that Clifton, the bank teller, went, too. Mother upped the sunblock to 45.

I peel an orange in the lodge kitchen. Coralee, a Chippewa woman who cooks and cleans for me, is pulling frozen strip steaks from the freezer. These she will grill in a Coca Cola marinade the guests fail to identify. Her husband is an old diabetic fishing guide — also Chippewa — with one kidney. Sometimes he still takes out rich white men in their Chriscrafts with the fish finders. For a fee he shows them one good minnow tree and one decent shoal where they can fish from the dropoff for just enough bass to keep them happy. He pees off the side of the boat.

Coralee loves him.

She stole, I believe, two of my crystal water goblets a week ago. She mentioned it was their anniversary, so the theft and the occasion dovetailed nicely. But the goblets are Orrefours. And mine. And not intended for the bottle of Moet that is also missing from the cellar. Paul says I may be mistaken. Mother tells me Coralee must have had a good reason. I watch Coralee inventory the baking potatoes for the evening meal. I am about to fire her.

We are the northernmost lodge on a lake in the lower forty-eight. Soon Paul will teach tennis, when the lines dry, and will actively promote what he calls the tennis component of Meridien. No other lodge at this latitude, he says, can offer tennis of this caliber. True. There are only five other lodges at this latitude. They offer moose hunting, which may have something to do with climate and demand. Unlike tennis. At Meridien, Paul is bellboy, handyman, skipper, and concierge, offering halfcocked fishing advice to guests ignorant enough to ask. I like serviceable men. As qualities go, it is as rare as Coca Cola steaks. The telephone rings. He takes the booking from a woman named Kitty Windle.

Over the winter, Paul's tan faded and he prayed none of the guests would want to go ice fishing. It was then he learned about the important places at Meridien — the septic field, the incinerator, the insides of my thighs. In bed the stories came, languid, like FM radio. I lay against him and watched the white and vascular frost on the window. There was the ex-wife who called him from her car phone two days before his last Virginia Slims tournament to say she was running over his lucky Head racquet. He had to listen as she described each exquisite crunch. Then she flung it once and for all off the Chesapeake Bay Bridge on her way to DC to find someone, as she put it, with more money and fewer pheromones.

There was a mixed doubles partner with leprous freckles who called him Clutch Clague — right there on the court — when a dishy little fraulein broke his serve in the fifth set. And there was what he insists was a fascist dyke line judge who ended his career with a bad call in that quarterfinal match against Borg. He called her a fat cow — which should have ended it — but the press came down hard on him, so he hid at resorts teaching flirtatious northern housewives who gave new meaning to the concept of follow-through. They came to him in their breathable tennis panties with their visors and wristbands and water bottles.

There was the former girlfriend from Raleigh whose hobby was clipping helpful household hints from the newspaper and gluing them to index cards. Things like what to do with leftover egg yolks. And how a lettuce leaf dropped into a pot of soup absorbs the grease at the top. From her he got herpes — blisters so painful he couldn't wear tennis whites or much of anything else for nearly three weeks. He couldn't even tolerate his bedsheets. He screamed into the telephone he hoped for her sake she had something on her index cards that could help clear up unwanted bruise marks from her windpipe. It was income lost at a time when he had to send alimony to the ex-wife now in DC who was discovering that the moneyed gents were there, all right, only she might have to have her mail forwarded to Riyadh.

I am cleaning cabins now that Coralee is gone. In eight, the farthest from the lodge, I change sheets, replace foil burner plates, sweep, mop, and swab the john. When I get back to the lodge, I watch Paul pour himself a glass of milk. *The Windle woman called to cancel*, he says, wiping his mouth with the back of his hand. *The weather report in Chicago*, he adds, *is for severe thunderstorms. She's afraid to set out.* Ah, I say. We all have our own deterrents. From the window overlooking the lake we see Briscoe, who cuts the engine to his barge, sidling alongside the dock. Paul goes down.

Briscoe has whiskers stiff and coppery as a wire brush and his union suit lacks buttons. On bad days he smells like old fish. On good days, like old socks. He delivers propane and removes garbage. In yesterday's paper was a list of local deadbeat dads: Briscoe was third from the top. *There are other sources of propane*, I tell Paul, *other barges. I won't have Briscoe any longer.* Paul says if Briscoe loses business his kids will never get the money. I tell him if Briscoe owned a fleet of barges and a closet full of Armani suits his kids still wouldn't get the money.

Briscoe tips the propane tank and rolls it to Paul. They laugh at a joke Briscoe tells. Everything glints in the morning sun. The tanks, Briscoe's fillings, Paul's watch. He checks the time and sees me coming toward them over the front lawn.

He laughs again, letting Briscoe enjoy one final moment as a fine raconteur. Both Paul and I know that the man is about to hear we no longer require his services.

The wind, I hear in town, is from the north. It fans the lake, pushing the surface into watery peaks. I have been gone from the lodge for five hours, banking, shopping, washing blankets in industrial machines. Back at the landing I load the groceries into the boat and park the Explorer. The clouds look milky and indefinite. Behind them the sky is mottled blue, lapis like Paul's eyes. I stop in front of a white Olds, dusty from the rough road, with North Carolina plates. Here in the remote northern center of the country we never see Carolina plates. They have their own water. Their own seafood. Their own wildlife. Still, here is a white Olds with Carolina plates. LOVE THEM HEELS says the bumper sticker. In the back window in gold letters outlined in black: MARY KAY.

I look inside. A pine tree car deodorant dangles from the rearview mirror. On the front seat is a road atlas opened to Minnesota. On top of it — I don't know why I step back — is the slick trifold I had a local print shop update over the winter, after I married Paul and added his name. And added the tennis component, even before the courts were built. Below the name Meridien Paul insisted on adding A RESORT, in small caps. I am uneasy. Surely it takes more than four Har-Tru tennis courts to call a place a resort. It takes a pool, a sauna, a Nautilus, fluffy towels, imprinted matchbooks, a nightly turndown for the consummately lazy, topped by a chocolate mint. What Paul says is *all in good time*.

Whose Carolina Olds? Whose map and Meridien trifold, where someone has scribbled *arrive the sixteenth, cabin eight, bring towels*? Today is the sixteenth. Only one guest was scheduled to arrive today: Kitty Windle. A faceless traveler who — according to Paul — didn't want to set out from Chicago in severe thunderstorms.

At the bait shop on the landing I use the pay phone to make a credit card call. She's on her way out, Mother lets me know, so it's not a good time to chat. I ask about the weather. *Aren't you having a severe thunderstorm warning?* The tapping I hear on the line is Mother applying yellow nosekote. *Storms?* she bleats. *Talk sense*, she tells me. *It's 78 degrees and the sky is china blue like that wonderful old set of dinnerware we had when you were growing up, do you remember it?*

Paul lied.

I have been gone from the lodge for five hours. The boy Benny who comes over from a neighboring island whenever he feels like earning a few bucks lifts the groceries out of the boat. When I ask where Paul is, *fish cleaning hut with the old guy from cabin four who came back with a twelve-pound pike*, he says, *a regular trophy fish*. I tell Benny to take the bags up to the kitchen. My smile feels like a face wound. I crunch down the gravel path by the row of housekeeping cabins. The saggy mother from Kenosha in cabin three calls out that they need more toilet paper and, if we could possibly swing it, a fly strip would be lovely. Letting myself into number eight, I stare at the brown silence. The bed is the way I left it, the chenille spread smooth. The bathroom is the way I left it, the blue Ty-D-Bowl undisturbed. No cups in the sink. No jacket in the closet. No racy paperback on the coffee table. Only the braided rug in the middle of the living area looks different. Askew.

Who is Kitty Windle? Why did she come to the landing in her white Carolina pine tree Mary Kay Oldsmobile when Paul said she lived in Chicago? When I was growing up with the china blue china my mother mentions I could not distinguish between hunger and nausea. The moods of my stomach were unreadable to me. It is hard to tell now, as I look around the uninhabited cabin, whether what I feel is alarm or relief. Suddenly I am ten and chewing creamed corn in a terror of uncertainty:

is it hunger? is it nausea? am I going to embarrass myself all over the Battenburg lace tablecloth and Noritaki? Is Father somewhere in a stomachless rolling paradise with Clifton where you never need deposit slips and paper plates are just swell?

Cabin eight. Has certain features. A separate dock, for one. A thicket of birch and cedars, for another. An entrance unobservable from the other cabins. Under the electric baseboard heater by the front windows is a glint of metal. Something that wasn't there when I cleaned this morning. It is a lipstick. I pick it up and turn the tube over in my hand, slowly, as though it is an Etruscan pot shard. Plum tomato is the shade. By Mary Kay Cosmetics.

Outside cabin eight is a rick of wood for the Franklin stove. And a large metal garbage can. I look around. For what, I don't know. The can is still empty. A garter snake — the watery green in nature that even Mary Kay can't reproduce in her eye shadow labs — slides under the cabin, away from me. The trail goes into the forest, where our slick trifold boasts you can still see old growth pine. And — I pluck what looks like a string from a clump of blueberry bushes — very possibly what's left of Kitty Windle. It is a length of nylon filament, used for stringing tennis racquets. I smell it. The wet, cakey smell of an oil-based foundation makeup. The sort of stuff women who don't live in the northernmost lake lodge in the lower forty-eight wear on their faces. And necks.

The incinerator. The can dump. The abandoned copper mine. Even the old dilapidated pit toilet, assuming you sprinkle enough lime. When you really stop to consider, there are many places to locate the hastily dead. Even around your own neighborhood. We, of course, have an advantage, namely a twenty acre island. Here I coil and pocket the length of nylon string. *Mother*, I say to the leafy air, *the Noritaki is safe, the Battenburg lace is safe, I am not sick, I am hungry, I can tell.* And her china blue china moves in. *Well*, I think before it eclipses that last strip of light we call consciousness, *he must have had a good reason.*

We are going across to Benny's island, Paul and I. There is a Lake Lodge Owners' Association meeting, where we will do what we always do: order desiccated martinis with olives and prattle with the others about dwindling tourism and difficult tourists. Paul plans on mentioning the new tennis component offered at Meridien. I wear a forest green top and a long crinkle-pleated rayon skirt. Weighted down. I wear no underwear. It makes things simpler for the return trip, after dark, when he cuts the engine and we drift. Will we be seen by other boaters? Will we hit a shoal? Paul is daring. So, I suppose, am I.

He stands at the wheel in his tight jeans and white polo shirt. From where I sit I wrap an arm around his thigh, flicking the inseam with my nail. He smiles down at me and opens up the engine. For him, it has been a good day. Despite the problem with the Windle woman, which seems to have altered none of the appetites that affect me. He is dreaming, I can tell, about a tournament at Meridien. Not this season, maybe, but next. Something classy with a top seed, some photo ops, and himself as tennis provider. Tennis guru. No more Clutch Clague. No more battered racquets. No more fat cows. Kitty Windle is one of those, I feel sure. It hardly matters which. His blond hair blows back in the headwind.

Paul, I wish I could say, you will really have to do something about the white Olds before too much time passes. He is busy negotiating the channel markers. From my pocket I pull a rock I have tied up with a length of racquet string. I hurl it, hearing the plop over the sound of the engine. He turns for a moment, wondering. *A loon diving*, I tell him. *Have you ever noticed* — I move my leg between his — *that when you get close enough, their eyes are actually red?* ∎

SIMON AVERY

LEAVING SEVEN SISTERS

Born in 1971, Simon Avery lives and
works in Birmingham. He has had short
fiction published in the anthologies
Cold Cuts 3, Last Rites & Resurrections,
Watch Fire, The Tiger Garden, and three
stories in Crimewave's sister magazine
The Third Alternative ('Blue Nothings' in
TTA8, 'Anonymity Walks' in TTA11 and
'Violent Cities, Quiet Towns and Settled
Homes' in the current issue, TTA25). He
also has a story forthcoming in Joel
Lane's subterranean horror anthology
Beneath the Ground. Simon would like
to thank Jay, Steve and Chris for their
help with 'Leaving Seven Sisters'.

She is flying across London in a taxi, euphoric; the streetlights a blur, the holdall filled with daddy's money, snug between her knees. Nothing going in; she feels distracted to the point of giddiness, full of adrenalin, coiling around her belly; electricity in her extremities. *Christ*, she thinks. *Jesus Christ*.

When she reaches her place in Earls Court, she hurries inside, rushes to the bedroom and peels off her clothes in a sweaty abandon. Empties all those non-sequential bills out onto the bed and rolls around in it. She's seen it in a movie, more than once; something she's always wanted to do but now it just seems silly. *Still*. She stares at the ceiling, listening to her heart racing, then puts her fingers between her legs and comes almost immediately. When she gets up there are fifties stuck to her back, between her thighs.

After changing and downing a couple of G&T's, she gets ready for Julian to arrive. Tonight would be perfect if they could just go. Just fuck off to France. But she can't. Julian will take the money and be a good boy. She trusts him implicitly because he's so young, and so in love with her, the poor little sod.

If she didn't have to kill someone tonight, everything would be just fine.

Dennis had always dreamed of coming to France. He had scenes in his head, pil- fered and reconstructed from books he'd read in his youth or on the inside: huddled beneath an umbrella in Marseille with an exotic woman whispering sweet nothings in his ear; on a train, speeding through a long corridor of trees, the ocean glittering in the distance; barefoot in a silent hotel, watching from a balcony with dawn breaking through the empty avenues. Now he was here for his final fling, he couldn't decide how to feel, except cold and tired to his very bones, a little bit past it. Yesterday wouldn't leave his head. As if the constant replay of its events might erase all the doubt and anxiety he felt the closer he got to that money. All that bloody *money*.

He'd been a minor felon since leaving school at fifteen. Grew up on a council estate in Peckham, all highrises and maisonettes. Almost everyone's dad had been inside for something. Mum would have a different bloke home every week. Sun bed tans. Closed curtains during the daytime meant the family was sharing out whatever they'd stolen the night before: TVs, stereos, video recorders, jewellery. It was a downward spiral from the get go; nothing to aim for really. A bit of breaking and entering, car theft, dope dealing, doing people over. By his twenties, he realised it had all gone wrong but he couldn't stop. No one would let him; everyone whom he'd surrounded himself with was as bent as he was.

But by this time he was finding himself at kitchen tables, sawing off shotgun barrels, sat beside virtual strangers. It was the whole nine yards: tights over the face; the car engine in danger of stalling out on the high street, with the alarm bells ringing; sweat in his crotch, shouting in the bank, a child wailing, too young to be mollified; Dennis thinking, *this is not The Sweeney. This is all fucking wrong*.

It was a long way from the picture that he kept in his wallet of Ingrid and himself outside an anonymous register office in Birmingham, in a tight old suit; the evening spent getting plastered with the in-laws; cake on paper plates, and then the drunken sweaty fumbling in a shabby B&B in Rhyl, both of them afraid to admit that some of the appeal had somehow gone from the other. They were already too familiar. They'd stopped kissing except during sex. The spark had gone without either of them really knowing how to pinpoint *when*. Ingrid had gotten pregnant, of course. One of them had been stupid enough to think that it might be the solution to all of their problems, but they'd already stopped talking, and Dennis had moved out by the time the baby arrived. Lizzie was a bright-eyed little girl, and by the time she was old enough to walk, she looked upon Dennis with the same suspicion and intolerance that Ingrid did. But she was precious; a little sweetheart.

She could still manage to make his heart jump sometimes. These were the good years that he was missing, he knew. One day she'd be an even more distant daughter once she knew just what a useless cunt her old man had been. But he didn't see what he could do about that. It seemed to be out of his hands.

Dennis had done a few stretches inside of course. The last time, Lizzie had turned five the day he went down. He met Potter on his first day inside. Shared a cell. Potter came from Peckham too; had mutual acquaintances, and they reminisced when they got tired of cutting out pictures from *Penthouse* and blu-tacking them to the wall by the bunks.

Potter had the heavyset build and thick-veined neck of a body builder, a cropped shadow of hair, and the dark furtive eyes of a small animal. When he smiled, Dennis could see the cheeky little smart arse schoolboy he'd been twenty-five years or so ago, and thought: *he would have bullied me every fucking day.*

Potter was everything that Dennis was not: where Dennis was slow and meandering, Potter was animated and edgy, as if he was permanently on speed and Pernod; where Dennis was inarticulate and frustrated, Potter was expansive and merely bemused at the whole fucked situation; where Dennis considered himself a bit traditional and strangely domesticated, Potter was obstreperous, footloose and fancy free: a shag in every city. But despite the shortcomings, Potter had gravitated toward Dennis with something like respect. Their background denied them any real sense of *closeness* — two hard lads from Peckham — but while Dennis suffered Potter, Potter went to work on him like he was a big blank canvas. *All those plans.*

"We'll go straight after this, Dennis. We'll be painters and decorators."

"I can't see you in overalls, Potter."

"What do you call these, Dennis? Fucking *Versace*? How about a pub, eh? Or a wine bar. A fucking *wine bar*, Dennis! *Luvverly.*"

Potter dealt with some lads Dennis owed money while both of them were still inside. Dennis didn't want them turning up on Ingrid's doorstep for the cash. He was already in too much shit with her as it was. Potter just told him it was sorted one day, *here, have a fag*, simple as that. Dennis was indebted, bound as he'd always been by some obscure criminal values. It was just another door, closing behind him.

Ingrid's solicitor contacted him a week before he was due out. Served him with divorce papers and a note from Ingrid. It said: *I'm clearing the decks, Dennis. Selling the house and starting all over again. You're not much of a father to Lizzie.*

He wondered who was. She sent a picture with the note of Lizzie in the back garden, which he stared at for days, feeling himself closing up like a dying flower. Her blonde curls were lit up by the sun. In her white summer dress and flip-flops, she was squinting up at the camera, trying to hear what Ingrid was saying to her, a childish tilt to her head.

Once he was out, Dennis stayed with Potter, who had bolt holes all across North London, and cabbed for some Turk lads with an old motor that Potter supplied him with. Somehow he always had five or six cars on the go: souped up engines, cranked up suspension; Potter would go on about it sometimes, but Dennis didn't have the foggiest. He just *drove* the bleeding things. The ashtrays would always be overflowing and the glove compartment filled with those cards you found in phone boxes with numbers for a shag. Potter had a penchant for grubby massage parlours, the grubbier the better; a fiver for a hand job in some places. Dennis abstained. Kept a stash of porn. Lived off kebabs and curries and cans of Coke. Talked to Lizzie on the phone; overcompensated wildly. At traffic lights he'd stare at his bony hands on the wheel, the wedding band still on his finger. Here he was, almost forty, living off another ex-con's charity, his only responsibility being a bit of maintenance to pay for Lizzie. But nothing else; no dog to feed, no real bills to pay, no burglar alarm to set on the way out, no babysitter to sort out at weekends. At forty, he thought, you shouldn't be so free, shouldn't have so little that it could be shoved into a holdall so you could fuck off at a moment's notice.

It had been late evening, yesterday. Dennis had been in Bethnal Green after dropping off some old geezer in a packed side road, with a girl half his age, dirty bugger. Potter had called him on his mobile, voice awash in static. "Where are you?"

"Bethnal Green." Dennis was watching the prozzie fumbling with her keys at the door to a converted Victorian three-high; the old fella glancing back at Dennis nervously as he counted out his change with the interior light on.

"I'm in Seven Sisters, Dennis. I'm in the shit. Drop what you're doing, alright?"

Seven Sisters was half erased with fog; streetlights gone soft; highrises fading away. The pubs were turning out the last of the piss-heads, singing and spewing in equal measure. But the streets were fairly empty; just the traffic lights to stop for. Dennis felt too much energy in his hands and feet, a cold sick feeling fluttering in his gut as he slowed through the clogged thoroughfares, the residential roads hemmed in with cars. He thought more than once about just turning round, going to get a take away, then sodding off home. But he didn't.

Potter was waiting outside by the bin bags on the pavement, his shirtsleeves rolled up over his thick, hairy forearms, a tattoo snaking from his scuffed knuckles to his elbow, a little bit faded like an old man's. He was smoking a tiny roll up, and when he tossed it beneath his heel Dennis could see his head shining with sweat between the bristles of his hair. "What have you done, Potter?"

But Potter was already chasing his shadow back into the tenement. "Just get *inside* for Christ's sake, Dennis." There was a smear of darkness on the back of Potter's shirt. Dennis couldn't be sure in this crappy light, but he knew what he thought it looked like. What it probably was. *Bollocks.* He felt a spasm in his chest, down his one arm as he crossed the threshold, trying to keep sight of Potter as he hurried up the narrow staircase into the gloom. He had to fumble with his hands on the walls and the bannister. Not using the time switches.

Potter's bedsit on the top floor was one of many. He seemed to have a place every couple of miles throughout London, all of them best recalled by their paucity of belongings. They contained the minimum for a night's entertainment. Sometimes they were just a storehouse for merchandise, or a place for mates to lay low from the old bill or worse, pissed off spouses.

But not this one. Not tonight. This was all wrong, all completely fucked, Dennis realised. The woman was half on the bed in an oyster pink slip, her hair still wet, a towel discarded across the headboard. Throat cut. Eyes wide open in a kind of sad resigned horror, as if in her last moments she'd viewed the sordid little scene outside herself. Tears were trapped in her eyelashes, waiting to dry. Dennis closed the door behind him, had to steady himself against it. He couldn't see anything but her. She commanded attention. Lips pale as wax; perfect flushed cheeks; too much blood on her face, her chest, the sheets. There was a roaring sound like a shell full of the sea in Dennis's head.

Van Morrison was playing on the portable CD player; forgotten now, playing 'Crazy Love' of all things beside two untouched glasses of wine. Potter switched it off finally. He was energised with grim distraction; moving around the pokey little room, breathing heavily, throwing shadows across the wall like a prize fighter waiting for all the right moves to return. Dennis kept dodging out of his way. He could smell the girl now: the smell of blood and semen and expensive perfume.

"Potter — "

"Here's what we're going to do," Potter interjected. He said it twice more, changing the emphasis from word to word each time. He stopped, pressed his fingers to his temples where the veins were bulging; stared at the woman as the blood pooled around her, congealing on the pillows.

She was a stunner, Dennis thought; one of those pretty butterflies in summer dresses on a Saturday afternoon, fluttering through Chelsea or Covent Garden with Gucci bags, Prada. Almost untouchable. Staring at her pale thighs, he imagined Potter watching her moving about this grubby little room on tiptoe, smoothing his palms over that oyster-pink slip, pausing on the soft generous swell of her breasts. Dennis could almost see her bending forward with a slight wry smile so Potter could pat her hair dry with the towel, and in doing so, revealing herself to him in a gesture that said more than words. Dennis thought about Ingrid then, started to feel his cock ache in his underwear. And his chest ached for her too.

"Who was she?" he asked finally, alarmed at the sudden dispassion he heard in his voice. When had he become the low life he'd always imagined he was only pretending to be?

"Some tart," Potter said, dismissive. "It doesn't matter. I want you to get rid of her for me, Dennis."

"Fuck off."

Anger flared across Potter's face briefly. "*Listen,*" he hissed, but then he lost the thread of it, and suddenly seemed deflated. "Listen. I'm *fucked* here, alright? You can see that, can't you, Dennis? She's fucking *dead*. *Jesus.*"

Dennis tried to fix him with his eyes, but he'd started to twist his wedding band violently. The smell was starting to get overpowering. They'd seriously need to open a fucking window soon. The woman's vacant eyes were following him around the room, like a portrait. "Should I ask why?"

"You know better than all that, Dennis, surely to Christ," Potter said stonily.

Dennis pondered over the untouched wine glasses. Paused. "You want me to sort your mess out?" The gravity of the situation was seeping into his bones slowly, like lead. How it always felt. Shotguns and getaway cars; stolen merchandise in the garage; doing over petrol stations in the small hours of the night; it was like a really poxy version of every crime film he'd ever seen. It made him sick to his stomach; it gave him the shits, and then he just needed cigarettes, some spirits warming him; some egress from who he was, who he couldn't stop being because of one mad fucker or another. Not even for Ingrid or Lizzie. For no one.

Potter lit a Silk Cut from the box that the woman had left on the bedside table, and exhaled slowly, fatalistically. Stared down at the butterfly like he was considering new tyres on a motor, ash crumbling onto her arm. "Just while I sort this out, Dennis. *One* fucking favour. You wouldn't have your kneecaps if it wasn't for me, mate. Think about Ingrid and the little one. Who sorted all that out for you, eh?" Breathless, steely eyed, Potter looked away finally. He'd never once come the heavy with Dennis in the past. He was ashamed of having to do it now, Dennis could tell. But he was scared too. This was something entirely new for Potter.

"You'll call the filth. And I'll still be here with my todger in my hand, standing over a fucking *corpse* when they finally kick the door in. What sort of stupid wanker do you think I am?"

Potter's patience looked to be ebbing. He was too edgy. Eyes darting around in his head, like there was some interior auto cue to follow in there. "I just need to sort this out. There's more to this, Dennis. I'm not asking you to shack up with her. I'll be back. You wrap her up and I'll probably be back before you have her downstairs. I'm not going to take you for a cunt."

He walked over to Dennis tiredly, put a hand on his shoulder. "You take your motor, bring it round the back. You get her all gift wrapped and downstairs — no one will see you — out the back door, down the alley and into the boot. It's pitch fucking black out there," he said, peering out through the curtains at the overgrown backyard. "You can sink her somewhere, can't you? A canal or something?"

Dennis nodded, defeated. The avenues were all closing down again. He let Potter go eventually, followed him out onto the street. Watched the tail lights as he vanished up the road, heading out of Seven Sisters. Part of him didn't want to go back inside again, once he'd parked the car behind the house. It was like being introduced and then left alone with a complete stranger: all those awkward silences.

Her name was Miranda Sinclair. Dennis had had her down as a Miriam or a Penelope; something along those lines: it was in the line of her nose, the high cheekbones, the upturn of her lips — upper class breeding. She was every bit the butterfly he had imagined.

Her handbag had slipped down between the bed and the wall, presumably during the struggle that had ended with Potter slitting her throat. Dennis slid it out, having noticed the strap, holding his breath when his face came too close to hers. He couldn't decide if her expression had altered since he'd arrived. Perhaps it was only some obscure relaxation of facial muscles that occurred post mortem, making her face look sadder by the minute, as if she were pitying him, or her killer, or the world. *Poor you.* You're better out of it, love, Dennis thought, trying to be cold, detached. But her tears dislodged then, and slid down the sides of her face.

He stared at her for a little while. After a minute of visualising it, he hesitantly ran his forefinger down her arm. Her skin felt clammy but impossibly smooth, like cold marble. He picked up a hand and ran the back of it against his face. Closed his eyes. Imagined her alive, putting her hand elsewhere. When he opened his eyes, her slip had slid away from her breasts. They stood up, small and perfect, even though she was on her back. Despite the blood on them, an erection had formed uncomfortably in his underwear. It wilted when he removed a glove and pressed a sweaty palm over her and smeared the blood, got it beneath his fingernails. He could hear his shallow breaths, swarming in his ears. When he stood up, he stared between her legs and could see Potter's semen, still slowly trickling from her vaginal lips. After that Dennis retreated to the window like a stung child, opened it and breathed in the still night air. Listening. The last bus, either coming in or out of Seven Sisters; some drunken cunt, singing at the top of his lungs a couple of streets away; two cats in the yard, arching their backs, hissing at each other, then crying like babies. Dennis looked at Miranda's blood on the tips of his fingers, then wiped it on his shirt tail.

After five minutes, he went and lit one of her Silk Cut and then stared at his mobile, willing it to ring. When it didn't he fished out a half empty jar of Nescafe from the kitchen cupboard, and made a black coffee in the one chipped mug on the drainer.

As he rifled through the purse from her handbag — finding her name, her address, her National Insurance number — he wondered absently if she'd screamed much; if Miranda Sinclair had cried louder at the point of orgasm or death. But he supposed that it didn't really matter. She was gone now, and these were her remains in his sweaty paws: a purse with no cash but several credit cards, store cards, even an organ donor card, which struck Dennis as peculiarly funny; a small make-up case and two different lipsticks: *one for shopping and one for shagging*, he imagined Potter saying in his ear; some keys to a house and car, a small VW key ring holding them together; a paperback novel, slightly dog-eared, a page folded in the corner, not twenty pages from the end. Dennis pulled out a postcard from a girlfriend of

Miranda's, holidaying in the Greek Islands ('I'm working up a glorious tan, Miranda, and I'm being chatted up every night by the Greek lads. They keep pinching my bum!' it read), then pushed it back in when he spotted a filofax. He slid out some glossy photos of Miranda in an evening gown, a few years younger perhaps, with an older man who seemed familiar but Dennis couldn't put his finger on it. In the other, she was alone on a sea front somewhere, laughing into the camera, hair flying in her face, seagulls wheeling in the distance over the sea. Pure happiness: Dennis could see it in her face. He looked back at her body again, sprawled over the bed, then back to the photo. This was how someone had lived, and how they had died. There was something to *know* here, he felt: some flower about to open and impart wisdom. But it wouldn't come. He didn't know enough. He put the pictures into his coat pocket and flicked through the filofax, looking for something else.

Addresses, phone numbers: satellites that had revolved around Miranda. Everyone had them in different variations and amounts. Dennis could have crossed them out. These people meant nothing now; they were just a funeral guest list at best. Here was a sister, a brother, here was the girl from the Greek Islands who enjoyed having her arse pinched. Here was daddy presumably, his card clipped into a page: John Michael Sinclair.

John Michael Sinclair.

Dennis suddenly had the sensation of falling from his chair in slow motion as took out the photos again. *Shit. Fuck.* The one of Miranda in the evening dress with the older man. That was daddy beside her. Dennis had seen him in the paper. Jesus fucking Christ, he'd seen him on the *telly*. He was a cabinet minister; minister for transport or agriculture or something. Dennis could feel his shirt clinging to his armpits, his back. He couldn't think clearly suddenly. Potter had murdered a cabinet minister's daughter. Jesus wept. The stupid *cunt*. He fumbled his mobile out of his pocket and phoned Potter.

"What is it, Dennis?" Dennis could hear Potter's fucked up fan belt squealing; Potter working through the gears impatiently. It sounded like he was racing a tractor.

"She was a fucking cabinet minister's daughter, you twat."

"Fuck off, Dennis. Just do your job, eh?" Over revving the engine. Braking. Dropping down the gears: traffic lights. "Just get off the fucking road, you tit." Muttering beneath his breath, then tearing away again. Waiting for Dennis to say something else.

"What was it, Potter? It must be something to do with *him*. Blackmail? What are you doing him for?"

"We're not talking about this, Dennis. We're not having this conversation."

Dennis looked at Miranda, the photos in his hand, processing it all. He was still absently fumbling through the rest of the handbag. "Was she in on it? Miranda, I mean?"

He heard Potter sigh. "You're making this very difficult for yourself, Dennis. *Very* difficult."

"You'll be an old man, Potter. If they put you away for this sort of shit, you'll be an old man when you get out. *If* you get out."

"I'm not going down for this, Dennis. You'll see to that won't you? You'll sort Miranda out and I'll sort the rest out. Otherwise it won't just be me going down for it." There was a pause where Dennis could see the inside of that cell again. He'd emptied the bag out except for one last thing in the side pocket. He slid out the small revolver and stared at it. Dumbfounded. Fully loaded. Not something that girls like Miranda just carried around with them, unless they had a bloody good reason to. He'd got to his feet but he had to sit down again now. He felt light-headed. "You can't trust them, Dennis," Potter said finally in a grim determined voice.

"Who? Women or sailors?"

"Rent boys."

Dennis snorted through his nose. Put the gun back in the bag. "I dare say you can't."

"Fuck off, Dennis. Do your job, eh? Be a good girl."

He'd intended to start wrapping Miranda up after that. Potter had managed to find some heavy gauge plastic sheeting that Dennis remembered his old man used to use instead of glass for his greenhouse. Clearly Potter had been prepared for this scenario — the sheeting was already folded up and wedged beneath the bed. Five rolls of masking tape too. Even some dumbells to weight her down with. What would he have said if Miranda had had a shufti under the bed beforehand? He knew Potter had the gift of the gab but there'd have been no bullshitting his way out of *that* one.

After ten minutes of getting it sorted, shifting bricks, he was knackered. He lit another cigarette and went for a piss, still thinking about the gun. Had Miranda intended to do the dirty on Potter? The idea made him smile.

Propping himself up against the wall, fag in his mouth, dick in his shaking hand, he found himself staring at a yellowed page clipped out of the *News of the World*, and taped over the cistern. It was an article on Miranda. Here she was in the picture, grainy and perfect, dressed down in leather trousers and a denim jacket but unable to deny those cheekbones, those pouting lips, the confidence of money in her breeding. Next to it was a smaller photo of daddy, the cabinet minister. Just seeing it confirmed brought Dennis out in a cold sweat all over again. He'd have to chuck this shirt away once he'd peeled it off his back.

As the pipes mumbled around the house, he worked his way through the article. He'd left his glasses in the car; couldn't be arsed to go and get them, so it took him a while. Eyes squinting, teeth bared; nose two inches from the words. This was really putting him off his piss.

So. John Michael Sinclair. Cabinet minister, mansion in Surrey, several hundred acres of land, inherited his father's fortune… Miranda Sinclair, estranged daughter, wild child — typical Sunday tabloid wording — on the arm of some pop star wanker or another, but here was the meat of it: Sinclair's wife had filed for divorce when Miranda was just seven, citing the usual 'irreconcilable differences'.

Dennis zipped himself up. Usually that meant the wife wasn't being bribed enough to forgive the mistresses or the fact that Johnny dearest enjoyed wearing her panties when he spoke to the PM.

But in the end mother and daughter didn't get much of a sniff of cash from the divorce, on account of Mrs Sinclair being caught having an affair that had begun at least five years prior to the divorce being filed. Her husband counter sued and won. She'd managed to write herself out of the deal. Possibly as a result, Miranda went from gilded youth to wayward daughter, half a Sloaney bird, half a druggie who'd ended up at twenty-one on methadone in a NHS clinic, somewhere in Fulham.

Had Potter read this article, clipped it and gone in search of the wild child, falling in love with all that deflected glamour into the process; blu-tacked the story in front of the karzi, so her face was always there when he whipped out his tackle? Or had she come with it — a press clipping from her filofax, no introduction needed; always looking for a chance to shaft daddy with all of his millions in some small way?

He imagined Potter, leaning on a bar somewhere, half glancing back at this posh bird, waiting for her table, the slash in her skirt going all the way up. Black high heels. Perfect calves. Not much left to the imagination.

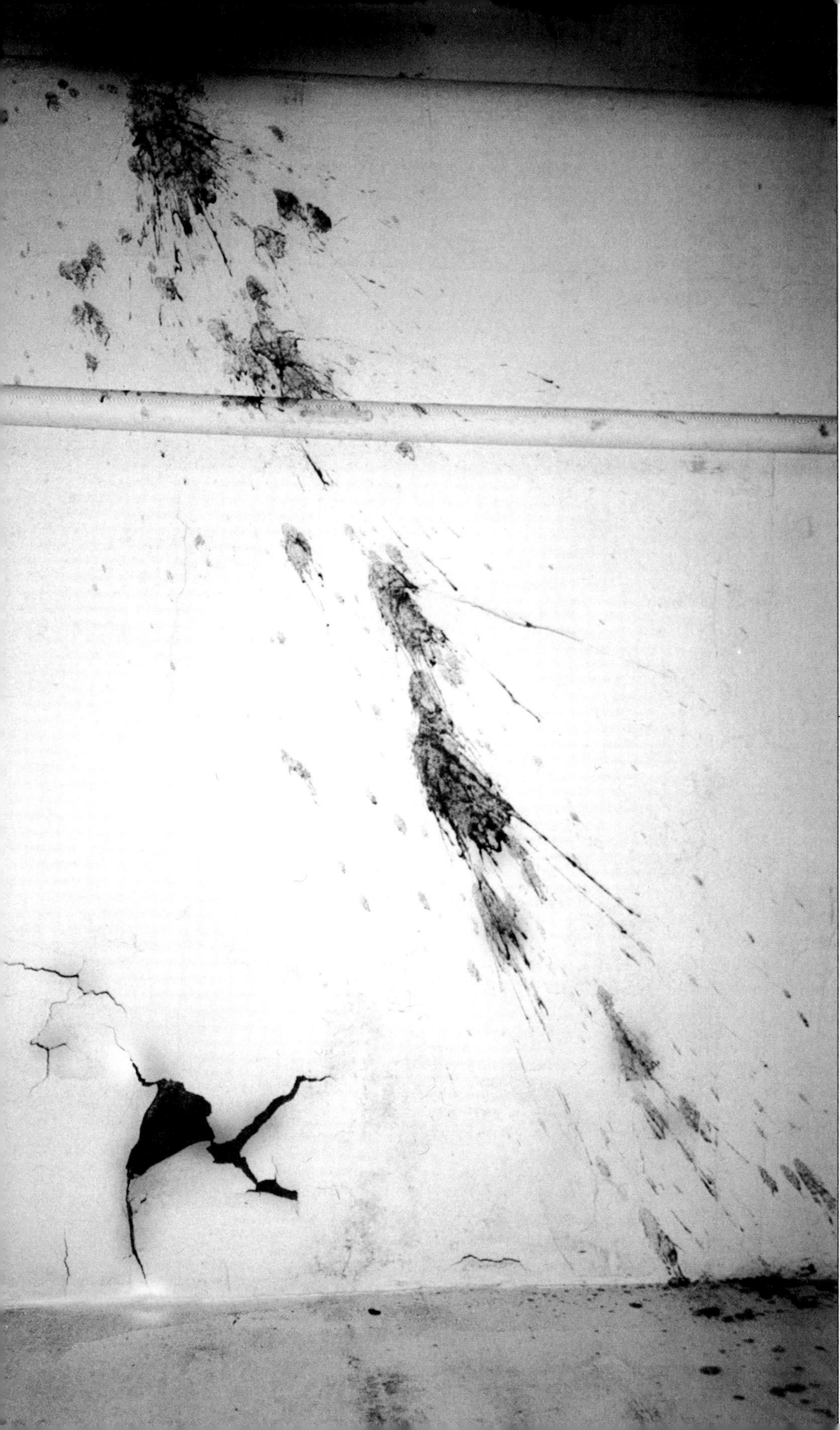

Dennis leaned against the doorframe, picturing Miranda with her hair worn up, tiny wisps of it curling at the nape of her neck. You couldn't resist kissing her in those places, then behind those pretty little ears, pale as porcelain. Potter had seen all that with the Guinness half downed at the bar, and gone over, introduced himself. Smooth as silk. He had the one Italian suit. Worked a charm every time. She'd have been like a deer in the headlights when he turned it on. Women like Miranda, they loved them smooth on the outside with a little bit of rough on the inside: East End bullshit. That was Potter all over; he'd have had her in bed before the evening was over, doing whatever he asked: *put it anywhere, sweetheart.*

Dennis crouched by the bed and stroked Miranda's hair, avoiding the places where it had gotten matted with blood. She stared glassily back into his eyes as he felt his erection pushing urgently against his trousers. Dennis held one of her breasts with a bloody hand, then pulled up her slip, trying to ignore Potter's spunk between her legs. Pale, perfect thighs. Tiny feet. By now he'd wrestled his throbbing prick out into his hand, and was working it furiously. But his body wouldn't stop shaking. Hollow in his gut. He kept seeing Ingrid outside that fucking register office, confetti down their necks. *She* wouldn't look at Dennis anymore, let alone Miranda. He had no moves, no patter. Just a wilting dick and blood on his hands in the place of spit. He crawled away finally to puke in the toilet, thinking *I'll never be Potter. Never be that smooth.* He didn't even have a fucking suit.

He had her weighted, wrapped and sealed and halfway across the carpet to the door when his mobile went. He could feel his back giving out as he straightened up. No fucking way was he going to be able to do this on his own.

"Where are you, Dennis?"

"I'm down the local wine bar, Potter. Me and Miranda decided to go out for cocktails."

"Fuck off, smart arse."

Dennis couldn't hear Potter's motor this time. No traffic. Nothing. Potter had gone quiet. Then something clattered. It sounded like furniture being broken, plates being dropped in a sink.

"She fucked me over, Dennis. Her and the rent boy. I think the cunt intended to do me in."

There was a pause and Dennis heard his own laboured breathing returning to his ear. *I fucking know she was about to do you in, mate,* he thought, but said, "What do you want me to say, Potter? Some spoilt bitch and one of your bum boys got the better of you? Why should I give a shit? I'm just your lackey." He felt some justifiable anger rising inside him, making his fists clench. *Good for you, sweetheart,* he thought, glancing at the body at his feet.

"I need another favour, Dennis. Last one."

Jesus wept. "Go on."

"I want you to go around to Miranda's. Leave her at the flat for now. We'll sort it out tomorrow night if we have to. I need to find this little fucker who's got my money."

Dennis smiled. He'd figured the scenario out from Potter's previous criminal endeavours. "Maybe he's still out sucking daddy's cock. Is that what he had to do for you? A few pictures of them in the act, couple of phone calls to threaten the poor old sod after. Miranda in the middle as the go-between; daddy's got no idea she's in on it. Am I right? Pictures'd look lovely in the *News of the World*.

"But then daddy's little girl turns out to be more than just a posh shag, but actually has the bollocks to go behind your back with your own rent boy. Christ, Potter, you must feel like a right *wanker.*"

Potter yawned for effect in his ear. Weary of it all, disaffected. But Dennis knew he was on the verge of defeat. "Just do this for me, Dennis, eh? Lock up behind you. Miranda's keys must be somewhere — "

"In her bag, I know. What do you want me to do if this rent boy shows his face?"

Potter sighed. "Detain him," he said.

Miranda had a flat in the basement of a Georgian terrace in Earls Court, three roads away from the station. Dennis parked his car on the corner and fished out his glasses so he could have a look up and down the street before making a move. The taxi radio stuttered at him until he turned it off. When the street seemed clear he crossed over quickly, hurried past the iron railings and down the steps, swivelling the wedding band through his glove as he went. There was a little bit of Miranda's blood on it now. He missed her face suddenly, as much as Ingrid's or Lizzie's, which just depressed him. He wasn't sure what he wanted. These roads were leading him in circles, one strange flat to another. Walking around in the footsteps of a dead girl. A clever dead girl at that. Given Potter more than the run around. It was a shame she'd had to go and get herself bumped off like that. It would have been a neat trick, someone fucking Potter over for a change.

The place was cold and full of shadows flung by streetlights on the pavement above. The smell of Potter's aftershave still lingered in the air. Dust suspended in the headlights of cars spilling by. Expensive furniture. Too much space for Dennis's liking. His shadow paced him around the room. He felt like he was still in that poxy film, the one he'd forgotten the ending to.

There was no thrill to walking around in someone else's house anymore. Breaking and entering was something you did at seventeen, not when you were knocking on forty. Still. He had the keys; he was almost a friend of the family.

He wasn't sure what he intended to do if the rent boy arrived. Probably shake the little bastard's hand. He had a grudging respect for anyone with an eye for the main chance, no matter how young they were. He picked up a few broken pieces of glass, presumably Potter's pissed off handiwork and left it on a table in the eventuality of someone turning up, then went for a nose around in Miranda's bedroom.

It wasn't until he'd rifled through her underwear drawer that Dennis noticed that the sheets on the bed were in disarray. When he bent to smooth them, smelling a hint of Miranda, he spotted the crumpled fifty that had dislodged from the pillow and fell to the floor. He smiled. Picked it up. Held it to the light.

"Ah, Miranda," he said to the silence, "I think I'm in love with you, sweet."

Dennis only discovered the message from Julian the rent boy once he'd stopped looking. With the fifty quid already burning a hole in his pocket, he'd gone through the bedside cabinet, then the wardrobes, the laundry basket, thinking perhaps the money had been stashed somewhere, and Potter simply hadn't had the patience to find it.

After quarter of an hour all he'd got was his shirt soaked to his back again. Cuffing sweat out of his eyes, he sat down in the pools of shadow on the floor, and stared up out of the window. A taxi stuttered by every couple of minutes or so, stealing his custom. Fifty quid probably didn't cover what he'd lost fucking around with corpses, cleaning up, running around for someone. He always seemed to be on the periphery; always the satellite, never the planet. He felt lost. Rootless. Suddenly he had the urge to simply see his daughter, spinning aimlessly in their old back garden, running after the dog, playing him up, grabbing his tail. A savage empty feeling in Dennis's gut assailed him, right there on the floor, and he had to put his hands down to steady himself.

His glove came to rest on a pair of jeans, crumpled and rolled beneath the bed. He saw Miranda, ever the butterfly, fluttering into this room just hours earlier, peeling off clothes, changing into the oyster pink slip that she'd died in, kicking off the discarded jeans, thinking about how she'd put Potter's lights out and keep the plan going...

There was a little piece of paper still inside her jeans pocket, folded into a tiny envelope. The pain momentarily forgotten, Dennis fished it out, fumbled his glasses back up the bridge of his nose. Initially he was disappointed. No 'Dearest Miranda'; no proclamations of undying love; no murderous blueprints for her to follow to the letter; no midnight fears confessed. Instead there was merely an address: a house number, a road and a town he couldn't pronounce, somewhere in France, and on the reverse simply the words: 'I'll be here. I will see you in a month's time. Julian'.

Dennis stared at it for a while, thinking. He hoisted himself to his feet then, and fumbled his way back into the front room. Julian wasn't coming. Julian was in all probability on a ferry by now, clutching a holdall full of cash. Dover to Calais, and away. Guts full of nerves at customs. English Channel churning his lunch up, over the side. Trying to think of Miranda. Keep her in mind. Just a month to wait for his butterfly. And all that fucking money to spend between them.

Dennis paused in the darkness. Hesitant. Uncertain. Potter might turn up soon, and there were things to be done that he could hardly admit to himself just yet. But this was it. Finally, this was it. Finally fitting the hole everyone had been trying to slide him into since his youth. It felt like stepping off a roof and finding you actually had some fucking wings.

After leaving a choked-up message on Ingrid's answer machine for Lizzie, he turned off his phone, locked up behind him and made his way back to the car. He had a bit of a drive ahead of him.

Julian is walking past the bookstore when he sees the headline on the English tabloid, nestled below the French broad sheets. He has to steady himself against the window, his legs threatening to give way beneath him. An old man, his face flushed with cold in his scarf and coat takes Julian's few francs from him, hands him the paper silently. His fingers are like wood, his skin like parchment.

Julian sits at a nearby cafe where the tables outside have chairs still upturned on them. His ears are roaring against the silence of the streets in the small town. At this time of the morning, they are as still as a churchyard. He can smell fresh bread somewhere. A bell rings in a courtyard down the avenue: it is ten AM. A cyclist passes him quietly and Julian feels an ache, heavy in his chest as he reads the headline. Miranda is dead. Murdered in a bedsit in Seven Sisters. He reads it twice, places his fingers over her picture. Everything is wrong now. Everything is fucked. Suddenly he feels tired and almost impossibly sad. He tries to remember the last words they said to each other, and remembers that they were, in jest, 'au revoir' of course. The cafe owner hovers nearby, slightly embarrassed at Julian's tears. Eventually he retreats without speaking.

Julian returns to the farmhouse which used to belong to his mother before she died: a small stone building in disrepair beside a river (where he'd intended to swim with Miranda come the summer) and a sudden sprawl of cornfields. The house offers no solace now; it will never house Miranda's scent; never have her shoes, kicked off in the hallway, her dresses tossed over a chair, her make-up in the bathroom. He is aimless again as he was when cruising the hotel foyers and bars, whoring himself to husbands and widows and God only knew who else, living off the *momentum* of it all.

The rooms are chilled with winter light. Julian stands over a radiator, beside a window with his hands clutching the cold iron. The rooms feel huge suddenly. There's no promise to them anymore, just the odour of stale tobacco, sweat and perfume. He feels as if his life has simply stopped.

When he looks out of the window he spots someone, a man moving away through the cornfield, towards the dark crowded roofs and spires of the town. He is too distant to see clearly. A sudden sense of alarm falls over Julian. He hurries to the bedroom, to the wardrobe, and finds the padlocks he fitted onto it last night forced open. He falls to his knees, pushes past his shirts and trousers, and finds with a sudden wash of vertigo that the holdall has been taken. By the time he bursts out of the house and into the cornfields, the man he spotted is out of sight. The money is gone.

For a time he cannot move, and so he simply stands there, his face in his hands. The air is fragrant. Birds are fluttering about the dovecote. A breeze ripples the corn, and it rolls like the sea. Then, Julian returns to the house, his every footstep huge and isolated in the empty rooms.

There is a photograph placed on the kitchen table, clearly left by the thief. It is a picture of Miranda that he took a few months ago. Taken in the sunshine at the seaside, she is laughing into the camera. Hair flying in her face, seagulls diving out over the sea. Pure happiness. It makes his heart swell until tears are rolling down his cheeks. He feels lost. Rootless.

Julian sits there all day, until the last of the light has gone from the rooms, and he can no longer see Miranda's face. Eventually he rises, closes the windows, locks the door and goes to the bathroom. He empties all of the pills he can find in the cabinet into the sink and takes them, a handful at a time. Then he falls into bed and wishes himself away to Seven Sisters. ∎

THE TTA LITERARY PRIZES 2000

£2000 IN PRIZES • CLOSING DATE 31/12/00

There is a first prize of £1000, a runner-up prize of £500 and five second runner-up prizes of £100 each.

No entry form is required, and writers may enter as often as they wish provided each individual entry is accompanied by an entry fee of £5/US$8. Cheques (including dollar checks), postal orders etc should be made payable to 'The TTA Literary Prizes'.

Stories will be considered within the categories of science fiction, horror, fantasy and slipstream fiction (eg crime with an element of horror, surrealism, etc). Entries must be no longer than 6000 words and must be original work in English which has not been previously published in any form. Entries must not be under consideration for any other competitions, under current consideration for publication or currently awaiting publication.

Stories must be typed double spaced on single sheets of A4/US Letter paper. The title page must carry the entrant's name, address and contact telephone number and/or email address. The title of the story must appear on each subsequent page, but no other author details must be shown. Pages must be clearly numbered.

Entries should be sent to Prizes Administrator Peter Tennant at 9 Henry Cross Close, Shipdham, Thetford, Norfolk IP25 7LQ, England, and must be received by the closing date of 31st December 2000. Manuscripts cannot be returned, so please retain a copy for your records. Stories should be accompanied by a stamped self-addressed postcard (self-addressed postcard with IRC for overseas entries) if acknowledgement of safe receipt is required.

A shortlist of stories will be forwarded by the Prizes Administrator to an independent panel of judges who will make the final decision. The judging panel consists of a professional author, a publisher's representative and a literary agent.

CLIFF BURNS

DAUGHTER

Cliff Burns has well over a hundred published stories to his credit, in magazines like Prairie Fire, Canadian Fiction Magazine, The Antigonish Review, The Silver Web, Prism International, On Spec and Gauntlet. In 1991 his short story collection Sex and Other Acts of the Imagination garnered excellent reviews and much praise. This was followed by various chapbooks and poetry/prose collections, and in 1997 by the full-length The Reality Machine (Black Dog Press). A second story collection, The Daddy Monster and Other Urban Legends (which will include 'Daughter'), will be published shortly, and he is currently working on a novel, feature films and radio plays.

Jasper comes in just as supper's nearly ready. The rest of us pick up on his mood right away and it gets really quiet in the kitchen, everyone waiting.

"We're moving out, Family," he says, trying to make like it's no big deal but meanwhile we're all looking at each other and thinking *here we go again*.

So we start packing everything up, supper and all, trying our best to ignore our growling stomachs.

Everyone has their job to do. Faye takes care of the kitchen and Little Todd and me load everything we own — which ain't much — into the one box we're allowed between the two of us.

"Quick, quick, my lovelies," Faye calls, but by now she should know better. Little Todd is only six but he works as hard as anyone and I'm already finishing up in the bathroom, grabbing the shampoo, Jasper's razor and whatever else in there that's worth taking.

Jasper waits beside the car, taking the stuff as we bring it out to him and shoving it all into the back seat. The trunk is too full with his things but, like I said, none of us has much anyway.

"All aboard," Jasper says, really pleased with how quick everything goes, how soon we're backing out of the driveway and heading down the street, leaving our problems (hopefully) far behind us.

I don't look back and feel no regrets about leaving. We never stay anywhere long enough to form any kind of relationships. That old house was just somewhere to live and after a few more moves I'll hardly even remember it.

Faye hands me some chicken, still warm, and I peel off a piece and offer it to Little Todd. Faye flashes me a real nice smile for being such a good sister to him but I can see from her eyes how tired and frazzled she is. And I'd say by the way Jasper keeps checking the mirror that he's jumpy too only trying not to let on because, after all, we're under God's special protection and that makes us completely safe from any kind of danger and tribulations.

Or so Jasper says and tonight, more than any other night, I surely hope he's right.

It's another long drive but Little Todd and me are real practised at sleeping on the road. Jasper never tells us where we're going and sometimes I get the idea he isn't sure himself, he's just following his nose or whatever. He says we go where we're guided and it's hard to argue when he puts it like that. And it wouldn't do you any good even if you tried. He can quote chapter and verse, prove he's right a hundred different ways from Sunday. Sometimes when he's drunk he makes us all get up and listen to him talk even if it's, like, three in the morning. It gets kind of scary. He speaks in different voices. Sometimes he nods off and drools down the front of his shirt. Faye says it's all part of being in the Spirit and sends us back to bed so she can deal with him.

Jasper asks her to sing him a song and Faye, tired as she is, is happy to oblige. Usually it's a song of praise but sometimes she surprises us. For instance, it's no secret that Jasper just *loves* Bob Dylan. We all know 'Like A Rolling Stone' by heart. I guess you could say it's kind of our theme song.

We drive all night long and on into the next day. Finally, in the early afternoon, Jasper gets the word (or whatever) and we turn off the highway into a town that looks almost *exactly* like the one we just left, same color and everything. He stops at a telephone booth near a gas station, looks through the Yellow Pages and makes a few calls. Then he hops back in and we're off again, Jasper getting us to help him follow the signs until we're pulling into a parking lot in front of an ugly, grey building with slits for windows. Jasper goes inside to arrange things and the rest of us are left to wait, sweltering in the sun. Little Todd is dozing again so we have to practically whisper: "What's the name of this town again?"

"Manley," Faye says, yawning, "just across the state line." Giving me another one of her soft as a feather smiles. "You tired of all this driving, Miss Jo?" Knowing how much I like it when she calls me that.

I stretch, jostling Little Todd's head in my lap — he grunts like a piglet but doesn't wake up. "I'm okay," I answer because in this Family we don't whine, whinge or complain.

She reaches back and runs her fingers through my hair. "Have to give you a trim. You know Jasper doesn't like long hair on girls."

"On *anybody*," I correct her, pointing at Little Todd's bristly skull.

Not much later, Jasper comes out the door followed by a fat man in a wide, blue suit and the two of them shake hands. They're both smiling like they got the better end of the deal. The fat man bends down so he can see through the windshield and waggles his chubby fingers at us. I politely wave back but Faye doesn't even bother.

Not only does Jasper have keys but also a hand-drawn map to our new place.

"Any trouble?" Faye asks him and Jasper grins.

"The Lord is our Shepherd and Protector," he says. "And not only that," he adds, waiting for us to join in like we always do, "He deals in cold, hard cash…"

Thanks to Jasper, devoted servant of the Good Lord Almighty, the Family's needs are always provided for. He's real good with his hands, Jasper is, in more ways than one. He can work construction, he can cut glass, he can fix almost anything except a broken heart (ha ha) and, as he himself puts it, he can steal like a heathen. Of course, as long as it's for the good of the *Family*, stealing is never bad or evil. It serves a higher power. I'm using Jasper's words because I've never figured out why it's bad for everyone else and yet all right for us. Jasper can give you about a dozen different reasons, depending on which day you ask him, so I guess it's all right but deep down inside I still think that a sin is a sin, no matter who does it.

I hear Jasper say that he paid the fat man for the first three months rent in advance and I have to grin because if we stayed anyplace for three months that would be some kind of a world's record for us.

When he stops in front of the house it's not bad. No broken windows or beer bottles in the front yard. Matter of fact, it looks quite decent and respectable, a house any ordinary family would live in. Jasper looks at Faye, waiting to see what she thinks and she leans over and gives him a kiss. "Aw, honey," she says, "it's *perfect*."

That afternoon, after I've put all my stuff away — which, let's face it, doesn't take very long — I'm sort of wandering around out in the backyard when I see her.

She stands on the sidewalk beside her house, wearing one of those backpack things, watching me, just staring kind of rude like. I pretend not to notice her. She must get the message because when I look up again, she's gone inside. Then I feel bad for chasing her away. Then I wonder how I ever got to be such a weird, screwed up kid.

I think in my heart I already know what's going to happen. I know that Jasper will see that girl and want her. She's nothing like Andie but she's pretty and perfect like Andie was. A little living doll.

Do you know the difference between a little girl…

Good old Jasper.

It's like somehow he knew she was going to be here.

Jasper comes in to say good night and that's when I tell him about the girl next door, thinking to myself, *well, he was gonna find out sooner or later...*

He asks a few questions and keeps his eyes on mine the whole time I'm answering. Neither of us mentions Andie's name but she's here in the room with us, all around, like clear smoke.

After she died we all became different people, smaller and meaner than we used to be. We each had our separate reasons for loving her and missing her. She was *his* special girl and *my* best friend. The closest thing to a sister I'll ever have.

Andie and me used to talk after everyone else was asleep. She was a year and a half older and nearly ready for a bra and easily the wisest, coolest person I've ever met. Like she always knew when Jasper was gonna start drinking again and what nights to make sure she slept with her jeans on under her nightie. Sometimes, during the worst of it, I'd hear her praying but so softly that I could never make out what she was saying.

After Jasper leaves I lie there listening to Little Todd snore. Somewhere in the house Faye and Jasper are talking, maybe about me, maybe about that girl next door. I'm glad she doesn't look much like Andie. I'm glad I already don't like her much. If she was more like Andie it would make it harder...because then it would be like she never actually got away, never gave up, never died, never *won*.

"How come you don't go to school?" Melissa asks me. We're sitting on the swings in her yard, just dangling our feet and still getting acquainted. I'm working very hard to make her trust me and like me so I put up with her questions, at least for now.

"Faye — my mother teaches me."

"Is that *allowed*?"

I bunch up my shoulders. "I guess."

"What does your dad do?"

"Fixes stuff."

"Like what?"

Another shrug. I'm already bored with her. "Everything." Then it's my turn. "How old are you?"

"I'll be ten this December." Andie's birthday was April 29th.

"That's good."

She doesn't ask about *my* birthday. Actually she's quite a bit stuck up and I don't like her at all. She's going to have some hard lessons ahead and a totally different idea about what being in a *real* Family is all about.

"Ya wanna go inside and play Nintendo?" This about the fourth time she's brought up her stupid, fancy video game.

"Sure." We leave the swings and head toward the house.

"Are you going to be staying in town a long time?"

I smile at the back of her head but she doesn't feel it. "Long enough," I tell her and that's pretty much all I'm gonna say on that particular subject.

Our Family doesn't have Nintendo or a VCR or a microwave oven even. I have one pair of shoes and two pairs of pants. I really like reading but I only own two books to my name, *Little Women* and *Harriet the Spy*. Little Todd can't read and doesn't seem too interested in learning. He has a couple of trucks and a bag of marbles and that's good enough for him. See, the Family doesn't care much for *things* and we pretty much spend whatever money Jasper brings home on food and bills and the rest we save for rainy days. When he can't find good, honest work, Jasper sells something out of our trunk. Once it was a brand new computer, still in its original box, and that was because we needed new tires for the car.

In no time at all I become Melissa's best friend and pal. Pretty soon she's telling me all about her life, stuff even her *mom* doesn't know. Or so she says.

Of course, I never let on that I couldn't care less about what's going on in her creepy little world. And just to get even, I tell Jasper *everything* she says. He seems really pleased with me lately. One night he tries to give me a whiskery kiss but I hold my old stuffed frog up between us and we both act like it's a joke.

I don't like the lovey-dovey stuff but it's good that he trusts me again. Ever since Andie died I've had the feeling that he's been *watching* me, though I guess that could be just my imagination. So I'm really giving it my best with Melissa, showing him that I'm still Family, ready to do whatever I'm asked with no questions or back-talk. With Jasper, you don't want him thinking it's any other way. 'Cause, you know, as far as he's concerned, there's *Family* and then there's everybody else in the world…

Faye and me are working in the kitchen when there's a knock on the door. We give each other a quick look to make sure we both heard it and then I go and see who it is.

Melissa is home from school early and wants to visit. Stands there with that look on her face, waiting to be asked in. So I guess I don't have a choice, do I?

But Faye and me pretend it's the most natural thing in the world and let on like we were just about to have tea. Meanwhile, Melissa's checking everything out, naturally seeing the boxes and the fact that we have hardly any furniture or knick-knacks and all.

After we finish our tea and cookies I try to get her to go outside but instead she decides she wants to see my room, so off we go. She stares at the sleeping bags on the floor and bare walls and Little Todd in his underwear, watching her, kind of frozen with shock. There's no clothes, no dresser, no *nothing*.

"Are you really, really *poor*?" she goes, once we're safely outside and perched on our swingseats.

"Not really. It's not like we can't afford things, it's just that we don't *need* them." Standing up for the Family just like I've always been taught to.

"But you don't even have a *TV*," she says, her eyes all buggy.

Before I can answer that, Jasper comes along, whistling to himself and, of course, he sees the two of us or, anyway, he sees *her*. "Afternoon, ladies," he calls, walking over to get a good, close look. "So you're Melinda, are you?" he says, acting really friendly and smiling with his eyes. "How do you do?" Melissa ducks her head down and Jasper gives me a quick little nod. Right then it's settled.

From that moment on, it's only a matter of time.

Andie always worried about what would happen if Jasper ever found out I helped her. Not that I did much. Basically, all I had to do was wait and watch (which was hard enough). I remember I held her hand. Once it was done I had to crawl back into bed and try to *sleep*, for God's sake, sleep like I had no idea of what I would be waking up to.

Andie never read *Little Women*. She told me the title alone scared her off. She asked me once if I knew the difference between a little girl and a little woman. Then, without waiting for an answer, she said: "The difference is, little *girls* don't understand…"

Jasper always says there's no such thing as luck, that the Good Lord Himself takes a personal interest in our Family. Well, I guess the Good Lord must have been looking the other way last night because, guess what, Jasper finally gets busted and we wake up to cops at our door at eight in the morning.

Turns out they're both young and really nice and polite, telling us that Jasper has been arrested and there are a number of charges. The bail isn't going to be too high, nothing our secret stash can't handle. The cops don't say much, just that Jasper was spotted creeping around in a lumber yard after closing and a 66-year-old security guard put the grab on him. They've impounded the car and are getting a warrant to search it. Faye plays it really cool, like she's sure there's been some kind of mistake, wondering if they could maybe recommend a good lawyer here in town... She even lets the cops come in for a quick look around. Not that we have anything to hide. After they leave, she calls the lawyer and gets the ball rolling. By the time she hangs up it sounds like Jasper is as good as sprung, but the final price looks to be pretty steep. Faye takes the shoebox out from under the sink, grabs a wad of money and gets me to call her a cab.

I suspect we won't be hanging around Manley much longer, so after breakfast I start Little Todd packing in our room while I box up the kitchen stuff, piling everything by the door. It takes us almost till noon but we pretty much finish the whole house. I'm sitting on the back step, taking a break, when Melissa comes home for lunch. She waves at me from the other side of the fence...but then she sees the boxes beside me and catches on to what's happening. "Are you *leaving*?" she asks, hanging her arms over to the fence and looking pouty.

"Yeah," I say, not bothering to lie because what's the point.

"Did your dad get a job someplace else?"

"He ain't my dad." She stares at me and I decide to cool it. "He's...kind of my step-dad, you know?" She nods like she does.

Just then her mom calls out the window: "Melissa? Ask your friend if she wants to join us for dinner." I can hear it in her voice: good ol' Melissa has been telling her how bad off and starving we are and now mommy wants to play the Good Samaritan...and maybe pump me with a few questions besides —

I hear a car pull up out front and right then and there make the decision, no time to think about it, hardly any time at all. "You better go inside," I tell Melissa, practically growling at her. "And tell your mom we ain't poor, we're just not stuck-up snobs about it." I can see I've hurt her feelings but maybe not enough. "Don't you get it?" I snap at her. "I can't be your friend any more, okay? We're never gonna see each other again so just...*go away*, will you?"

She sort of stumbles back from the fence and halfway to her house has to cover her face with her hands. Once she's inside she must really cut loose because through the open window I can hear her mom again, asking her *what's wrong, honey, what's wrong*.

Faye and Jasper come walking around the side of the house, talking, laying plans for our daring escape. He nods at all my hard work and gives me the keys to the car so I can start loading.

Now that I know Melissa won't be coming with us, I feel a lot better about things. I have to admit, sometimes it gets lonely and it would be nice, you know, to have someone to hang out with and talk to...but then I think about how hard it would be for her, getting used to a whole new Family, living an entirely different life, everything else becoming just a dream.

I wonder if her parents would ever stop looking for her. I wonder if they would ever forget their precious daughter. I wonder if they would still be able to recognize her, years later, and call her by her real name. ■

MARION ARNOTT

PRUSSIAN SNOWDROPS

Marion teaches English and History at St Andrew's Academy, Paisley and writes short stories because she's mad about the form. She has three children who are currently showing her how to operate a computer without terminal despair setting in. Her work has appeared in a wide variety of magazines.

Traudl arrived with the spring, which was sudden that year. Karl was taken
unawares by both, startled awake one glittering white night by the sound of the
spring thaw; the river cracked like a pistol shot and, in the shivering dark, began
to move through sundered ice. Karl's hot water bottles were flabby and chill as fish
on a slab and he cursed between chattering teeth: spring nights in Prussia were
noisy with crashing ice and gurgling water, howling wolves and the drip-drip of
melting icicles. He longed sleeplessly for the soft air of Berlin, gently gilded and
scented with hyacinths.

He longed even more once he met Traudl. He was crossing the square to the inn
that Sunday, when he saw what looked like a bundle of rags on the stone bench
beneath the statue of the Teutonic knight. He peered through fluttering sleet and
saw that the bundle was a woman, ugly, lumpen, and scowling ferociously.

"Your pardon, Gnädige Frau," he said before he walked on, shaken both by her
malevolence and a painful yearning for cheerful girls in stylish hats.

"Who was that, Ernst?" he asked when he joined the little company in the warm
corner beside the fireplace.

"Traudl," the schoolmaster said, tamping down his pipe.

The postmaster nodded. "I thought she had given that up. It must only have
been the winter kept her away."

"She reminded me of that story," Karl said. "You know, 'What big teeth you
have, Grandma!', 'All the better to eat you with, child'. I thought, any minute she's
going to spring and tear my throat out. Why is she sitting out there in the cold?"

"Waiting," the teacher said. "And before you ask what for, no one knows. She's
from the asylum — quite incoherent. All she'll say is that she's waiting. Every
Sunday afternoon she waits until darkness falls. And then she goes home."

The postmaster smirked into his bierstein. "I did hear one story. A man gave her
a kind word thirty years ago and said he'd be back soon. So she waits in hope."

Karl sniggered. "That face never had a hope and has always known it."

"Well, then," Ernst said. "Hopelessly ugly, therefore no story to tell, therefore
not to be written about in *Tales From The Village*. Now who's for another beer?"

Karl was amused by the attempt to influence his articles; the teacher's status as
most educated villager, and the only one who had joined the Party *before* the Führer swept to power, had gone to his head; or rather to his flat cheeks which puffed
out like a hamster's whenever he recalled that fact. He insisted that the Tales reflect well on his village, and Karl made sure they did when he whiled away long
Prussian nights with schnapps and purple prose. The villagers, he had written,
helpless with laughter at the thought of the schoolmaster's coterie of turnip-witted
farmers, were purest Aryan stock, a living link with Germany's heroic past; soul
brothers of the men who had fought Roman, Turk, and Russian and poured their
blood into the soil, making it theirs forever; of the same Germanic tribe admired by
the noble Tacitus for virtuous beautiful women and merciless moral men.

Blood and soil and heroes made the schoolmaster's spectacles mist with emotion;
Karl never knew how he kept his face straight while the tedious little man polished
them clear. Even funnier, the Führer himself had proclaimed the Tales inspirational,
which only confirmed Karl's opinion of the Führer, and since then, the villagers
had bombarded Karl with local legends of the Knights of the Teutonic Order, heroic
resistance to Jew landlords, and of Aryan bloodlines untainted since the Dark Ages.

Karl put them all in his column. They were his living, and possibly a ticket
back to Berlin, hurriedly abandoned after his coverage of the Führer's reception
for the world's ambassadors. The sight of booted blackshirts displaying courtly
manners and a knowledge of fine art — the Führer had issued a general order
that they should — was hilarious enough, but when they got drunk, groped the

French ambassador's wife and dumped her in the fountain along with her protesting husband, he lost all sense of self-preservation and reported it. Half Berlin sniggered, the other half wanted his blood. "What you must remember," his editor said, "is that Nazis have no sense of humour. East Prussian office for you until things cool down." "But there's nothing to report there," Karl protested. "Find something," the editor said, "something not funny." Karl found *Tales From The Village*.

Karl sighed. The schoolteacher was telling him of his plans to revive an ancient summer solstice festival: bare-breasted blonde Valkyries holding sheaves of corn, together with bare-chested blonde Titans wielding swords, would re-enact an authentic pagan sacrifice in the water meadows.

The flow of scholarly claptrap was interrupted by the arrival of the beer. "My round, meine Herren," Karl beamed. The answering smiles displayed broken brown teeth and cavernous gaps. The sight plunged Karl into despair: you'd think there'd be dentists, even in East Prussia. He averted his eyes, and through the sleet blooming on the window pane, glimpsed Traudl, solid as a boulder wrapped in a blanket. The prospect of dozens like her displaying their all among the wheat sheaves rendered him speechless, and the schoolmaster, mistaking his silence for interest, began describing an entire calendar of pagan festivals. Karl sighed heavily.

Traudl was under the statue every Sunday. Karl always met her unwavering stare with a polite bow and a "Good afternoon, gnädige Frau." This was brave of him because her intensity made him nervous, and it provoked the schoolmaster to pontificate on the subject of degeneracy. He would steeple his fingers under his chin and say, "And now if I may move on to matters esoteric," and serve Karl, the only man in the village with sufficient intellect to understand him, a dollop of Nazi science.

The day that Traudl first spoke to Karl, the schoolteacher passed the afternoon blaming the high incidence of imbecility in East Prussia on the proximity of the Polish border. Karl struggled not to laugh as he imagined diseased Slavic wits drifting across the frontier like dandelion seeds seeking out a hapless Aryan womb to root in. Ernst claimed that Traudl was a mongrel produced by a Polish father and a morally degenerate mother, and that in spite of the best efforts of the Party, that kind of unregulated breeding would continue to degrade Aryan bloodlines until the Führer's programme for purifying racial stock was carried out —

Karl smothered a yawn and the schoolmaster rebuked him mildly. "Sometimes, Karl, I don't think you take eugenics entirely seriously."

"On the contrary," Karl smiled, "I was remembering the last time the Führer spoke on the subject. We ended the rally with the *Horst Wessel Lied*. It was most moving. You know, Ernst, we must get you to Berlin so that you can experience it all for yourself."

The teacher, who never cared to be reminded that he had never personally witnessed the Reich's ceremonies, resumed lecturing. He had devised a course on eugenics for his village pupils: responsible breeding, the duty of individuals to the race, sterilisation of the unfit and so on, and he thought perhaps that Karl might care to write a little something about his work.

Karl nodded enthusiastically, stopped listening, and thought about the rally. He and Siggi and Friedrich had been as drunk as lords and bawled out the first verse of the *Horst Wessel Lied* because it was the only one they knew; then gradually they realised that everyone else knew all the verses, every last turgid one, which seemed to them hysterically funny. "They're word perfect," Friedrich said. "No one but a man of genius could have inspired them to it. We have underestimated the Führer." Siggi said that the Führer would rise in his estimation when they could all sing in tune and as he spoke, the arc lights which blazed a cathedral's vaulted ceiling across the night sky were suddenly extinguished, and they found themselves giggling into a black void, unable to stop.

Karl looked out of the inn window to hide another grin. Traudl was out there as usual, sitting in the shadow of the knight, waiting. She could have been a statue herself, she sat so still, except that sometimes she tilted her head as if she were listening. Karl followed her gaze. She had a view along the river and the road which wound beside it; and in the far distance, the ruined church in the water meadows, its collapsed tower, its roofless walls, its screen of naked trees piercing the pale glassy sky. She was looking at nothing and listening to nothing and waiting for something to come of it all, which, he decided, made her no more feeble-witted than half Germany.

It was night when she spoke to him. He was weaving unsteadily back to his lodgings in the thickening darkness, slithering across icy cobbles, when she stepped out of an alley and stood in his path. Her accent was coarse, her voice harsh. "Mein Herr, I have been waiting for you."

She was nervous, but determined. Karl bowed, trying not to notice her troglodyte eyebrows. "Gnädige Frau, it is late and very cold. Some other time."

"A word. Only a word." Her face in the acid light of the wrought iron street lamp was yellow and surly. "A word can't hurt, can it?"

No, he thought, and a smile wouldn't either. Then, seeing the heavy bony face darken to jaundice, decided that it wouldn't help in the slightest. "Another time. Next Sunday."

He made to pass her by, but she seized him his arm with surprising strength.

"Not in the village. They wouldn't like that."

"Who wouldn't?"

"The schoolmaster. The postmaster."

Karl hiccoughed and reclaimed his arm. "Gnädige Frau, the schoolmaster may like or dislike as he pleases. It is a matter of impreme sudifference to me. Supreme indifference." He giggled and shook his head.

"Are you laughing at me?"

"Not at all. I am drunk, as you see. In no condition for a gossip. Gnädige Frau, good evening."

She came after him, her heavy boots thumping dully on stone cobbles. "I have money. You can have it all." She snatched at him, but he twisted away, fell, and lay dazed while she fumbled in a woollen stocking cap which she fished out of her pocket. She was breathing heavily and he was suddenly afraid — *what big teeth you have, Grandma* — but it was only money she pulled from the cap, wads of *Reichsmarks* tied up with string. She loomed over him, yellow-fanged and panting, trying to push the notes into his hand. "All for you," she gasped.

Her excitement alarmed him. He had heard of women possessed by erotic fantasies; there had been a case in Berlin, a bloodied knife —

She hauled him up by the lapel of his coat. "The money," she said. "Take it. You do something for me. An easy thing."

"Please," he said, thrusting the money back at her, "there's nothing I can do for you."

"A letter. Write me a letter. That's all."

He blinked and swayed. "Gnädige Frau, what on earth would I write to you about?" He laughed and stepped back.

"*From* me. You write a letter from me."

"Why?"

"Because I can't write!" Anger flared like lightning in her dull eyes. "You write lots of things. It's not much to ask." Her voice deepened in desperation. "I can pay."

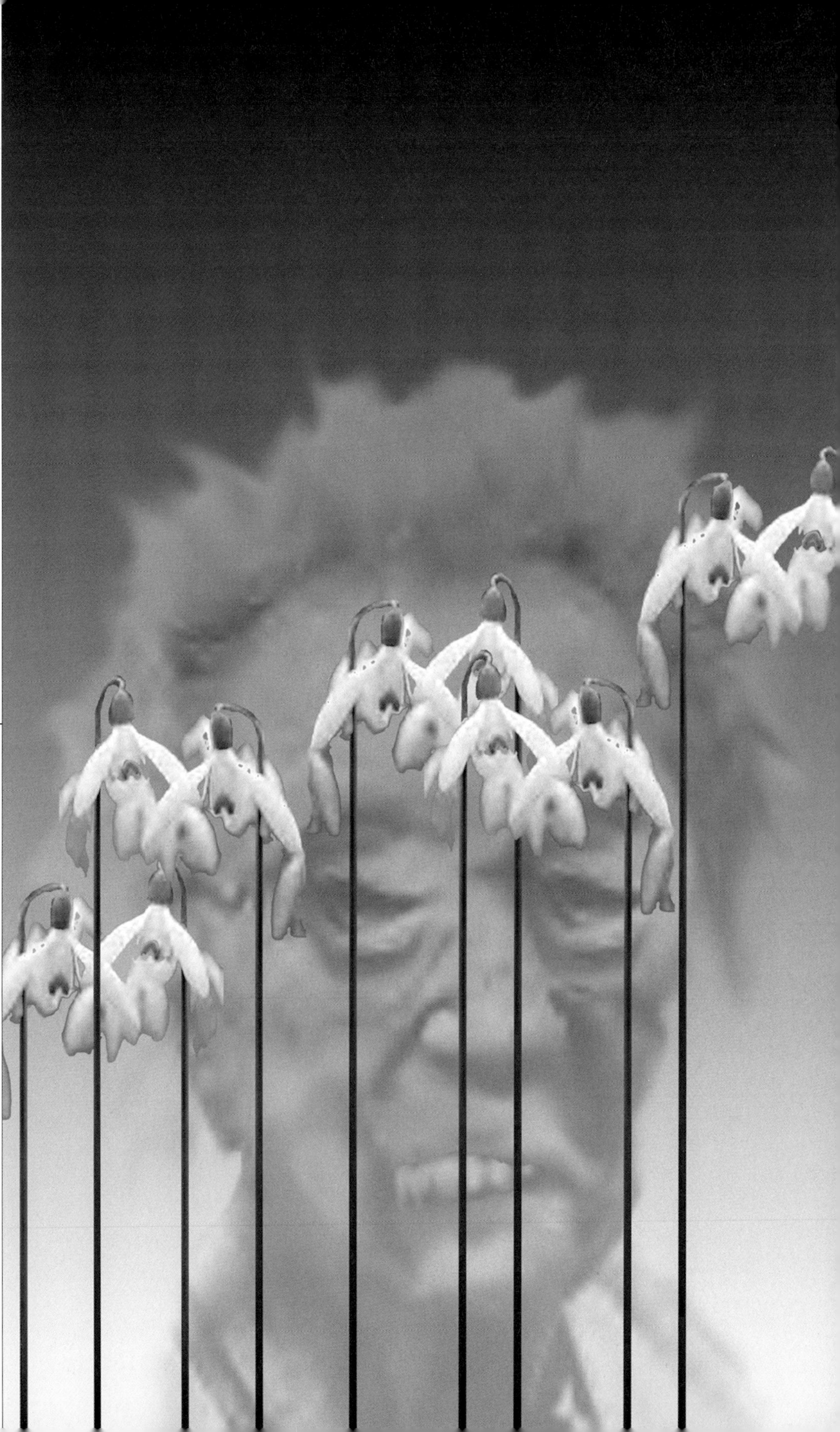

He hardly knew how he came to agree, but he did, partly from pity, partly because she wasn't going to go away unless he did, and partly from a humiliating fear of her flickering urgency. He salvaged his pride by grandly waiving payment, and then was in such a hurry to get away that he forgot to ask what kind of letter she wanted.

Karl wrote to Friedrich about the mystery of Traudl's letter: he imagined pleas to the Lost Lover to return, advertisements for the marriage columns (*I can pay!*), and postcards for display on the noticeboards of dubious nightclubs (*Honestly, I can pay!*).

His cousin's reply was prompt and full of Berlin gossip and their friend, Siggi, who was the subject of most of it. Siggi was in 'this-time-you've-gone-too-far-trouble' with the editor. He had drawn the weedier Party leaders — round shouldered under the weight of masses of silver braid and deathshead insignia — demonstrating the etiquette of saluting Nazi style: the full stiff-armed salute, delivered along with a stentorian 'Heil Hitler!', was given by inferiors to superiors; the half salute from the elbow, palm up, with a drawling 'Heil Hitler!' was a sign of very high rank; and a half salute, palm down, was terribly, terribly sweet and greeted with whistles and cries of 'Hello, darling!' from the prettiest boys in town. Respectable citizens were worried about giving the wrong impression, and Doktor Göbbels was incandescent with rage. Siggi could not see what all the fuss was about and felt he had, after all, shown considerable self-restraint by not drawing Göring in his Chinese silks and green nail polish.

Karl laughed at the cartoon which Friedrich had thoughtfully enclosed with his letter. The Party leaders reminded him of Ernst in his Sunday best SA uniform, self-important nonentities with an awesome talent for talking bilge. Siggi often said that listening to them was the penalty for living in the Age of the Common Man; he doubted that the Reich would last the promised thousand years, but judging by the amount of speechifying that went on, it was going to feel as if it had.

As for the Troglodyte, Friedrich wrote that there was hope for her yet: the Führer had promised every Aryan female a husband and decreed that it was a civic duty to breed for Germany. Siggi was ecstatic about it: all over Berlin, patriotic women were throwing themselves at men, pleading to be impregnated. The SS, flower of Aryan manhood, were the favoured target and Siggi was desperate to join but didn't think they'd let him in after the saluting business.

Karl's homesickness was particularly acute all that week.

On the following Sunday, Karl waited for Traudl at the appointed place and time: at the back door of his lodgings after his landlady had gone to church. "No one must see," Traudl had said. "No one."

He led her into the parlour. She was intimidated by Frau Haar's brutal cleanliness and would not sit down until the third invitation, and only then after she had stretched her woollen scarf under her boots to protect the linoleum. She hunched silently on the edge of her chair, staring at her big red hands lying loosely in her lap.

"Gnädige Frau — "

"I'm not married."

"Gnädiges Fräulein — "

Her quick upward glance revealed dull brown eyes lit by a reddish glow. "Are you laughing at me?"

"Your pardon?"

"That's how the Doktor speaks to the rich relatives. Me, I'm just Traudl."

"It was a courtesy, but…Traudl, if you prefer."

She stared him full in the face, making up her mind, and he was absurdly relieved when the light in her eyes faded to the colour of old stone and she resumed the study of her hands.

"You wanted a letter written, Traudl. Shall we begin?"

"I don't know how."

"What do you want to say?" he said, whittling a pencil to a point with a penknife. "And where do you want to send it?"

"I don't know."

An hour later, he had worked it all out: Traudl wished to notify her former employer that her services as a laundress were still available. The difficulty was that he had decamped in the night without leaving a forwarding address, a course of action with which Karl could sympathise if Herr Doktor Reichardt had been often exposed to Traudl's efforts at conversation. He told Traudl that without an address, it was impossible to write to the Doktor.

"But he must be somewhere."

"He could be anywhere."

"You're clever. You could find him."

"He could be anywhere. And perhaps he doesn't wish to be found."

She shook her head. "No. He was looking for the patients. To bring them home."

The mystery deepened. First, a mislaid Doktor, then mislaid patients. How careless Traudl had been! "I think, Traudl, that if the Doktor wishes to employ you again, he will be in touch."

Her heavy brow furrowed with the painfulness of thought. "How? He knows I can't read. And the telephone at the hospital doesn't work any more."

Unpaid bills, Karl decided. The good Doktor had fled his creditors. "Perhaps you should seek some other employment until the Doktor is settled again."

"He left me in charge," she said, shaking her head. "I have to look after his dog."

"Without an address, I can do nothing," he said kindly.

Her protests turned her complexion an ugly brick colour as she repeated over and over, "But he must be somewhere. You could find him."

Her disbelief and his denials collided across Frau Haar's hearth rug. Traudl rocked backwards and forwards in her chair, her fists clenched in her lap. "He told me he'd be back soon!" She made a sound somewhere between a growl and a whine. The scene was becoming distasteful.

Karl rose and crossed to the door. "I'm sorry, Traudl. Try the police. It is their job to find missing persons."

Her rocking stopped suddenly. "No!" She pounded her fists on her knees. "No! No! The Doktor said not to talk to them. They're bad."

"Then I don't know who can help you." Karl opened the door wider. "You must go now, Traudl. Frau Haar will be back shortly."

She lunged out of her chair. He sidestepped quickly, but she only swooped over the pencil shavings and scooped them up. "She likes things tidy," she said and blundered past him to the kitchen door. He heard the heavy boots thumping across the vegetable patch, then the creak of the back gate. When he looked, she was gone.

The morning wasn't entirely wasted; it gave Karl the opportunity to tease the schoolmaster. The little man drew Karl aside as soon as he arrived at the inn. "Karl," he said heartily. "You look well today. You have colour in your cheeks. The spring air?"

Karl nodded. "Delightful, isn't it? I didn't have to break the ice in the wash basin this morning and the electricity supply reappeared in the night. Suddenly life is full of promise."

"Karl..." The schoolmaster removed his spectacles and polished them, then folded his handkerchief neatly into his breast pocket. "The strangest story has come to my ears. Rumour has it that you were consorting with Traudl this morning."

"Consorting? What a quaint expression, Ernst."

"Of course, I said I found that hard to believe."

"That was thoughtful of you."

"An unlikely tale, isn't it?"

"If you say so."

"You're fencing with me, Karl," the schoolmaster said with a tight smile. "Is there any truth in it?"

"I don't know, Ernst. It depends what you mean by consorting."

"Then she did visit you this morning?"

"Yes, she did. I'm relying on you to keep that quiet, Ernst."

"Too late for that. People are wondering what you could possibly want with her."

"My business, surely?"

"Nevertheless, people are talking."

"There isn't much else to do on a Sunday afternoon." He took the schoolmaster by the arm and drew him over to the fire. "Except to sit in the warm and have a beer and some good conversation."

The schoolmaster returned to Traudl's visit several times, but Karl refused to be drawn and Ernst was reduced to a series of irritated harrumphs.

Karl wrote to Friedrich that night. 'My learned friend was so cross that he didn't mention his beloved Valkyries and pagans once. With any luck, he's going to ban me from attending his festivals. He did give some fatherly advice about keeping bad company. And a little lesson in eugenics. Because of her Polish blood, Traudl can be violent; because of her mother's depravity, she can be promiscuous. I'm not sure whether Ernst fears most for my virtue or my life.'

He had to end the letter there. The light flickered twice and went out and he couldn't find the matches to light the oil lamp. The drumming of the river filled the room; it seemed louder in the pitch dark. So did the wolves.

His next meeting with Traudl came after he heard from Friedrich again. 'Tell the Troglodyte,' Friedrich wrote, 'that her Doktor is dead. He committed suicide in the foyer of the Ministry of Health at Tiergarten No.4. Before he pulled the trigger, he said, "I can't live with the guilt." No one knows what he meant and, interestingly enough, no one wants to know. He was a respected psychiatrist and his death didn't even make the Stop Press. Siggi says the importance of a story can be measured by the silence it engenders; this silence is ricochetting round Berlin and everyone's running for cover. Even Siggi's friends, who are always in the know even when they aren't, declare to a man that they haven't heard about the very public suicide of Herr Direktor Reichardt or his guilt complex. They've never heard of Tiergaten 4 either. Since most of them pass it on the tram home, Siggi has concluded regretfully that they are all lying in their teeth. He is now in pursuit of what he is sure is a very nasty scandal.

'He has found a charwoman who saw Reichardt hanging around the foyer for days before he died. Every official was too busy to see him. That didn't surprise the char. She didn't approve of his unshaven appearance or his stale shirt or the way he paced up and down the foyer pushing his fingers through his hair. More than once she had to ask him to move so that she could mop the floor; he won her good opinion when he apologised charmingly for being in her way, but the poor gentleman didn't have make a mess of the marble tiles when he blew his brains out. Siggi wants you to quiz Traudl. He feels suicide is a massive over-reaction to an unpaid telephone bill. You're to find out how he lost his patients and what was worrying him. If necessary, you're to sacrifice your virtue.'

Karl knew Siggi was like a hound after truffles when it came to scandal. Accordingly, he left the inn early the following Sunday afternoon and waited in the alley, intending to startle Traudl for a change.

"Traudl!" he hissed and leapt out into the lamplight.

He felt foolish when she only hesitated for a moment before walking on. He fell into step beside her.

"Traudl. We must talk."

She plodded onward with a sulky bovine tread which made her chins tremble. Only East Prussia could produce such a creature, he thought; perhaps there was something to the schoolmaster's theories after all.

"Traudl, are you angry?"

"No."

"Yes, you are. No time for a chat tonight?"

"Nothing to say."

"You had lots to say last week."

"*You* didn't."

"I have now."

He could not see her expression. They had moved out of the circle of light under the lamp and the shadows had erased her features. She turned off the main street and took the narrow path down to the river.

"Where are you going, Traudl?"

"Home."

"May I come with you part of the way?"

They trudged along in silence. There were no lights beyond the village and Karl soon lost sight of her in the icy dark. The path sloped sharply downwards and was slippery with deep sucking mud. He clung to bushes and skeletal branches to steady himself.

"Traudl! Slow down!"

Her heavy tread never faltered, but her voiced floated back to him in the darkness. "Go back! I don't want to talk to you!"

"But it's about the Doktor!" The wind threw his words back at him — Doktor! Doktor! — and startled him. His foot caught on a root and he plunged headfirst down the slope into a cold slime of rotten leaves. He lifted his head and smelled the airy cleanness of open water nearby. There was a rustling movement in the inky darkness, and then Traudl was standing over him. She stooped and dragged him upright.

"Did you find him?"

"Let me catch my breath."

"Did you?" She tugged at his arm and swung him back and forth like a rag doll. He remembered big square laundress's hands which could wring blankets dry as easily as twisting a kiss curl. He could not tell her that the Doktor was dead, not out here in the lonely dark. There was no telling how she would react.

"I have news," he said. "Come to Frau Haar's and I will tell you."

"No, now."

"Frau Haar — "

"No. Not her house. Here."

"But — "

"Where is he?" she shrieked, shaking him harder.

"Berlin. He's in Berlin."

"Is it far?"

He laid a hand on hers and patted it tentatively. "Oh, yes, Traudl. Very far. And you don't know the way." He could feel her thinking and he grew cunning, remembering Friedrich's hopes of a spectacular scandal. "The Doktor's in trouble, Traudl. He needs your help before he can come home."

"The patients. Are they with him?"

"No, they're still lost."

"He said they'd be back. Like last time."

"Last time?"

"Yes. They all came back."

"But they haven't come back this time, have they?" Karl improvised wildly. "And everyone says it's the Doktor's fault." He detached himself carefully from Traudl's grasp. She stood immobile, gazing up at a black sky flecked with sparks of steel, and tilted her head as if she were listening. "Don't you want to help the Doktor, Traudl?" he asked softly.

She wrung her hands and shuffled from foot to foot. "I'm not to tell. The Doktor could get into trouble. Me too. I helped."

Karl moved closer to her. "But he's already in trouble, liebling."

She cracked her knuckles in her agitation. "Do the police know what we did?"

Karl felt one of his headaches coming on and wished he knew what they were talking about. "They've locked him up," he said desperately. "He must have done something bad to the patients."

"Not him. Never."

"Well, then, tell me about it. I'll write in the newspapers that he never did a bad thing, ever, and the police will let him out."

She whirled suddenly and stumped along the path. "No, I promised not to tell." She barged down the path, arguing with herself.

"Traudl! You must help me help the Doktor!"

She halted abruptly when she reached the river bank. "Is it help if I tell about the last time? The time they all came back? That's not a secret. Everyone knows. They only say they don't."

"I think it might help, yes."

Traudl decided quickly. She flopped down on to one of the large rocks which littered the river bank. "All right," she said and chewed at the cuff of her mitten. "All right. He didn't do bad things. The hospital was a good place after he came. He wasn't angry like the one before. No hitting with wet towels. No electric wires on us."

"Oh, that was kind," Karl said, taken aback. "Now, what was the 'last time' you were talking about, the time when they all came back?"

"That was later. He let me work and gave me money for it. I learned to be tidy and wash things. Nobody made the sheets as white as me." She halted on a note of coy pride until Karl murmured admiringly. "I ironed the little cloths for his breakfast tray. I never forgot. That was the first year he came."

"What trouble are you and the Doktor in, Traudl?"

"He said I was his best laundress. And a good talker too. I never talked before he came but he helped me. I don't talk to everyone. Just him and some of the patients. And you."

Karl silently cursed the good Doktor. Traudl was going to talk mountains of trivia — he knew the signs. And Siggi would kill him if he didn't listen. He gathered his coat around him and perched on the rock beside hers. She began talking and continued all through the night.

On his way home, he saw that dawn had turned the horizon ice pink on the far side of the river. Birch trees, black lace against the skyline, speared the new morning. What had she said? Little Heinrich was afraid of the birch trees and she always had to hold his hand to calm him down.

Frau Haar kept a respectable house and preferred that he keep respectable hours. Karl slipped into the house by the back door. In the hall, he put out a hand and touched the silver framed photograph of Frau Haar's grandchildren on the dresser. This was the frame Traudl had described, silver, etched with a pattern of feathers. It had been Elvi's frame, and Elvi had searched everywhere for it, crying for her mother's photograph. Frau Haar was the housekeeper and she was angry with Elvi for losing the picture the way she lost everything, the careless stupid halfwit, it was no wonder her father had had her locked up. Traudl knew all the time that Frau Haar had taken the frame — she liked pretty things — but she didn't say anything, because Frau Haar had a bunch of heavy keys and she often hit Traudl for staring too hard, or Elvi for crying and getting on her nerves.

Karl considered Frau Haar's love of pretty things. He tiptoed quietly to his room so as not to disturb his landlady. He didn't feel up to a smiling grandmotherly re-proof this morning.

He spent most of the day writing it all down for Siggi and Friedrich. Traudl's story had been like a country ramble down winding lanes and through thickets of detail, but he summarised it ruthlessly: 'In the summer of 1933, men came to the asylum. They were uniformed and had long boots and guns. The Doktor had argued with them for a long time in the hall, but they showed him papers. The Doktor telephoned to Berlin while the patients were being brought out; he shouted a lot until the man with the papers pulled the telephone wires out of the wall and asked which patients could work He didn't want any dangerous or very feeble-minded ones.

'The Doktor wouldn't tell, but Frau Haar took the men into the office where the files were kept. One of them stood in the doorway and called out names: Elvi and Maria and Detlef and lots of others. He called Traudl's name too, but the Doktor said she was an employee, not a patient, and the man burst out laughing. "Oh, I do apologise, Gnädige Frau."

'All the patients in the locked ward were left behind, but the rest were taken away. The men shouted and shoved them to make them go faster. Elvi cried and cried and one of the men said she was a pretty little silly who should play it smart and not make herself red-eyed and ugly. Then the Major came out in his old uni-form jacket with the Iron Cross on a ribbon. The man looked at his card. "What's wrong with him?" he asked. The Doktor told him the Major had shell-shock and that he was a war hero. The man with the white card saluted and told the Major to stay in the hospital because he had already done enough for Germany. All the soldiers smiled, but the Major was upset. His bad dreams came back and he scream-ed all night long. The Doktor said it was because of the guns.

'One other thing happened that night. Frau Haar said the patients wouldn't be spoiled where they were going. The Doktor slapped her face hard and told her to get out. She just stood there with her hand on her cheek and her mouth flapping open. She never came back again and the Doktor let Traudl be housekeeper, but there wasn't much work. There were hardly any patients left…'

Karl put his pen down and leaned back in his chair. Apart from a hiss of excite-ment at the telling of the slapping of Haar's face, Traudl might as well have recited a railway timetable. He had asked for details, but her memory was a repository for irrelevance: she didn't know the name of the man with the cards, the surnames of the patients, the date of the visit, or the name of any of the Berlin personnel that Reichardt had contacted. But Friedrich would out. This was going to be the Tale From The Village to end all Tales. Ernst was going to be furious! Karl picked up his pen again.

'And that's when she first started waiting,' he wrote. 'The Doktor got the phone fixed and phoned Berlin. He was promised his patients back when the road building season was over. He told Traudl they would come home soon, and all that summer on her afternoon off, she sat in the village square, watching the road for them. Little Heinrich had taken his flute and she listened for him piping the others home along the riverbank. She watched and listened and waited.

'They came back one frosty night in autumn in a big lorry. The Doktor came downstairs in his plaid dressing gown and signed papers and then opened the big front door. The patients came in quietly and stood in the corner looking down at the floor. None of them said hello. The man with the papers said they had been good little soldiers once he'd knocked the nonsense out of them. The Doktor told him to leave and he went out laughing.

'The Doktor didn't laugh. He walked up and down the line of patients in the corner and didn't say a word. Elvi began to cry and the others shouted at her to stop before they all got into trouble. She stuffed a rag into her mouth and cried without noise. "Good little soldiers," the Doktor said, and then he sat on the stairs and cried. Then they all did.'

Karl stopped writing again. Traudl had almost criticised her Doktor then. "What was the use of crying?" Heinrich was blue with cold without his shirt and Detlef had a broken arm and Elvi was walking on the carpets with dirty bare feet. Traudl had to see to everything all by herself because the Doktor only cried and pulled his hair. "I can't believe that this has happened," he kept saying.

But Traudl believed. She knew the things that happened in the world. She was the first to know that Elvi and Maria were pregnant. She knew about Maria because she was sick every morning. She knew about Elvi because she sat rocking on the floor all day, saying her alphabet over and over. She thought her mother might come for her if she could prove she wasn't stupid. Traudl guessed from the rocking that she would have a baby soon, because she had rocked too when a bad thing had happened to her. She had rocked and rocked but she didn't know her letters and so she had sung a little song. That was when they put her in the hospital. The three men didn't get put anywhere, though. She had seen Karl drinking with them at the inn. No, she wouldn't say their names because they'd get her locked up again. And what did it matter? These things happened all the time. She didn't understand why a clever man like the Doktor didn't know that.

Karl chewed his pen, thinking of Traudl and her three men. She had hummed her song for him, tilting her head and tunelessly crooning a cracked counterpoint to the shrieking wind which drove the clouds away from the moon and whipped at her scarves and wrappings. He decided to censor that little tale from his letter. No one would ever believe that the Troglodyte could attract three men. He thought of the farmers he drank with in the inn — no, not even in East Prussia could any man be that desperate. This was clearly the erotic fantasy of a madwoman, and would cast doubt on her truthfulness if it were known. But the fantasy didn't mean that she had lied about everything else. The tale of Reichardt had the ring of truth, was even touching in its way. And his death was a verifiable fact. But for the life of him, Karl couldn't think what the Doktor had to reproach himself with. 'And,' he wrote to Friedrich, 'we may never know, because Traudl refuses absolutely to discuss the second time the patients went away.'

It was a week before he heard from Friedrich. 'Traudl must spill the beans,' his cousin wrote, 'for Siggi's sake. He has been afflicted with moral outrage. We all thought it was some new joke at first, but now we fear the case is genuine and irrecoverable. Siggi is earnest and never amusing and no one can stand his company

for long. He darts like a firefly all over Berlin, enquiring about forced labour and vanished lunatics; he pins T4 clerks to walls and bribes them to bring him the contents of their superiors' waste paper baskets.

'So far he has gleaned that the Ministry at Tiergarten 4 researches eugenics, fertility, and insanity. They distribute grotesque photographs of the insane to demonstrate the effects of degeneracy on racial health. Siggi produces these gross pictures without the slightest provocation, even at the dinner table. He rages that his zanies have been rounded up and put into labour camps along with politicos and other undesirables. He considers it a harrowing fate to have to dig roads and be lectured at by the politically committed.

'Certainly, some sort of forced labour programme was in operation last year, and yours is not the only report of non-return from labour duties. All enquiries are met with referrals to other departments and officials — there are dozens of them. The Führer breeds them like rabbits and they are all alike: they know nothing and they write down in triplicate the names of people who want to know. Siggi makes them spell his name aloud three times in case they get it wrong.

'He is full of high purpose. The editor refused to print his latest cartoon (he's still apologising for the saluting business), but Siggi persuaded him. You should have heard him: "Of course it will embarrass the government! Why else are we here?"; "Someone has to worry about the poor lunatics digging roads while being preached at by socialists and trade unionists. Why else are we here?"; "The cartoon is *not* mocking the Party. It isn't the slightest bit funny."'

And it wasn't, Karl had to agree when he looked at it; it was chilling. It showed the Pied Piper of Hamelin with a deathshead face and a flute at his mouth, dancing a ragged file of grotesques up a wooded mountainside. One by one, they disappeared into a narrow cleft in the rocks while the deathshead grinned and fluted. 'Where are they now?' the caption underneath read.

It was a grim flight of fancy, but Karl chuckled. Moral outrage! Not Siggi! More likely he was suffering from a prolonged hangover and plain old-fashioned guilt. He had a sister confined in an institution. He had mentioned her once at the end of an evening of inventive depravity when he was reviewing his life through the bottom of the glass: "Shh!" he said. "Today is someone's birthday, but I must not say her name. My father forbids it. She brought shame on us by being peculiar, you see, and so forfeits her place in the family and the world. All day long she hears the voices of angels and devils, all kinds of voices, but never ours. Her photographs have been removed from the mantelpiece and the lock of her baby hair from my mother's jewel box. No one remembers her. Except me." He grinned slyly and drew letters in the beer slops on the table. "You see? Her name." He rubbed it away with his cuff before Karl could read it. "Shh!" he whispered. "Her name must never be spoken; her absence must never be noticed. Have you any idea how much effort it takes not to notice someone who isn't there? But I keep her here." He had knuckled his forehead so hard that Karl pulled his hand down and pinned it to the table.

Karl frowned. Siggi was odd sometimes. Perhaps there was a family weakness.

The schoolmaster had regained his good humour by the following Sunday. "I brought you my lesson plans," he said, basking in the rosy firelight beside Karl. "Eugenics. Perhaps your readers would be interested. Berlin should know that we are not all backwoodsmen out here."

"Very thoughtful of you, Ernst. The electricity, plumbing, and church gargoyles may be mediaeval, but the village is in the vanguard of the new science. Your influence, of course."

The schoolmaster flushed with pleasure. "I try. One likes to pass the torch of enlightenment to the next generation."

"Your lesson plans may well be of interest, Ernst. There is a Ministry in the Tier-garten entirely devoted to — "

"Oh, yes, I know. I send for all their public information pamphlets. But I believe I have refined the theories to a consistency suitable for children to digest. I have devised a programme..."

And he was off. Karl waited patiently for a break in transmission. When the schoolmaster paused for a swallow of beer, he said suddenly, "And did you ever have contact with the asylum here, Ernst? To increase your understanding of the problem?"

"Goodness, no. It's seven miles outside the village and you know these places — closed doors and no outsiders, please." He placed his empty stein carefully on the table. "What makes you ask?"

"I wondered if the patients were the inspiration for your studies."

"No, not really. We occasionally met the better behaved ones in the village, exchanged a good morning and so on. They were not inspiring."

"I understand the hospital is empty now."

"Yes. The Direktor abandoned the place once the inmates had gone."

"They're not coming back then? The patients? I believe they left once before and returned."

"Oh, they didn't exactly leave that time. They were temporarily seconded to a labour-therapy squad. The programme was successful, I believe."

"But that's not why they left the second time?"

The schoolmaster's spectacles misted over. "They didn't exactly leave then either, Karl. There was an outbreak of typhus. Most of them died, the rest went home, and the Direktor abandoned the place."

"The Direktor shot himself."

The schoolmaster blinked rapidly. "Really? How sad that is. But, you know, the man was as unstable as his patients. Ask anyone in the village."

"He had something on his mind. He said he couldn't live with the guilt."

"Perhaps he neglected the hospital drains." The schoolmaster emptied his glass. "The interesting question is, does psychiatric work attract the unbalanced, or do they become like that through contact with the insane?" He signalled to the bar-maid. "Did I tell you that I am planning a trip for the children? To Nürnberg for the autumn rally? We are all so excited."

Frau Haar was even less communicative than Ernst. She said nothing about life in the asylum except that she had been like a mother to those poor souls. As for Reichardt's suicide and the fate of the patients, she knew nothing at all about what happened there after she retired. But she would pray for the good Doktor.

Karl concluded regretfully that they were both lying in their teeth.

Wednesday's weather was milder, if not quite springlike. Karl wrapped up warmly, and with Siggi's cartoon in his pocket, set out for his tryst with Traudl. He had persuaded her to show him the snowdrops at the place where the patients had their happy-days, and the birch trees which had frightened Heinrich. He put it to her that it was the least she could do if she wouldn't tell him her story.

The air was crisp and the sky a glassy blue. Karl enjoyed the brisk walk past gardens sparkling with frost until he turned down the path which wound beside the river. It was like entering a dank tunnel. The path was overhung with branches, bushes and trailing grasses, which rotted mournfully in the mud. He took his mind off his discomfort by planning how to make her talk.

He was wet and filthy by the time he reached the little white style where Traudl awaited him, swathed in shawls and scarves. "The snowdrops are this way," she said, and without another word led the way across the water meadows. They waded knee-high through grass crunchy with frost, and only halted when they reached the birch trees which palisaded the edge of the meadow. She waved her mittened hand. "The birches," she announced. "The ones Heinrich was afraid of."

She clearly expected a reaction. He struggled to find one. "Ah, yes," he said at last, "where Heinrich lost the race."

She nodded. "Every summer. Heinrich kept up with Detlef when they ran across the meadows, but Detlef always won because Heinrich stopped at the trees. They frightened him. He wouldn't go in the woods unless I came and took his hand." Traudl gazed dreamily into the leafless thicket.

"Is this where Heinrich played his flute, Traudl?" He had to ask her twice.

"Not here," she said at last. "He didn't like the trees whispering to him. Or Detlef running off through the woods. He could hear Detti's sandals getting further and further away — " She clapped her mittened hands together in a light rapid rhythm. "Like that. Slap. Slap. Slap." She clapped again and added helpfully, "The path is hard like biscuit in summer. Slap. Slap. Further and further away until Heinrich couldn't see him any more. 'Oh, Traudl!' he shouted every time. 'Where's Detti? Where's he gone?'"

Karl was amused to find that just for a moment he felt Heinrich's dread of the silent forest closing in over the sound of invisible running feet. Traudl was still speaking. "But," she said, "he was all right when I carried him."

"Carried him?"

"He's small for his age."

"How old — ?"

"Ten. But small."

"Ten? In an asylum?"

"Since always." Traudl grinned wolfishly, pushed her eyelids into a slant, and sank her chin into her shoulders. "He's funny looking. The snowdrops are this way."

The clearing was a long way into the forest. He arrived panting and overheated. Traudl was well ahead of him. "This is where the happy-days were," she said with a sigh. A tiny ruined chapel stood to one side. Birches crowded spikily upwards from inside its roofless walls. The clearing was studded with flat table tombs, each carved with a great crusader's cross, symbol of the Teutonic knights, the flower of the Aryans. He sat on a tomb and lit a cigarette. His feet were buried to the ankles in a thick carpet of snowdrops which trembled thick and white in the breeze.

Traudl tramped round the perimeter of the clearing, slapping her arms to keep warm. "Is it pretty? Do you like it?" she called to him.

He nodded. "Very pretty. And peaceful."

"The Doktor said the snowdrops were a sign that winter was nearly over. We all — "

Karl flicked his cigarette into the snowdrops and heard it sizzle. "I have something to show you, Traudl." He held out Siggi's cartoon. "Look. My friend drew this. It's in the newspapers."

She began circling the clearing again. "Heinrich didn't like it here."

"Traudl, come and see."

Her speed increased to a lumbering trot.

"Traudl!"

She turned and ran in the opposite direction.

"Why didn't he like it here, Traudl?" He patted the space beside him. "Come and tell me all about it."

She stood still. "I told you. He didn't like the trees. Or those." She pointed at the tombs. "There's dead people in there. See? Pictures of their bones."

Karl glanced at the table tomb; it was carved with skulls and scythe-bearing skeletons, their bony fingers pointing at a Latin inscription: *Memento Mori*.

Traudl came closer. "Heinrich heard claws scratching to get out from under there."

Karl grinned. "Heinrich had a vivid imagination."

Traudl pouted sulkily. "He heard them scratching like rats." Her whisper was like the rustle of dead leaves. "He thought the trees grew out of their bones." She pointed skywards. "See their fingers? And their arms?"

The birches, naked and slick with ice, soared dizzyingly above their heads. Twigs were like fingers flexed in frozen anguish, branches like arms uplifted to Heaven, and the wet silver bark which covered them looked like rotten dead flesh. Or so a little boy might think, Karl thought with a shudder.

"Woo! Woo!" Traudl screamed suddenly. "Woo-hoo!" She leapt at him and he tumbled backwards off the tomb. She slapped her thighs and laughed. "The Doktor fell off too. Every time. Good joke, isn't it?"

"Yes," he said, brushing wet debris off his trousers. "I can see why you call them happy-days."

"Yes. Heinrich laughed and laughed and then he wasn't frightened. He asked questions. Why do trees grow upwards? Why do snowdrops grow in circles? I didn't know, but the Doktor did. Do *you* know why?"

Karl seated himself and lit another cigarette. "I don't think I do, Traudl," he said patiently. "What did the Doktor say?"

She recited carefully. "Trees and snowdrops are just like people — each grows according to its nature." She pursed her lips. "That's clever talk, isn't it?"

"Yes, it is, Traudl. Wouldn't it be wonderful to have the Doktor back?" She nodded and dropped her eyes. "I think I know how. Will you look at my picture now?" She sidled nearer. "See, Traudl? The patients are being led away. It says, 'Where are they now?' My friend is worried about them. He would bring them back if he knew where they were."

"I don't know where."

"Did they go with the soldiers like before?"

She kicked idly at snowdrops. The smell of smashed stalks rose green in the air. "The picture's wrong," she said. "Heinrich had the flute, not the soldiers. And they didn't walk. They went in a big lorry."

"So the soldiers did come again? You know, liebling, if we tell about the soldiers, then the Doktor will be let out. And we'll make the soldiers tell where the patients are. But if we don't tell, then maybe you'll never see any of them again."

Snowdrop stalks snapped and squeaked under her boots. "I could get into trouble. I don't want to be locked up."

There was real terror in her eyes. Karl patted her arm. "Traudl, tell me about it. If it will get you locked up, then I'll keep it a secret. If it won't, then I'll put it in the papers and find the Doktor. Is it a deal?"

He was frozen to the marrow of his bones by the time she agreed, and even then the ordeal was not over — she insisted he accompany her to the hospital because she had to give Fritzi his dinner.

"I thought all the patients were all gone away," he said.

"Fritzi's the Doktor's dog," she said.

"Oh. Sorry."

She grew confidential. "Fritzi gets his dinner early or he makes a pest of himself when the patients are having theirs."

"But there are no patients."

"It's still Fritzi's dinner time."

There was no arguing with that.

It was about four miles through the woods to the hospital. Karl stumbled after Traudl while she barked amusing anecdotes about Fritzi over her shoulder. The animal was, apparently, every bit as remarkable as the Doktor. He gasped admiration whenever he could summon the breath and swore inwardly that Siggi was going to pay for this.

The hospital was a gracious old hunting lodge with carved wooden gables and a solid square frontage half-hidden in red creeper. He might have admired its prettiness if he hadn't been exhausted. They entered by a side door. Traudl stood commandingly by the oak coat-stand in the little hallway. "Overshoes," she chanted. "Coat. No drips, please. I polish the floors on Wednesdays."

He divested himself of wet garments while she removed layers of shawls and scarves and an old military greatcoat. Her hair, he saw, was iron grey and cut short with a side parting scraped back in an enormous diamante clasp. The effect was oddly childlike. She smiled her wolf's fang grin and touched her clasp. "Pretty, isn't it? The Doktor won it in the Christmas lucky dip. He said he would give it to his best girl. That's me. I'll feed Fritzi now. You can watch if you want."

The kitchen was warm and bright and the little daschund frantic with joy. Karl restrained him while Traudl filled his bowl with meat. He pulled a chair close to the stove. "Tell me about when the soldiers came."

She said it was like the first time: the soldiers, the papers, the shouting, the lorry. Elvi was hit with a gun to shut up her screaming. And they pushed the Doktor to the floor when he tried to help her. The soldiers walked right over him. "My God," he kept saying, "what have I done?" But Traudl didn't tell.

Karl was bewildered. He studied the coffee pot in front of him. "But what could you have told, Traudl? None of this was the Doktor's fault." She was suddenly busy, mopping up a coffee splash, muttering under her breath. He waited patiently.

"They took the Major with them this time."

"They didn't before. Why did they this time?"

She polished furiously at the bass taps shining over the sink. "Because of what the Doktor did. And me."

She left Karl in Reichardt's office while she took Fritzi for his walk. Slowly he began to make sense of what she had told him. The phone, black and gleaming on Reichardt's desk, had rung two days before the soldiers came. A voice warned Reichardt he was about to be visited again. He shut himself in his office all that day.

Traudl knocked at the door after everyone had gone to bed and brought him sandwiches. What a mess the room was in! The drawers in the filing cabinet were open and there were little white record cards all over the desk and the floor. He was typing and Traudl asked if she should send for Fräulein Harkus, because typing was her job, but he said he couldn't trust her and gobbled down his sandwiches.

"But I can trust my best girl, can't I, Traudl? Not clever Harkus or my loyal nurses. Only you. You must never say anything about this, Traudl. It could mean big trouble for us both. You can keep your mouth shut, can't you?"

Karl stood in front of the desk where Traudl must have stood that night. The desk was wide and covered with green leather. There was a green shaded lamp to one side. He imagined Reichardt, pale and unshaven, in a splash of light among the shadows, peck-typing and wolfing down sandwiches. His eyes would have been bright and feverish when he told Traudl his plan. "It's a paper game," he told her. "Paper gives them power over us. We shall fight paper with paper." Traudl hadn't understood, but she'd fetched the garden refuse sacks, and while he typed, obediently shredded all the little white cards he pointed at, then filled the sacks with them.

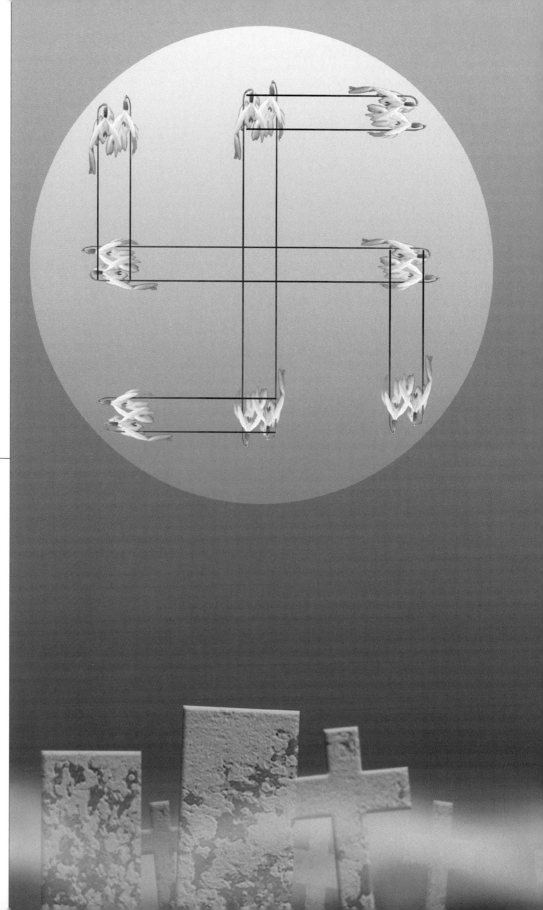

He had a pile of new cards beside his typewriter. "What shall I say about the Major, Traudl? And Elvi — we can't let them take her, not after last time."

Traudl couldn't remember what he said about the Major and the others, but she had allowed Karl to look through the filing cabinet. Maria Barbel, Elvi Polk, Heinrich Reinke, Major Beck — according to the records, they were all suffering from multisyllabic psychiatric illnesses, presenting as hallucinations, delusions, violent outbursts, and a total incapacity to follow a disciplined regime. In short, unfit for work.

Karl understood. The soldiers hadn't wanted the severely disordered the first time and so Reichardt had transformed his patients, working throughout the night to produce records showing false diagnoses and hopeless prognoses. Traudl kept him going with coffee and burned the old records to wisps of ash in the boiler room furnace.

Karl stood entranced, seeing it all happen by the light of a green shaded lamp, hearing the quiet flip of a card across the table, the rip as Traudl tore it to pieces, the tap-tap of the typewriter. He saw Reichardt yawning and filing his new records so that everything was in order, proper and correct.

When the soldiers came, Traudl hid in the cupboard in the hall. They were smiling and polite this time. So was the Doktor as he regretted that he had no patients fit for work. The soldiers were delighted to hear it. It was the unfit they had come for this time. "What for?" Reichardt demanded. "What use are they to you?"

"None at all," the soldiers said. "They are being relocated."

The Doktor turned chalk-white then. He said they couldn't do that, but they showed him papers and said he should be pleased to be rid of the troublesome ones. They were going to a special hospital for people like them. Reichardt fetched his coat and said he was coming too, but the soldiers locked him in his office and told him there were enough doktors where they were going.

From her hiding place, Traudl saw a scene from Hell. The patients were screaming and running everywhere, trying to get away from the rifle butts. Elvi hugged her baby and cried. One soldier was kind and stroked her hair. "Do you think we are monsters, liebling? Would we hurt our little Elvi?"

Reichardt hammered on the door of his office, shouting that he was going to report this, but the soldiers only laughed. Traudl let him out after they'd gone and he spent the next two days on the telephone. But it was no use. "No one can say where they are, Traudl," he said. "Due to staff shortages, the paperwork has been held up. We will be informed in due course." He laughed till he trembled. "They've been lost like parcels in the post. I must go to Berlin and see these people face to face. I shall make them give our people back."

When Traudl returned with Fritzi, Karl told her firmly that her story must be told. There would be no trouble. The newspapers would protect her. Once people knew what was going on, the soldiers would be in trouble and Doktor Reichardt and the others would be brought back home. He would be proud of his best girl and know he had been right to trust her.

"I shall send the story to Berlin, Traudl. I'll show it to you first, of course."

She shrugged. "I can't read." She fiddled frowning with her diamante clasp.

"I'll read it to you. Would you like that?"

"I don't have much free time," she said almost coquettishly.

"You can polish the floors while you're listening," he laughed.

"Will the Doktor read about me too?"

"Definitely."

He was half way home and tramping through the snowdrop clearing before he remembered that Reichardt was dead. With a stab of pity he pictured again the pale unshaven man in the green lamplight. Karl rested on a tomb for a few minutes and sat thinking and smoking. Snowdrops glimmered ghostly white around his feet in the fading light; they were everywhere. His eye travelled along jagged lines of them into the long grass under the trees while he planned his exposé, and his future. There was no telling where this would end. Governments had fallen for less and the credit would be his. Reichardt had done his best and he would mention that — but for the life of him, he still couldn't understand why the man had shot himself.

There was a letter awaiting him at Frau Haar's. Karl sat stunned on the edge of his bed when he'd read it. Siggi was in hospital after a drunken brawl with some blackshirts. The details were sickening. Siggi had been identified by his press card which had been the only recognisable thing about him. His friends had prayed that he would live, but now they prayed he would die, so severe was the damage to his brain, which was slopping around in his skull like mashed pumpkin.

Karl hugged his knees to his chest, sick to the pit of his stomach. Friedrich said that Siggi had been delighted by the response to his cartoon. Furious relatives of patients denied that the patients were missing — they had died of typhus and they had the medical certificates to prove it. The trouble was, there were hundreds of them, all dying of the same disease, in the same span of time in places scattered all over Germany. Now the relatives were asking hard questions about the conditions the patients were being held in. The editor had been summoned to T4 and been harangued by an official about the distress that Siggi's cartoon had caused the recently bereaved, and about Siggi's relentless badgering of T4 staff. The official was moved to question the role of the Free Press in a civilised society. The editor had apologised profusely, swore that it would never happen again, returned to the office and told Friedrich that Siggi had been right all along and they were going to prove it. Friedrich advised Karl to break the story before someone else did; for Siggi's sake, he'd added, or he'll come back and haunt you.

Karl spent the rest of the day planning how to introduce the patients to the public. He would have to make them interesting. The hard facts about their removal from care and subsequent ill-treatment would send shockwaves round the Reich. In tribute to Siggi, he would head the story 'Where Are They Now?' Everyone had heard rumours about the conditions in labour camps. The Party had as good as infected the patients deliberately with typhus by sending them there. He would lead the crusade to bring the survivors home and make his reputation forever.

He laid out his typewriter, carbons and paper and began. Words had never flowed so easily before. Reichardt must have felt like this the night he changed the patients' records: or no fatigue or hesitations, no stumbling after the right phrase. He worked on through the night, sealed his scoop in a large brown envelope and took it to the postbox at the end of the street.

Dawn broke as he turned back home. The river rushed noisily through crystalline light and made him think unexpectedly of Traudl. He considered the unexpectedness of things that happened in the world: who would have thought that a dismal night spent on a riverbank with a Troglodyte would lead to all this? He shook his head in disbelief and when he reached his lodgings, plunged straight into a deep sleep.

He woke suddenly with the crack of a pistol shot echoing in his ear. "But they don't!" he cried out. He sat bolt upright and snapped on the light, but the room was empty and quiet: no pistol shots, no sandals slapping across earth baked hard as biscuit, no flute piping off-key. Shivering, he pulled his blankets round his shoulders. Such a strange dream: bright sunshine and screams, a blue and golden summer day, and thousands of snowdrops, splashes of out-of-season frost, zigzagging through the grass towards the trees. And above the screams and shots, a child's voice, clear and sad like a flute's: "Why do snowdrops grow in circles?"

"But they don't," he said aloud.

And they didn't. He was back in the clearing by mid-morning. On one side, snow-drops formed circles like ever-widening ripples round the trees and tombs; on the other side, the ripples were broken into jagged lines, as if the earth and the bulbs clinging underneath had been disturbed. His eye followed the jagged lines and traced a pattern of grassy rectangles humped side by side among the snowdrop circles.

He lit a cigarette and slumped against a tomb. He saw it all now. The patients had been permanently relocated, and much closer to home than anyone had thought, right under the birches which had terrified little Heinrich. Perhaps he'd had a pre-monition. Maybe Reichardt had too when he'd turned white at that word 'relocated'. "What have I done?" he kept asking. Had he sensed he'd signed their death warrants? He couldn't have — such a thing was beyond guessing. But he found out somehow. Then he shot himself.

Suddenly, the rotting dead flesh of the birches nauseated Karl and he crashed through the snowdrops, out of the clearing, and went running home. He had an article to rewrite.

The schoolmaster was sipping tea from Frau Haar's wedding china when he arrived. "Karl!" he called cheerfully as Karl made to slip upstairs. "I was about to send out a search party! Come and have some tea. You look frozen."

Karl took a seat by the fire; it would be a comfort to feel warm.

The schoolmaster looked pointedly at his boots. "You've been walking, I see."

"Yes. I needed the exercise. I've been lazy lately."

The schoolmaster's cup chinked in his saucer. "Lazy, Karl? A little bird told me you were working all night." He stirred his tea, smiling gently. "Frau Haar was concerned, especially when you went out so early this morning, and then went out again without breakfast. Some tea?" He turned to Karl's landlady. "Frau Haar, when you're in the kitchen, tell the boys I won't be much longer."

Frau Haar left the room, and through the open door, Karl glimpsed three burly brownshirts sitting at the kitchen table. A finger of unease stroked his spine.

"We're on our way to a meeting," the schoolmaster said. "But there was some-thing I wished to discuss with you first."

Frau Haar returned with a cup and saucer. Karl beamed warmly at her. "You've been baking, Frau Haar," he said, "This looks wonderful."

"Then eat," she said coldly as she went out again. Karl took a piece of stollen cake. He had to sit with it in his hand. Frau Haar had forgotten to bring him a plate.

"So, Karl. Where did your walk take you?"

"Down by the river."

"Really? Wilhelm says he saw you in the woods."

"Did he? Well, nowhere is very far from the woods around here." Karl bit into his cake, but the icing sugar clogged his tongue like sawdust and he couldn't swallow.

"You look weary, Karl. But if you will burn the midnight oil — the work must have been very important."

Karl shrugged. "The usual, Ernst. A little Tale From The Village."

"You're too modest, Karl. The chief charm of the Tales is their variety. They dot here and there, into the distant past, the recent past, back to the present, and cover all sorts of subjects on the way. There's no telling what you'll come up with next, except that it will be vivid and interesting. That's a great gift. Come. Indulge me. What is the new Tale?"

Karl swallowed hard and looked for somewhere to put his cake, which was growing sticky. He laid it on the embroidered tablecloth. "You'll see when it's published, Ernst."

"This sounds mysterious."

"There's no mystery. It's just that — oh, I can see I'll have no peace until I tell you. But you're spoiling your own surprise."

The schoolmaster's teaspoon clinked cheerfully. "Surprise?"

"Yes. The Tale concerns your calendar of pagan festivals and ancient rites."

The schoolmaster smiled briefly and nudged the leather coat which lay across the arm of his chair. There was an envelope, large and brown and addressed in Karl's handwriting. It should have been well on its way to Berlin by now.

"That was an unworthy lie, Karl." The schoolmaster laid the envelope across his knees. "And a stupid one. The postmaster is a devoted Party member. He helps me keep an eye on things. I have said it before, Karl — you don't take us seriously enough. One cannot put an old head on young shoulders, but someone of your intelligence should have a firm grasp of the realities of life. Your friend, Siggi, is another such, although I fancy he has a firmer grasp now. Don't frown, Karl. We read all your correspondence to and from Berlin." Ernst stared steadily at him through gold-rimmed glasses. "I am glad you found us all so amusing."

There was a short painful pause while the schoolmaster collected himself. He steepled his fingers under his chin and for one hysterical moment, Karl thought he was going to say, 'And now if I may move on to matters esoteric', and if he does, he thought, if he does, I'll giggle and won't be able to stop.

But the schoolmaster was concerned with reality today. "Your friend stirred up a furore. He was warned several times. Did you know that? But he was stubborn and wilful and inflamed by the gossip you sent him. Oh, yes, Karl, you bear some responsibility for what has happened." He blinked rapidly. "I hope you will accept that it would grieve me should a similar unpleasantness enter your life. But there's no reason it should, is there? Your friend let emotion overrule his intellect and his own best interests. I fancy that you are not a man of that stamp."

The pause this time was longer and much more painful for Karl. It only ended when he dropped his eyes. The schoolmaster carried on gently. "A young man of your talents has much to offer the Reich, but you do need guidance, Karl." He tapped the envelope on his lap. "This article is what I would have expected from you — angry, full of appeals to popular sentiment. Well, a young man should have heart and feeling — that is to his credit. One would need a heart of stone not to feel for little Heinrich and pretty Elvi. Do you think I have a heart of stone, that I cannot feel?" A sense of grievance pursed Ernst's lips. "I thought you knew me better. If I had no feeling, would I be talking to you now like a Father? Now, don't lie to me. You went to the clearing yesterday with Traudl. And you went there again today. May I take it that the secret is no longer a secret?"

Karl's heart lurched and he sat very still, uncomfortably aware of the deep rumble of brownshirts' voices in the kitchen. He pictured a brain like mashed pumpkin and felt the colour and warmth drain from his face. The schoolmaster nodded. "I thought as much. And you came racing home to write about it, full of outrage and popular sentiment." He steepled his fingers again. "Why, Karl, do you think a quiet schoolmaster like me, with some pretensions to culture, is involved with this unsavoury business? You see? I am trusting you. I admit I played my part in it. Do you understand why? These unfortunate creatures are a threat to us all, a virulent bacteria in the bloodstream of the race. Just as a doctor takes drastic action, such as amputating a diseased limb so that the rest of the body may thrive, so we take action against them. Sometimes, Karl, awful things have to be done for the higher good, things that one would shrink from if left to oneself and mere human sentiment." Ernst gazed thoughtfully into the fire. "It takes a brave man and a strong one to recognise that truth, to take action when he bears no malice, to rise above natural inclination and engage with necessity — "

"A merciless moral man?" Karl asked, and thought, my God, he believes all this. He lives according to his nature and thinks it's a philosophy.

"That's what I admire about you, Karl, the apt word, the telling phrase. The Party has need for that talent. You must consider your future. Next week your newspaper is being bought over. In the time you have been writing the Tales, you have touched a chord in thousands of hearts and the Führer himself admires your work People identify with the noble simplicity of your stories. A thousand texts by our philosophers and scientists could not win us the converts you have."

Something shrivelled in Karl as he listened: he knew he was complicit; knew he could never be a Siggi or a Reichardt; knew he was already considering his future. He loathed the schoolmaster for understanding these things about him.

"It is only because of your potential contribution to the Reich's success that I make time for you now," the schoolmaster said. He held up Karl's envelope and tore it in half. "Look. As a gesture of goodwill, I will destroy this." He tossed the halves on to the fire. "See? All gone. Some things are better left unsaid, unwritten and unread. Now it is your turn to show goodwill. You could write that piece you spoke of — my calendar of festivals and their importance in the Aryan tradition. Do it well enough, and you will make both of our reputations in Berlin."

Karl nodded.

The schoolmaster rose and put on his coat. "Good. I shall collect the piece on the way home and post it myself." He turned in the doorway. "By the way, does Traudl know about...?"

Karl shook his head.

"All the same, she remembers more than she should. We must arrange her silence. Don't look so stricken, Karl. Nothing dreadful is going to happen. We shall organise another institution for her, one where no one will listen to her ravings."

Karl decided the wisest course was to believe him. He wrote the article and pulled out all the stops. Ernst's spectacles must be made to mist with emotion.

Traudl waylaid him in the alley the following Sunday night. "You didn't bring my story." Karl stared. There appeared to be two Traudls. He had drunk too much again.

"Gnädiges Fräulein, how nice to see you again."

"Did you put it in the papers?"

"Oh, yes, liebling, that's what I do. Put things in the papers."

"You didn't read it for me." She was electric with excitement.

"No, I've been busy. But I have it here."

He produced a Party pamphlet Ernst had given him. The front page was devoted to an explanation of euthanasia, and its other name, mercy. And it listed all the categories of people who would be better off out of their misery.

They were standing under the light which burned at the end of the alley. It was the last lamp before the path turned down to the river and the smothering dark. Karl felt as if he were standing at the edge of the world. Traudl was in her listening pose: head tilted sideways, gaze fixed on the stars above. Her woolly scarf slipped back to show her diamante clasp dazzling in the lamplight. It wouldn't do any good to warn her, he thought, because where could she go?

"The story is on the front page, Traudl." He improvised wildly. "'The mystery of the disappearance of thousands of mental patients was solved today thanks to the courage and kindness and honesty of a woman named Traudl...'"

Traudl was radiant. He had never seen her smile before; this must be a happy-day for her. He gave her his most deathless prose. It would be cruel to short change her. ■

STEN WESTGARD

GUNSAFE

Sten Westgard went to the 1995 Clarion East writers workshop but didn't let that discourage him. He has been published in Tomorrow, Odyssey and Altair, but he hopes it wasn't his fault these magazines ceased existence soon after printing his stories. Fortunately, his fiction has also appeared in Realms of Fantasy, Titan Webzine, Lady Churchill's Rosebud Wristlet, the Datlow & Windling edited fairy tale anthology Black Swan, White Raven and a story called 'Contracting Iris' is in the current issue of The Third Alternative. Sten lives in Norwalk, Connecticut with his wife Jill, where they are eagerly awaiting the birth of their first child. He has gone back to graduate school to pursue a degree in computer science.

As the alarm woke Pierce, he reached into his pillow holster, wrapping his hand around the .38. Adrenalin dispelled his sleep; he pulled the pistol free, scanning the pre-dawn darkness of the room. Pierce knew he could only rely on his wits for protection, not the electrified dust ruffle or the reactive bedposts. He glanced at the clock: 5:48AM.

"Honey?" Terry murmured beside him, safe beneath the kevlar comforter.

"Shh…" Pierce said, holding his Special Snubby in both hands, defensive position. "Plug in."

Pierce heard Terry grope through the nightstand drawer. She put on her headphones, adjusted the voice mike, and plugged in. As soon as Terry drew her Lady Smith, he slipped in his own earpiece and clipped a mike to his shirt.

Terry read from the nightstand console. "Block watch lists a disturbance two streets down."

"Details?" Pierce murmured.

"Origin unknown."

He cursed silently. Damn screen-watchers. They could wake him with their updates and alerts, but they never stepped away from the keyboard to check things out for themselves.

"What about the house?"

"Nothing on the scopes. Security fields read normal."

"Bollocks," Pierce said. Last week the neighbor's girl snuck in after curfew without so much as a murmur from the monitors. Convinced the computer she was rain. Pierce's father, rest his soul, used to say that men who relied on security fields died.

Pierce slid out of bed, crouched low to the ground in his domestic camouflage pajamas, still holding the gun two-handed. A few quick steps to the master bathroom. He had to be sure it was safe before he could check the rest of the house. His brother Claude had neglected that precaution *once* and paid with his life. About two years ago, Claude's ex-girlfriend let herself into his apartment and waited behind the shower curtain, hiding. Claude came home, checked the rest of the house for intruders. Then the call of nature called Claude to his death.

With his left foot Pierce kicked the bathroom door, leaning his shoulder on the doorframe to keep the gun steady in his hands. Rushed into the darkness. Slashed the shower curtain back. Nothing.

"Bathroom's clean," Pierce muttered into his microphone. His eyes sought out the commode. The .45 Taurus sat waiting for him, holstered securely next to the toilet paper. Eight in the magazine, one in the chamber. The safety nutsies said house guns should be kept in Condition Three: chamber empty, loaded magazine. Pierce didn't believe in wasting precious time. He had vowed on his brother's grave that he would never be caught with his pants down.

Terry's voice came through his 'phones. "Infrared scan complete. No foreign heat signatures."

"Don't bring up the floodlights yet. Check electronic emissions," Pierce returned, grabbing the Bull-pistol and dropping the Snubby into his pajama pocket.

Pierce turned to the bathroom sink. On the counter, beside his laser shaver and Terry's curling rod, lay the extra ammunition for the Taurus. He checked the rounds: a mixture of Domicile Defense load and White Elephant points. Perfect for urban defense — one-shot certainty that wouldn't damage dry walls. Generally he preferred Ku Klux Klammo, but they were hard to find in stores. He slipped the magazines into his other pocket.

He hesitated. Closing his eyes, he ran his next moves over in his mind. Other home owners used infrared goggles or other nightsight-wear. But not me, Pierce told himself. The best way to stay alive was natural nightsight. See 'em straight, shoot 'em straight. No filters, no enhancements, none of that sissy stuff. Besides, Pierce hadn't graduated from Thunder Ranch just to strap on something that killed his peripheral vision.

"All right, I'm coming out," Pierce warned. He scuttled out, still keeping low to the floor. Taurus in one hand, the other hand on the floor for balance.

"Vigilante net has confirmed the alert," Terry said, her voice hurried and insistent. "But they can't pin down the number of criminals."

"I'll check the kid's room," Pierce said, as he switched the master bedroom door to manual and slid it back into the wall on its silent, painstakingly-oiled track. The hallway looked clear. He moved forward on the plush Wearever/Soundnever carpet.

Pierce triggered the door to the kids' room, pushing a button on the outside of his earpiece. He tensed, recalling the last episode of *911 Knights*, with its recreated scenes of a point blank shoot out in a colonial style broom closet. Took a breath, let half out. Waited for the intruder. No one emerged. Pierce stepped inside.

The room was sparse and empty, as it should have been. A disused bunk bed, faded pictures of Craig and Ellen at Freedom Camp, each smiling, posing with their airguns, holding riddled paper targets so the afternoon sun shone through the holes. International Rifle posters still hung on the wall. Neither child was in the room, of course. Craig lived in a log cabin on Judgement Estates, nearly two hundred miles away. Had been up there for five years, living off the web, the grid, off everything. Pierce missed Craig's steady hand, his reassuring cover-fire, but he knew when the Big One came he would be thankful he had somewhere to retreat.

Ellen was another story. While attending Magnum College, her roommate had a 'cleaning' accident — polished a soft-nosed bullet with her head. Ellen had a kind of breakdown, and ran off with some Nonviolent freak — name of Paul or something. They dropped out together. Now she fooled around with all that tangle-gun/taser/pepper-spray crap. Lived in the Regulated States. Pierce and Terry had disowned her immediately, taken her off both the Christmas and protection list.

"Kids' room, clear," Pierce said. "Gimme a full house check. System by system."

Terry answered, reading off the console. "Security fields: normal. Infrared: normal. Electronic emissions: normal. Starlight scopes: normal. First floor eye-beams: normal. Foyer metal detector: normal. Should I call for a sweep?"

"No," Pierce said, keeping his voice just below a whisper. They had a one-year subscription to Suite Security, courtesy of Terry's worried parents. He didn't care if his in-laws subscribed, but he wasn't about to let any suburb soldiers guard his house. His mother had died that way. One night her alarm sounded, notifying the First Alarm Inc headquarters. Wasn't anything but forgetfulness — she had gotten home from the senior center and hadn't deactivated the alarm. When they showed up, they gave her such a scare: flashing lights, stun grenades, masked men with their skin blackened to avoid giving any glare. Her old heart gave out; she was dead before they realized she was the subscriber. The alarm might as well have summoned the funeral home.

Pierce walked over to the kids' closet. The door was open, as he had left it last night. A few boxes lay stacked along one side. Sunday dresses hung from the rack. He pushed those aside, ducking under and slipping into the back. It was almost pitch black in the closet, but Pierce knew his way by feel. His fingers found the catch of the disguised secret panel. Hooking his fingers in the catch, he swung the panel out, revealing the hidden crawlspace behind it — and the ladder.

Pierce's uncle Nick hadn't had a ladder. One summer night there was a big thunderstorm, a window-rattling, wall-shaking, burst-of-lightning classic of a boomer. Spooked his wife, who spooked Nick. Alarm went off; they heard noises downstairs. So, with Glock auto-pistol in hand, Nick padded on his sneak slippers into the hall. Must have been quite nervous; they found his robe with patches of sweat in the armpits and back. So nervous that he paid more attention to the possibility of an intruder than to the stairs. Without looking, Nick planted his foot down on Tiger, the family cat, stumbled and fell the entire staircase. Put three slugs through his chest on the way down. Died before he reached the bottom of the steps. All because thunderstorms frightened Tiger; she had forgotten about her tiny cat door and broken in through the screen.

Pierce had built the ladder a month later.

"I'm going downstairs," he whispered over the 'phones.

He slipped off his robe, tucked the Taurus into the back of his pajama bottoms. He couldn't hold the gun and go down the ladder safely. For one moment, he had to move without the meaningful weight of a firearm in his hand. As he squeezed himself into the narrow crawlspace, he felt the clammy darkness swallow him up. He couldn't see. All he felt were the worn two by fours beneath his hands and feet; the elastic of his pajamas straining against his waist from the burden of steel; and the friction of his Taurus scraping lightly against the plaster whenever his back flexed.

"Police net just issued an APB," Terry said. "Initiating a sweep."

His breathing increased. He told himself it was only fifteen steps — only the distance between two floors. But it was too fast, too panicky. He lost count of his steps. One moment, the unseen walls were closing in. Another, there were no walls at all; he was caught on a ladder that went down and down forever. As the fear rose in him, he tried to remember the training he received in the Parent Teacher Reserves: panic is the deadliest killer; people don't kill, fear does. Fear makes you slip up — it gives them the advantage.

Willing discipline into his lungs, Pierce regained control of his breath. In-out. In-out. Match the rhythm of the hands and feet. Breathe in, move the hand. Breathe out, move the foot. Work the diaphragm.

At last his foot touched the floor. He was in the kitchen pantry. The smell of potatoes and onions reassured him. He put his hand out and felt along the shelves of canned goods until he found the door.

"I'm at the bottom," Pierce said.

"I've got you on the scope," Terry said. That meant the downstairs thermal detectors were working. "Doing fine," she added. "Don't slow down now."

Nothing to worry about, Pierce told himself, shivering as the sweat cooled. I have nothing to disarm, no code to punch, no counter-measures to turn off. There are only rooms and doors, no man's land and cover.

Not like his father. Spike had walked down into his kitchen for a midnight snack, forgetting all about the Claymore tripwire he had set only four hours ago. Got a mouthful of steel.

Pushing the door open on soundless hinges, Pierce brought out his Taurus again. The breadknife lock was still in place. A black box sat next to the food processor, just as Terry had left it. It opened quietly as he pressed his palm to the top; the Colt .45 still lay inside. A good sign.

"Kitchen clear," Pierce said. His chest, back and armpits were damp with sweat now. He felt the cold wet in the creases of his eyes. And the beginning of fatigue as the adrenalin threatened to wear off.

The dining room seemed fine. Kneeling down, Pierce caught sight of Saturday night special taped beneath the table, beside the chair where he normally sat. Never let your guard down during the meal.

"Dining room clean. I'm going to check the front door."

"Still no signs. No reports. No signatures. No emissions, either. 6:04. Keep moving, honey."

As he edged toward the front door, sidestepping so his feet never crossed each other, Pierce felt his nerves pull taut. An onslaught of memory overwhelmed his focus. Yesterday, he had heard about Enfield, his brother-in-law who worked at Custom Holsters. He got plugged in a supermarket as he bent down for a case of Classic, his jacket drooping to show the Derringer he kept strapped to his chest. He seemed too close, too menacing to the woman getting Caffeine Free. Other shoppers were amazed at how fast she drew her Ruger. The cops were more amazed that she was able to fit a .357 into her purse.

Too many mistakes. Horrendous blunders or dreadful fate, perhaps a doomed family karma. He needed to be so careful.

Pierce's eyes twitched, squinting, but not because of the darkness. He pressed the concealed foot panel ten feet from the front door. Instantly, the door slammed down, the heavy bulletproof panels dragging it to the waiting sheath below. His clammy hands tightened on the Taurus.

There was nobody there.

As the door groaned back into place, the fear surged in Pierce. "Go to radio silence," he said. If the criminals had jammers…

"Let me — "

"Quiet, now!" Pierce shouted. He threw his earpiece to the floor and ripped the mike from his shirt. The new E-warfare backpacks chewed up house systems for breakfast, they said. Could triangulate a headset in less than a second.

He heard footsteps behind him. A slow, stealthy padding.

"Terry?" he whispered, heart pounding like a machine gun.

On the stairs, the Snare-Step creaked, just as advertised. He turned, saw the flicker of movement, a gun barrel glinting in early dawn. He fired. Blind shot. Make 'em duck.

The intruder returned fire. Plaster and paint exploded beside him. He rolled right, firing wild. In the muzzle flashes, he glimpsed a shadow: long hair and a Lady Smith, a fluid body in motion. Terry?

Hologram hoax, his training cried. Take no chances. He shot again, shredding the bannister. In the burst of light, he thought he saw steel-blue eyes. My enemy? My wife?

The light above him shattered, raining glass on his head.

Responding to the shots, the floodlights came up. Shadow turned to silhouette. A woman's figure. His finger pulsed on the trigger, pointing the gun at her heart. A one shot, just like the targets at the range.

For a moment they stared at each other, frozen on the ends of each other's barrels. He saw the predator's stare in her narrowed eyes. Mother of my children. Motionless target.

The words choked in Terry's mouth. "A false alarm. Squirrels on the wires."

"The house is clear," he sighed, peeling his finger from the trigger. The gun dropped to the floor. He brushed the sweat off his face. It dripped off the back of his hand onto broken glass.

Terry fell to her knees. Her body, once locked in iron stance, now shook.

"You get the broom," Pierce said as he walked up the stairs. "I'll notify the Police net."

He would deal with the rest later, Pierce figured as he mounted the stairs. After the evening sweep, he'd patch the walls.

And keep an eye on that Terry. ■

THE 3RD ALTERNATIVE

'The most exciting new work is being honed on the cutting edge between mainstream and genre. TTA stories are definitely the best of contemporary short fiction' **Time Out**

CHAZ BRENCHLEY

JUNK MALE

Chaz Brenchley is the author of nine thrillers, most recently Shelter, and the major new fantasy series The Books of Outremer. His novel Dead of Light is currently in development with a film company. He has also published about 500 short stories of various genres in magazines and anthologies. Chaz lives in Newcastle and is writer-in-residence at Northumbria University.

If we are all, all of us star-stuff, composed of the atomic residue of a light long gone to nothing — and we are, believe me, we are — then it follows necessarily that we are all, all of us also nuclear waste.

I like that. Glory turns to stinking ash, and the ash gets up and walks around and does things. I guess you could call it the corruptibility of man.

I was lying on one of the lads' bunks, idly scanning a newspaper, essentially do-ing nothing; keeping just half an ear on the sounds and scuffles of the fresh young waste behind me, the occasional thud of footsteps overhead.

I'd been stupid that morning, sent Scuzzy running off to do the shopping. That boy can hardly read, but he knows what he likes, better than he knows what's good for him. So he'd come back with the *Sun*, along with the milk, the eggs and bacon for my breakfast. So he was still sitting very quiet, very still up front, nursing his bruises; so I was picking through nudie-pics and soap stories, trying — not too hard — to find anything that might masquerade as news. Trying for the second time: we'd only just come out of a long darkness, one of the major tunnels on our route. I'd lain there listening to the boys howl at the echo, hadn't bothered to switch the lights on.

A vicar had run off with a bishop's wife; it sounded like a joke, but I wasn't sure which might be the straight man. A helpline had been set up in the States, for women called Monica Lewinsky; there were probably dozens of 'em, all freshly deed-polled, hot in pursuit of notoriety. It seemed to be what they did best, the Americans, sought reasons to make a public display of their uninteresting selves. Another of them, a millionaire this time, Stephen Learfoot, was holed up on his yacht in Great Yarmouth harbour, with wife Roxanna and two-year-old child Stacy; notoriously reclusive — for the sake of contrast, no doubt, for the sake of the constant pursuit — and claiming to be phobic about lenses, they hadn't been seen on deck for days. Photo of blank deck, to prove it. I wondered why they didn't up anchor and away if they cared so much, if they were so anxious to escape the banks of paparazzi on the shore; but no doubt there'd be more wherever they touched land. No doubt if there weren't, they'd come back to give these a second run. What kind of damage would that kind of lifestyle, those kinds of lights do to a kid…?

I didn't even envy them the boat; I had one of my own, that I liked better. And a hand-picked crew, and privacy, that I liked better yet. I stretched out happily, thought about going up to check on what kind of damage my own sweet boys were showing, this time of the afternoon when I hadn't been watching them for hours. I'd heard no serious fights, though, no men overboard. I could probably afford not to watch 'em for a little while longer.

Just then, though, the noises changed outside, above, around me. There was a breathy call from the bow, and that was Scuz; he wouldn't dare to call above a breath, for fear that I might be sleeping. I'd even heard him try to shush the others in the tunnel. A moment later, anxious mutters from the boys at the back as they woke up to whatever Scuz was seeing. The engine-noise cut to a sudden murmur, startlingly quiet after the steady rumble that had been at my back since lunchtime, since I'd handed the tiller over and come below. Just a lock, I thought, most likely; any minute now there'd be a clatter and a whoop as the boys gathered up lock-keys and leaped ashore, wild yelling as they raced ahead to open the sluices.

Except that that didn't happen, only more quiet talking. I was just picturing the afternoon's route in my head — tunnel to pub where I'd meant to step off for an hour and no, no locks between — when the hatch swung up behind me, and one of the lads came padding down.

"Uh, Skip…?" Geo: big, solid, sensible, worried Geo. Vice-captain, and no pun intended; the boys hadn't got it, anyway. Sharp they were, my latest crew, but bright not. Bright made for problems; I didn't look for bright.

I'd told them not to disturb me before the pub. If Geo thought he had to disobey, he was probably right. I lowered the paper, propped myself up on one elbow and said, "Well, what?"

"There's another boat," he murmured, shuffling bare feet worriedly on the lino, rubbing sweaty hands on his jeans, the weight of responsibility visible on his naked, sun-scorched shoulders. "Wedged right across the canal, we can't get past..."

"Stuck, are they?" It happened: holiday-makers, incompetent with a heavy boat in muddy shallows. "Take the poles, then, and help to push 'em off."

"We can't see anyone, Skip, it looks empty."

"They're probably shagging inside." I'd known that happen too, where the moorings slipped and happy humpers simply didn't notice. "Have you tried shouting?"

"We didn't like to..."

Sometimes I thought I trained these boys too well. My fault, if so; I didn't blast him for it. I just sighed, let the paper drop and rolled easily to my feet. Gave him a slap to get him moving, and followed him up the steps and out into dense sunlight, the tense silence of my waiting crew.

A smile would have resolved their doubts in an instant, but I didn't give them that. I glanced around — Benjy on the tiller, Michael and Domino perched on the taffrail, all three in their uniform T-shirts, *cabin boy*, *mutineer* and *scrubber*, all three warily watching me — and then turned to gaze forward. With Scuz in the bows, there was only one missing from that roster; he was standing on the roof, staring straight ahead and right in my line of sight. He was stripped down to swim-shorts, catching more sun than Geo; I gazed at the lean bones and the honey-brown, money-brown skin of him and almost did let that smile loose, though I kept it out of my voice. "Shift, Shabby."

"Sorry, Skip..." Shaban scuttled to the side, and I had my first clear view of what lay ahead.

As Geo had said, it was another narrowboat lying athwart the canal at an angle, her bow buried in the reeds on the port bank and her stern strayed all the way over to starboard. As I'd suspected, she was a holiday hire, decked out in company livery. Not a full sixty-eight footer like my own *Screw Archimedes*, closer to forty, but long enough to block this narrow waterway. Her engine was still turning over; I could see the dark water threshing into froth around her stern, as the screw drove her slowly deeper into the soft, crumbling bank. I called out once, twice, but there was no reply, no movement. "Must be the *Marie Celeste*," I grunted.

"Skip, it's called *Daffodil*, I can see from here..."

"Never mind, Shabby. Listen, I'm going to bring us up to her bows," waving Benjy away and taking charge of the tiller, stretching one hand to the idling throttle and pushing it one notch forward to give the *Screw* some weigh, "and try to nudge her out of that reed-bank. You and Geo are the boarding-party. Stand by to jump across as soon as we're alongside; switch that engine off, then see if there's anyone aboard. If not, bring her to the bank and tie up. Understood?" If she was a drifter, I'd just have her moored and leave her; let the idiots who'd let her drift track her down, or explain themselves to the owners.

"Yes, Skip. Sure..."

It took more than a nudge to free the *Daffodil*'s nose, with her engine pushing her ever deeper into the bank. I nudged, backed off, tried again harder; ended up having Scuz busy in the bow with a barge-pole, just to fend us away from the reeds to be sure we didn't join her as I flung the *Screw* forward full-throttle. I think I heard him yelling "Ramming speed!" as we advanced.

One thing about narrowboats: with a quarter-inch steel hull, they're hard to bend. I've done it, but never in the *Screw* and only against a concrete abutment, which came off considerably worse.

It was the mud beneath the *Daffodil*'s bow that gave way, as it had to: with a sucking sound and a swirl of filth rising to the surface, an almost visible stench that had Scuz suddenly choking and clowning a faint, staggering around and almost losing the pole, almost falling in to join it.

A double thud told me that the boys had leaped over and landed safe as the other boat swung free. We ran slowly parallel for a short way, till Geo cut her engine; I knocked mine back to idle and we waited, no one speaking, while Shabby opened up the hatch and went below.

He was back in short order, looking oddly grey in the sunlight. He glanced at Geo, his mouth working wordlessly; then he turned towards me. "Skip, you'd better come…"

"What is it?"

He couldn't tell me, he didn't have the words. I handed the tiller back to Benjy, and bounded lightly across the gap. Shabby's eyes moved between me and the hatchway; this close, I could see that he was shaking.

I took the steps quickly, lowered my head below the hatch — and saw immediately what he had seen. It was dim down there, but there was no mistaking, no fooling myself. In the little kitchen area lay a woman's body. A couple of flies were buzzing around the dark pool that surrounded her dark head, that glistened a little in the available light.

This was death, there was no mistaking it. I went in anyway, calling needlessly to the boys to stay outside. Crouching above her, not quite reaching to touch, I saw that she was young, little more than a girl; and I thought her hair had been blonde once in its matted dreadlocks, before the blood had matted it further. Her face was almost gone, it had been so brutally battered.

As I rose slowly to my feet, I caught a movement in the shadows at the far end of the boat. "Who's there?" My voice was sharp and rising. No one answered. I couldn't see a figure, and there was nowhere big enough to hide a man; I was sure of what I'd seen, though, and moved forward slowly, making softer, encouraging noises in my throat. I was expecting a pet, a dog or perhaps a cat. What I found instead, huddled in the furthest corner, mattered more. It was a child, a toddler, a stout and sturdy little boy with huge eyes, his hair cropped roughly, inexpertly short with a pair of blunt scissors by the look of it.

I could have left him, left her, buttoned the crew's lips and moved on; but canals breed dog-walkers, cyclists, lovers. It's better to break news than to be broken. I hoisted him out, held him in my arms; tried an unaccustomed smile and said, "Hi, kid. What's your name?"

"John," he whispered, as the air filled with a rank and familiar odour.

I sighed and said, "Okay, John. Don't worry, you're safe now. We'll look after you, till we can get you home. Come on now…"

I tried to hold my body between him and that other on the floor, but it wasn't necessary. As we passed her, he buried his face in my shoulder, both arms clinging tight around my neck.

It was an effort to disentangle him as we came out on deck, but I managed it at last, thrusting him into the arms of the gaping Geo.

"His name's John," I said abruptly. "He's your charge, for now. Get him cleaned up, he stinks. If you're lucky, you'll find a nappy underneath those dungarees."

They were cheap and looked grubby, like the T-shirt he wore beneath; that fitted, I thought, with the girl below.

"Uh, what shall I..."

"I don't know. Improvise, use what you can find. You'll manage, Geo."

With that vote of confidence, he nodded and reached for a boat-hook to draw the *Screw* closer, so that he could step across safely. Geo had looked after kid brothers in his former life, before he'd left it; he tended to mother the other lads, when they'd let him. That was why I'd made him vice-captain, it wasn't just a joke.

All the boys knew now what lay out of their sight, I could see it in their faces. Shabby must have found some way to tell them, in my absence. I had as much of their attention as I was going to get, what wasn't busy imagining the scene below; I gave orders, snappily.

"Benjy, take the *Screw* and moor up, as soon as the bank gets firmer. Domino, you jump ashore and run ahead; there's a pub less than a mile on. Phone the police, tell them where we are, say we've found a body. Then come back."

"Skip — what about your mobile?"

I just looked at him, for a moment; then, wearily, "People have scanners, they listen in. The police have scanners too. If I call this in on my mobile, they get the number; if they overhear any other messages from the same number, they know who made the call. We don't want that. Do we?"

"Er, no, Skip."

"No. So run. I'll bring this boat behind, Benjy, and moor alongside." I looked for the key to get the engine started, and checked suddenly: it wasn't there. "Hold it!" Just in time, just as the *Screw* started to move away. "Scuz! Over here, now!"

He looked startled, then clambered up onto the roof and ran back to a point where he could jump over. The *Daffodil* rocked a little beneath his sudden weight.

"What's up, Skip?"

"No key. Think you can get her started?"

He bounced down onto the deck beside me, glanced at the control-panel and grinned. "No problem, Skip." I hadn't expected one. Scuz could get into a car, past its immobiliser and away in thirty seconds; I'd encountered him first in my own BMW, with about ten seconds to spare.

He forced that boat's ignition with a penknife, in five seconds flat. I put her into gear and motored slowly in the *Screw*'s wake, until we found a stretch of solid bank. Domino had already made a wild leap to shore, and was barely a dot along the towpath; that boy was the fastest thing afloat.

Ten minutes after we'd tied up he was back, breathing hard, his T-shirt clinging damply to his skinny copper body. "They're coming, Skip. Told us to wait, not touch anything..."

"All right. Just tell them what you saw, all of you," as I scanned their taut, anxious faces. "Nothing more than that. Okay?"

Tight nods, from every one of them.

"Good lads. Here, Benjy, share these around..."

I tossed him a pack of cigarettes and went down into the *Screw* to make sure that Geo was up to speed. I found him quietly cradling John, whispering nonsense into the kid's ear.

"How is he?"

"He's fine, I guess." He was clean at least, wearing one of the boys' T-shirts, its bagginess knotted into a tail between his legs. I wondered briefly what arrangements Geo had made beneath the knot, and decided not to ask. "Except, he's not talking..."

"That's no surprise, Geo. Given what he's seen." His mother battered to death, most likely, and then her motionless body for however long afterwards. Small wonder, if he found nothing to say about it to the strangers who'd plucked him out. "You just keep him happy, till the police come."

He nodded. "I think he's happier down here, away from the others."

I was sure of it. I slipped him another couple of cigarettes for company and left him, going up to keep an eye on my high-wired crew. Thoughts of the police might quell them, but not for long; they could turn dangerously hyper, if I didn't watch them. Indeed, Scuz was already daring Domino towards the *Daffodil*: "Go on, one quick look..."

"Leave it, Dom. You, Scuz — do you need another lesson in common sense?"

He flinched from the memory of that morning, when he'd brought me the wrong kind of newspaper. "No, Skip."

"No. Good." Come to think of it, his bruises were showing; I added, "Go below — quietly! — and put a shirt on. Fetch one for Shabby, too. And shoes for everyone who needs 'em." I'd have my crew looking spruce and ship shape, before the police turned up.

When they came, they came in waves: at first just a couple of officers who'd parked up at the pub and walked down, to check that this wasn't a hoax. They took one glance inside the *Daffodil* and called for support; that followed half an hour later, in the form of a plain-clothes inspector and a bunch of uniforms. The inspector was quick and easy with the boys, who after all had little enough to tell him; inevitably, he took more time over me.

"Mr Stewart, I confess that I'm a little confused. I gather that none of these boys is related to you?"

"That's right."

"Can you explain exactly what your relationship is, then, how you come to have charge of them?"

"Surely. A friend of mine runs a hostel in London, for homeless lads. They're persistent runaways, all of 'em; troubles at home, of course, and sometimes other problems, drink or drugs or whatever. He takes them in off the streets, gives them food and a bed, a place of safety. So he has a houseful of difficult adolescents, I have a boat; he talks me into giving some of them a week's holiday, come the summer."

I had the paperwork to prove it, and showed it to them. That's the advantage of Mickey's place, it's all very official and above-board. That's one reason why I always go back to Mickey when I'm looking for a new crew; the boys know the score, and so do the authorities. They just don't know that they're singing from a different score-sheet.

Once the police were content with my credentials, they moved on to what they thought were more relevant questions. If anything, though, I was less help than the boys: I'd been below decks for a couple of hours before we'd met the *Daffodil*, so no, I'd seen no one on the towpath. No dog-walkers, cyclists or lovers — certainly no one who might have recently abandoned a boat, a boy and a body. I confirmed that the *Daffodil's* engine had been running and the key missing; they should check their records, I suggested, see if any holiday-makers had reported a stolen boat. They'd done that already, they said, and had turned up trumps. An elderly couple had tied up for lunch at a canalside restaurant a few miles back, before the tunnel; when they made their way back to their mooring, the *Daffodil* was gone. It wasn't unknown for youngsters to pinch a boat for an afternoon's joy-ride; you can start one with a penknife, they said. Really? Fancy that, I murmured…

They were keeping an open mind, but their best guess lay along those lines: a couple with a kid, from society's margins to judge by her appearance and his, indulging a reckless temptation that was perhaps fuelled by drinking. They took the *Daffodil*, perhaps against her objections; an argument led to violence and the man fled, abandoning boat and child together. It was unfortunate that none of us had noticed him on the bank, but not surprising; he would likely have run on ahead, rather than turning back. There was no towpath through the tunnel, and no footpath across the hill it bore through. They would ask questions at the pub, they said, and of any fishermen they found along the way.

I asked if I could take the *Screw* down as far as the pub, and tie up there for the night. They'd know where to find me, if they had any more questions.

That would be fine, they said. Don't let the lads inside, they said that too; I nodded wisely, and assured them that I wouldn't.

Geo handed the kid over to the care of a policewoman — difficult for both of them, I thought; the little boy struggled and clung, the big boy looked like he wanted to do the same: I heard him giving her instructions, "He doesn't talk, except that he says his name, he says 'John' when he needs the toilet. Usually too late. I guess he's potty-trained, except that he's so shocked he's half forgotten" — and we went that extra mile at a slow chug. We'd lost half a day on the journey, which meant we'd also lost a full night's work; I spent the time on the phone, making rearrangements.

The sun was setting, by the time we'd moored. I set Scuz and Domino to cooking, then went to the pub alone; had a couple of pints while I pondered myself and what I'd done that day, what others had done before me. Then I headed back with bounty for my loyal crew, a carrier bag bulging with carry-outs. The police were a watchful presence in the pub, on the towpath, parked a little way up the road and talking to everyone. Clearly they hadn't caught their running man; likely, I thought, they didn't even have a witness yet. Certainly not a reliable description, or why work the night-time crowd so hard, so hungrily? They'd be here still to-morrow, I thought, and staging a reconstruction next week, as like as not. The girl had looked like a traveller; while students often looked the same, deliberately dirty, they didn't often have little kids in tow. And travellers travel, in borrowed boats or otherwise, and have holes all over to hide up in. I thought their running man might have run far by now, far indeed, and be seriously difficult to trace. I though they might have trouble enough just putting a name to the corpse...

I let the lads sleep late next morning; now that the schedule had been changed, we had only a short day's journey ahead of us. When they were up and we were moving slowly through the heat, I lay as before on a bunk with a newspaper that I'd fetched myself from a village down the road. A sensible broadsheet this time, it made only small mention of an unidentified girl's body found on a stolen boat on the canal, a toddler at her side. The tabloids might be full of it, as the pub had been full of journos and photographers — another reason the boys had got a carry-out, not to have their pretty pictures on page two: I knew I couldn't trust 'em not to point the finger at themselves, so I kept them below decks all night — but I wasn't curious enough to care.

Neither was my interest piqued by the trouble stirring again in Chechnya, nor the leaking rumour that yon US millionaire's baby was missing, lost or kidnapped or gone overboard. Bombs and bullets far away, who gave a fuck? Dead bodies close to home could cost me time and money both, but not a distant war. And missing kids I knew all about already, their care and resettlement not a speciality but a sideline of mine, a hobby really. Like many hobbyists I took more pains than the professionals, I thought; I did the thing precisely, did it well.

As witness my boatload of boys, moving serenely through the summer's day, dozing and smoking and soaking up sun while they waited for the long, long summer's night to come...

When we came to the appointed place, there were hours yet to kill before our first appointment. I set the boys to scrubbing up, to mopping and polishing inside and out before I let them think about showering themselves. Clean bodies in a clean boat, that's how I like my crew to be presented.

They were starting to show first signs of nerves by now. Nothing unusual in that: I watched, counting variations on a theme: how this one would go very quiet while that one ramped, how one would pause unexpectedly in his work to gaze at some unseen horizon while another focused intently on his hands and what they did, on a world he could touch and feel.

Nerves were good, I liked to see a boy on edge, so long as he didn't topple over. That kid yesterday, I thought, had toppled far and gone. Too scared even to shit himself, until Skip came reluctantly to the rescue; I wondered if he were talking yet, and doubted it extremely. The paper had one thing wrong, that he'd been found at his mother's side; he'd been as far from her as he could get, and not a drop, not a speck of blood on his dungarees that I had seen. No blame to him for that. I thought of Greyfriars Bobby and remembered a dog I'd killed once, a bitch that had run into the road too foolishly close to my wheels; driving back later, I'd seen her body in the gutter with a clutch of puppies pressed close. Trying to suckle, trying to wake her or simply trying for some last snatch of cooling, carrion comfort: animal instinct was one thing, human shock it seemed was something other.

I kept a careful eye on my charges, as the sun sank. Fed them on bread and cheese, not to fill the *Screw* with smells of cooking; sent them one by one into the shower and let her fill instead with scented steam, shampoo and body-wash. No deodorants. The boys knew this routine. They milled quietly in jeans or boxer-shorts, rubbing towels through wet hair and flicking them at bare backs, arguing over the contents of my jewellery-box, adorning themselves with ear-studs and cheap gold chains while they jigged and sang along with what music played from the boombox in the corner.

JUNK MALE

I left them to it once I was sure of their mood, going up on deck to double-check the solidity of the gangplank while I waited for the first customer of the evening to come along the towpath. Wouldn't want him to slip; slip-ups were bad for business.

He came on time, big and brisk and cash in hand. I waved that aside. Payment on delivery was my policy, always had been; satisfaction guaranteed, or I'd know the reason why. Besides, if they paid upfront they were less scrupulous about tipping the lads after, and I took fifty per cent of any tips.

He went below; I listened to the murmur of soft voices coming up through the hatchway and knew how the boys would be preening, posing, trying to catch his eye. The first score of the night was a challenge to them, they laid bets on it; I bet with myself, but only after I'd seen the punter. This one, I thought it would be Domino who got to lead him through to the front cabin, where my double bed was neatly made up with fresh sheets and flowers. Big men went for slender boys, more often than chance would allow.

The lads only kicked up a racket when they were licensed to do it, I'd trained them that well; they were all but silent when a client was aboard and busy, knowing that I would tolerate nothing less. I heard the shuffle of cards, an occasional protesting whisper, nothing more. And smiled, and thought about being *in loco parentis*, as people always assumed that I was, as the police had. What else, with half a dozen ripening lads all of an age, who couldn't possibly all be my own…?

And frowned, and chased that thought a little before I shook it out of my head, no concern of mine.

After a while I caught the scrape of a match clearly in the night's hush, and the whiff of tobacco smoke that followed it, wafting back from the bows. There was no smoking below decks, on a working night; only a boy who'd done his stint was allowed a cigarette, a rest in the open air before he rejoined the others.

So I was ready when the customer came out, a minute later. He settled up, thanked me gravely and went his way; I checked my watch, heard movement in the boat as Geo went forward, heard Domino's bright laugh as he helped to change the sheets. Score one to me, I thought, and smiled lightly as I watched the towpath for another man alone without a dog.

The next was older, sadder; he'd take Scuz, I thought, for that boy's sullen pout, his air of taking on the world and always losing.

I took the pipe from my pocket, for a peaceful blow. As I cleaned it after, my drifting mind remembered something I'd read about gas-companies having a machine that made its own way through their buried pipes, to seal leaks from the inside. That notion triggered another, that I held for a while in my head.

One man left and another came, at steady intervals through the long late evening and well into the night. When the last of them was done and gone off happy, I rewarded my willing, weary boys with crisps and beer and a final smoke before I bedded them down and went through to the forward cabin. Geo had changed the sheets one final time, for me; and had done his best as well against the lingering odours of musk and sweat, opening the windows wide and lighting a rose-scented candle.

I undressed, lay down and thought a little more while I waited for sleep to come: thought of parents and missing children, of boys lost and found, of puppies pressed against the cooling body of their mother.

In the morning, we motored to the nearest town and moored up for a while. I sent Scuz and Shabby off to find a launderette, to wash and dry the sheets; warned the others to behave while I was gone, and went to find a phone. Just for the joke of it, to stamp myself with virtue.

I called the police, that same inspector who'd interviewed me and left me with his number; I said, "You're asking questions on the wrong side of the hill."

"Beg pardon?"

"Try the other end of the tunnel. That's where they abandoned the *Daffodil*: put her bows into the tunnel's mouth and jumped ashore, left her engine running. She'd go through on her own, bang the walls a bit but nothing worse than that, they'd knock her straighter every time she did it. You can't get stuck in a tunnel, it feeds you through. It wasn't till she met the curve of the canal on this side that she ran into the bank."

I heard him grunt, I could almost hear him think; I knew the question that must follow before he asked it. "So who are they, then? 'They', you said..."

"That's right. Is the kid talking yet?"

"No, he's not."

"No." I didn't think he would be. "That American couple, with the yacht in Great Yarmouth — it's true, isn't it, that their little boy's been snatched?"

I heard him breathing slowly, in and out. "How did you know?"

"He says 'john' when he needs the toilet."

"I'm sorry?"

"He had to be American, when I thought about it. It's hard to hear an accent in one word, but it is there. And I bet she's not a Yank: blonde travellers with dirty dreadlock hair, it's a very British thing. And he hadn't been near her, and show me the kid who could do that, who could see his mother killed and keep that distance, never once go up to touch, to claim her back..." And no wonder he wasn't talking else, when he'd been snatched by strangers into a life quite unlike, quite brutal in comparison to what he knew; when that life had abruptly turned brutal for real, under his eyes, a girl battered to death in front of him; when even his rescuers wouldn't call him by his proper name. It must have felt like we were talking to somebody else. He might learn to take shelter in that when he was older, if he remembered this at all. Some of the lads who washed up at Mickey's certainly did; they had their *noms de guerre*, and what had happened to the boy they used to be had happened to a stranger. Or the other way around sometimes, that what they did under their new tag was all acting, all unreal while their true self, their true name was sealed up and hidden deep below. I had both, I thought, aboard my boat right now.

"There are two problems," I went on sententiously, enjoying myself enormously, "two moments of greatest danger when you've kidnapped someone. One is picking up the money; the other is handing back the victim. Money's not so hard now, these days of electronic transfer; you can send it round the world a dozen times in minutes, with the help of a dodgy bank or two. Lose it in charity accounts, wash it whiter than a sheet. People aren't so handy. But say the ransom's paid, the parents want their kid back; what better than to tell them he's in safe custody, the cops have got him already, up the other end of the country? Dump him with a dead girl, some stray you pick up on the road, who won't be missed for weeks; of course people will assume that she's his mother. Pick the right girl, the autopsy will confirm she'd had a kid or two. No one's going to think of DNA tests, not for a while. They'll just go chasing phantoms, a mother-and-child and a father too, and none of them ever existed." It was brilliant, I wished I'd thought of it myself, I loved it.

He did not. "Why go to all that trouble, then, why not just kill the kid if you're prepared to kill a girl?"

Because there was honour among kidnappers? Because no one would pay up a second time, if the victim died the first? Perhaps the one, perhaps the other; but I hoped that neither of those was true.

"Where would be the fun in that?" I asked him, and hung up. ∎

RAY NAYLER

CUTTING WOOD, CARRYING WATER

Ray Nayler was born in Quebec, Canada, and raised in California, where he still lives. Over the last few years he has had short stories published in Lines in the Sand, Deathrealm, Onionhead Literary Quarterly and the Berkeley Fiction Review, with others upcoming in Ellery Queen's Mystery Magazine, Hardboiled and other magazines. He recently completed his second novel, and is currently working on a third set in Toronto.

This was just before I killed him. I was lying in our cabin, on the bed, staring at the ceiling and thinking about things. I felt very calm. I wasn't angry — or at least I didn't feel angry. I felt still. I knew I was going to do it, but all the emotion that had driven me was gone — as if I had already killed him, and now everything was better. I was just lying there, all bundled up in my parka and with my boots on, listening to the snow tapping softly on the windowpane, smoking a cigarette, and thinking about when Cassandra and I first came to the Hot Springs.

Cassandra had been very excited about it. I had just been released from the hospital, and I was in her bathroom, shaving. She told me about how her friend owned the Jackson Hot Springs in Oregon. This friend had called her up and invited her to stay there over the winter, when it was closed. The friend needed someone to look after the place — keep squatters off the property and make sure nobody vandalized the buildings.

"It would be ideal. You have a little money from the lawsuit, and I don't need much. It'll be just the two of us, lounging in the hot tubs and sitting by the fire in the lodge. What could be more perfect?" She paused, and I could tell she was trying to gauge what my reaction would be to what she was about to say. "It'll give you the time you need to get better. All the way better."

"I feel all right." But of course I didn't feel all right. I had to concentrate just to keep my hand steady while shaving.

"I know you do, baby. But don't you think it would be better for you to just relax a bit? By Spring you'll feel so much stronger."

So we drove up to the place. Or, I should say, *Cassandra* drove up. I was still having panic attacks when I got behind the steering wheel. Sometimes I even got them while I slept. I would dream the whole thing over again, only I was looking down on it, floating above it.

It had begun to snow already. There was a light dusting of it on the ground and on the roofs of the little cottages.

I liked the place right away. It was kind of run down — just a building with the pool and hot tubs and lockers, a dozen chipped-paint cabins, and a score of empty tent sites. The smell of sulfur from the mineral springs carried in the cold air. Cassandra skipped through the thin layer of snow and managed to scrape together enough to pitch a snowball at me. There was a note taped inside the office door, telling us to let Mark Ciroc in when he showed up. He was the handyman Cassandra's friend had hired to fix the place up for the spring.

After unpacking, we went to the main building and climbed into one of the private hot tubs. We left the door open, just because we could, and I took her, all wet with the sulfur water, her hair steaming, her breasts against the hard tile. She was a bit of a hippie. A feminist. She didn't shave her armpits or her legs. I remember when I fist glanced under her arms at the hospital, and saw that dark fringe of hair. I had thought I wouldn't like it. But I did. It reminded me that she was an animal, a human being that I was inside of, a hippie white girl I was ramming myself into. She bit my brown fingers when she came.

The air seemed almost brittle with cold after the tub. She arranged our things in the cabin while I stumbled around lamely in the dusky half-light, looking for wood for our first fire.

I stabbed the cigarette out and lit another. It wasn't quite time yet. Right now they would be in the hot tub — like we were that first night, only with the door closed. She needed some 'time away from me'. They were 'just friends'. "He knows the same things I do. We think the same way. It's just good to talk to someone who has the same politics as me, the same values."

We'd been there about a month when he showed up. By that time, the cold had gotten worse. She didn't seem to mind it, tramping around in the snow in her big fleece-lined parka, pointing out the sharp black birds to me, the cold-footed raccoons foraging in the snow. The Jackson Hot Springs were just outside of town, but we never went anywhere except to the bright-lit Safeway to buy supplies.

In the bitter cold of the morning, I would strip down in the chilly locker room, run to the heated pool and jump in, drifting in the cloudy water that seemed ready to freeze in my hair each time my head broke the surface. And one morning, when I surfaced, he was standing over me.

"Nice morning for a swim, man."

I was naked, of course. I felt suddenly ashamed, especially of the scars along my neck and shoulders, where they had dragged me across the pavement.

He had one of those even, Dudley Do-Right smiles, and huge knotted shoulders packed into a flannel shirt. He would have looked like a picturebook lumberjack, except for the dreadlocks framing his square face. He reached a broad, flat hand down to me and we shook. "Name's Mark. I just got in. Beat the storm that's coming. But you guys know about that…"

"Yeah," I said. I hadn't known anything about the storm. "It's good to meet you. I'm Sal."

I got out on the other side of the pool, away from him, wrapping my towel around myself. On my way into the locker room I bumped into Cassandra, naked, going for a swim. "We'll have to start wearing swimsuits. The handyman's here."

She gave me a condescending smile and patted my head. "I know. I met him on his way in. And it isn't like he hasn't seen a naked person before. He was telling me about the naturist colony that he practically grew up in, Sal."

"Well, anyway…"

She was already walking past me to the pool, her breasts taut from the cold, the skin dimpled and tight across her thighs and butt. I didn't want to make an idiot of myself by going back out to the pool and playing the overprotective male. I scraped myself dry in the locker room and threw on my clothes.

I had to walk by the pool fence to get to the woodpile, and I saw them talking. She was standing in the shallow end of the pool, the water lapping across the swell of her breasts. He was squatting, that same bright smile on his face.

I hacked at the frozen logs, but they turned the ax-blade away like stones, the impact vibrating up my cold-numbed arms.

Later Mark used the same blunt ax to split them into even quarters, and built our fire for us in the main building. He brewed a bitter Chinese tea over the fire. The wind snapped snow against the building while we sat there wrapped in blankets, the fire crackling. They talked about the WTO and Mark's work in Nicaragua, building houses for people who look like me.

I went to the window. It was still snowing lightly, the snow spinning and drifting across the ground. I watched Mark come out of the main building, closing his coat across his chest, a dark blur against white, making his way around to his cottage.

A conversation in the dark, beneath the piled blankets, her slick thighs wrapped around my leg. I can hear her heart tapping behind her ribs.

"We should…invite him in. Don't you think? Make him feel welcome, instead of like an outsider."

"What do you mean?" Immediately I am tense, alert.

"I guess I don't know, Sal. I don't know how *open* you are to new things. But since we're all here, and alone…" I could hear her heart quickening. "I mean, I'm sure he would be respectful of your boundaries. And it's not like he hasn't done things like this before…"

"I have to go to the bathroom."

"Sal…"

I was up, throwing on all the clothes I needed for the short hike to the bathroom and showers, fumbling for a flashlight in the dark.

"I'm just going to pretend you didn't say that to me, Cassandra."

"It's not like it's anything *I* haven't done, Sal. If he were a woman, I would want the same…"

"I'm not hearing you."

"I love you, Sal. I would never…"

But I'd snapped the door shut behind me. The flashlight made a dull circle on the blank snow.

"Hey buddy."

I looked up from the map I had been studying. I had been thinking *I am definitely lost*, over and over for the past hour or so. Now I was stranded in some bland town in the foothills of the Sierras, sitting in the parking lot of an IHOP.

The kid standing at my car window was Bic bald, a skinny white boy in a black flight jacket with an American flag sewn to the sleeve. I didn't see the ten other kids just like him, crouched behind the other two parked cars in the lot. I rolled the window down. That's the last I remember. The rest is a catalogue of injuries: broken femur, broken wrist, two broken fingers, three cracked ribs, dislocated shoulder, broken nose, eight teeth knocked out, concussion, fifteen stitches in eyebrows and lips.

My world jump-started itself again on my third day in the hospital. Cassandra was sitting next to my bed. She was the one who found me, after they were done with me. She called the ambulance, and cradled my bleeding head in her lap while the sirens approached. She came to visit me every day while they put me back together again.

I had no idea I had been beat up because of my race. To be truthful, I didn't think about my race much. I speak no Spanish. My parents spoke no Spanish. I have green eyes. My grandfather was White. And where I grew up, nobody said anything about the color of my skin — at least not where I could hear it.

So I was surprised when the papers called it a hate crime, surprised when the ACLU attorneys showed up at the hospital, and shocked when the boys' families paid me restitution. I sat in court with plaster up to my hip and my handsome all-American face. Four members of the jury cried. I didn't. By that time I had other things on my mind — like Cassandra, her hands beneath the sheets at the hospital. Our relationship was perfect. She got to feel political and justified. I got to give it to those White boys, again and again. And they liked it.

When I got back to the cabin she was gone. I knew where she was. I could even have stopped it from happening, but I didn't. Instead, I lay in the dark and let myself get angry.

The biggest storm of the winter hit a few days later. It was a warm one, full of wet, sticking snow that clung to your cheeks and turned its brothers to brown slush on the ground. She didn't stay with him. He cut wood for our fires but left us alone while they burned. I would watch him walking in the snow, crouched against the wind like a wolf, going from building to building, fixing things. My leg still ached where it had been broken, and I spent most of my time soaking in the dark, sulfur-stinking tubs. Sometimes Cassandra would come in, naked, lowering herself into the cloudy water, finding me with her hands.

I would bend her over the lip of the tub, my hand at the back of her neck, her cheek against the rough tile.

"You can't control people, Sal. You have to understand that. People need to be free. They need to do what they want."

I shoved the cabin door open. Snow spun and drifted in, falling across the rough wood floor. I dug into the snow outside and found what I was looking for — the ax handle. While cutting wood in the cold, the metal head had split, shearing like glass. But the ax handle had that perfect heft to it, like an extension of my arm, its flat wood head like a blade itself.

My boots squealed in the snow. Somewhere in a stand of trees one of the big branches gave way under white weight and came crashing down.

She was right about the place. I was feeling better. My muscles were lean and hard and animal. What I had lost in the hospital had come back in thick ropes around my arms and legs. I moved with all the grace that had once made me proud, when dancing to the thud-thud-thud of my people's melody-less music. Back then, I was always immaculately dressed, my hair a thick black mass, perfectly contained, like my ancestors' in Los Angeles, when they came at us to tear our clothes and beat our pearl-handled switchblades from our hands.

I could almost see her, opened up to the dark water, sweat and sulfur in her hair, the taste of him on her lips.

People need to be free.

He was asleep when I did it. Once, when it was almost over, he said something with his broken mouth. It might have been *stop*.

Afterwards, I dropped the bloody ax handle in the snow. And waited. ∎

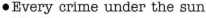

ZiNE

The definitive creative writers' guide to the world's independent press, with
detailed contributors' guidelines, competitions, articles, reviews, news and views

ALIENS
SEX
VIOLENCE
DINOSAURS

FROM THE PUBLISHERS OF CRIMEWAVE

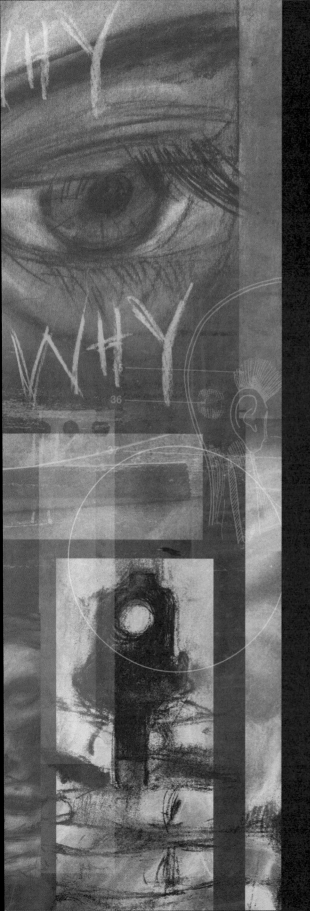

BRIAN HODGE

MILES TO GO
BEFORE I WEEP

Brian Hodge is the author of seven novels ranging from horror to crime-noir, most recently Wild Horses, a highly-lauded lead title from William Morrow, who won its rights in a spirited auction. Never before published, 'Miles to Go Before I Weep' is the seed story for that novel. Brian is nearing completion of his next novel, Mad Dogs. He's also written around eighty short stories and novellas, many of which have been forced at gun-point into two acclaimed collections, The Convulsion Factory and Falling Idols, with a third one in the works. He lives in the shadow of the Colorado Front Range, where he periodically locks himself away with an ever-growing digital studio of keyboards, samplers, didgeridoos and assorted noise-inducing gear, for an alter-ego recording project dubbed Axis Mundi. All of which, on the whole, beats working.

The air conditioner in Dickory Doc's wheezed like a horse ready for a bullet in the head, and we were all sweating our drinks out as fast as we could pour them down. The heat makes people crazy…but then, for most, it's not too hard a push.

This seemed as righteous a truth as any I'd thought lately, one of those things to cross your mind for no good reason, then before too many ticks of the clock, along comes somebody to prove it. I'll watch, not often one to ignore a good object lesson.

"See those two?" This newfound friend and confidante that I'd never see again after a few more drinks pointed along the bar. His finger was aimed at a blonde barmaid and a redheaded customer who looked to be having a race to see who could grow their roots out quicker. Likely this wasn't the source of the aggravation mounting between them, but my new bleary-eyed friend and I sat too far away, and the jukebox wept too loud with lament over no-good lovers gone away, so we didn't have a clue what it was all about. Just didn't much like breathing each other's air, I guess.

My friend, forgotten name and all, waggled his finger at the bar in front of us. "Next round says those two'll be scratching eyes out inside of five minutes. Okay?"

"Bet," I nodded, but knew the loss would be mine, because I just had to lay it down once more in favor of human decency. It was a faith thing, and some days we all need a little of that sort of exercise in our lives.

So we settled in for the wait, see what five minutes really feels like when you're waiting for something to break, be it the peace, a window, or a bone. Feels like eternity, and, not for the first time, I wondered why we couldn't all just live out our days five minutes at a time. Why, we'd all feel like we had forever in front of us.

Though I'll concede that, for some, that might be the very worst thing to stare them in the face each morning.

So we waited and mopped our sweat with napkins already soggy from the bottles and our foreheads, all that tension like a loaded gun at the other end of the bar and only a handful of us aware of it at all. The others in their own little lost paradises, desert rats and cowboys and bikers, and their women. They converged here like the varied breeds that come to a watering hole on the African savannah: drink, for drink you must, but drink knowing you run the risk of turning into somebody's lunch.

As much a charm school dropout as the redhead already looked, she started to look meaner still over some new volley of insults exchanged across the bar, tried to get in the last word once the blonde's back was turned by throwing one of those little pickled cherries — used — at her. It missed by a foot, splatted into the wall where it popped like a devil's eye.

"Too damn hot is all," I said. "Now if we were in Canada, say, this wouldn't even be happening."

"If we were in Canada," said my friend, "she'd've thrown a moose pie."

"Sorry, I beg to differ. A cooler climate leads to cooler heads. Eskimos? They don't even have a word for war." I paused with my bottle at my mouth, reasoning this through. "You know…another Ice Age just might go a long way towards world peace."

"Vikings," he said, and rather resembled one himself. "You forgot about Vikings. There goes your whole theory right there."

"Damn," I said, and wasn't it always just this way? Brutal facts intruding on what seemed for the moment like a revelation, perfect and honest. It wasn't any easy thing, saving the world.

And I was truly sorry a minute later when my friend won his bet, when the whole stewpot of strife and bad blood at the other end of the bar came to its inevitable boiling head, and the rest of the scenario played out uglier than a hemorrhoid.

Harsh words led to a shove, the shove led to a slap, and the slap was the pin on the grenade. The redhead decided to try using the blonde to wipe her own bar, and glass went crashing while men grabbed to salvage what drinks they could, then cleared aside to give them room to fight it out. Dickory Doc's roused with a mighty roar by the time the blonde landed a solid punch to the redhead's jaw and went scrambling across the bar.

I've never yet seen a catfight that wasn't a spectacle of awe and horror. This, I suspect, because such fights wear the masks of both comedy and tragedy. There isn't the brute strength of men out to bust a head — and often a lack of the finer coordinations — and so it's almost funny, those wild roundhouse swings and the feral faces that only furious women can make, and when the makeup goes it only exaggerates things more. But then again, there's all the pure animal viciousness of tooth and claw, and that dark red-eyed bloodlust to not give up until one tears out the other's throat, and maybe drinks harsh foaming whiskey from the loser's skull.

They kicked and they gouged, tore loose flaps in each other's clothes, bit when they could. When they weren't grunting in fierce rage, they called each other names that no man could employ and get away with. In time they flung each other out the door to land beneath the sky of this burning Newby, California night. The air was still and only the bravest stars shown through LA's leftover smog, the city's only bequest to this desert town where rivers and dreams and old dogs came to die.

"I don't guess anybody calls the sheriff, do they?" I asked.

My friend shrugged his big Viking shoulders. "Friday night, no high school football, now what do you think?"

Desperate people with desperate hopes cheered as those four mean little fists pummeled away, or yanked out a dangling scrap of dark-rooted hair and flung it aside like a puny scalp. Locked in a deathgrip, the beautiful sweaty harridans went rolling across the gravel lot, through a dirty oil slick left by some heaving engine, and came out looking like negatives shot at a Kabuki theater.

When she gave her rival's head a good knock against the lot, I thought the blonde might've been able to snatch victory from what was looking like defeat, but then the redhead reached up to bum a cigarette from some burly truck jockey, and went to work on the blonde's shoulder. She burned in one tight round hole after another, through the tattered T-shirt and then skin, and the blonde barmaid started to yelp as if she'd only just discovered what true pain really is. For the redhead it was like scenting fresh-spilled blood, and her fingers jabbed forward, going for one wide blue eye but missing by a fraction, hissing out the cigarette against the blonde's cheekbone.

There was no shortage of admiring cheers for that trick, although if my voice was heard at all, it would've been a groan of sickness. There was no comedy left, only tragedy, and I felt it all the way down to my gut; deeper, even, in some dark place where the soul cowers, protected in its final refuge. And I remembered when I used to try to intervene at such times as this, playing the peacemaker, before I got taught the true value of a smile and an empty hand.

It didn't take long for the redhead to finish things, all open-handed slaps and bitter bloody grins and rabbit punches. Two final kicks in the ribs, and the blonde curled up like a question mark at the end of her life's sentence. She lay in the gravel and the dust and the oil, not moving except for the labor of sore ribs as she tried to breathe. The redhead was up and swaggering back to the bar to nurse her own wounds, drink her just rewards, celebrate victory. Something to tell her grandkids about someday, on lazy Sunday afternoons at the trailer park.

The sated crowd was swift to break, following its champion back inside. All of them like chickens with their pecking order, strutting away to leave a bird-sized lump of feathers and blood heaped in the dirt. To the rest I guess she didn't exist anymore, barmaid or not. Peculiar, but then I'd never much liked Newby, coming through here. I always get the feeling I should've stayed at the motel.

I paid off my bar mate and told him he'd have to drink the spoils of war alone, and he didn't seem insulted as he went back inside with an unsteady saunter, and next thing I knew the lot was empty but for the final two of us, breathing the ghost of a smelly breeze from the west. I crunched over to where the blonde lay in her pain and defeat, went down on one knee.

"Do you need any help?" I asked, as gently as I could.

She lay in shadows, and her eyes didn't open. After a moment her backhand flashed with clumsy accuracy and a big chip of gravel ricocheted off my forehead.

"Well put my eye out next time." I fumed a few seconds, even if her pride was the last thing she had to guard. "Anybody I can call for you, then?"

She struggled a moment, raised on one elbow, and started to snicker when she saw me covering my face with crossed arms. That little bit of a laugh did her face some good, battered as it was. Nothing but tangled hair and dirty scrapes, trickles of blood and swelling, and that crusty hole on her cheek like a wound from a .22.

"No. Not a soul," she said, looking as if she wished she'd never gotten up that morning, maybe all year. "Pretty sad, huh?"

I'd lowered my arms by now, and pulled a red kerchief from my pocket that I sometimes used as a bandanna. "It's clean," I said, and gave it to her. She went scooting backward to sit against a dusty fender and dab away at the damage.

"You know, what I can't figure out is, how come nobody moved in to stop it, you coming from behind the bar." We both knew what I meant. In every bar I'd ever been in, with any personality — good or bad — it was the Eleventh Commandment: thou shalt not mess with the barmaid. Break it and unshaven angels would be dancing on your head in seconds, if only to save themselves from prolonged thirst.

The battered woman gave a spiteful look at the closed door. "Loretta? She's local. I'm not," and that said it all. "You must not be either, if you didn't know."

I shook my head. "No. I'm not."

She huffed with a short low whiskey laugh. "Well, looks like your IQ just shot up by forty points."

I grinned down at the gravel. "You're sure there's nothing you need?"

Her hand dropped to her side, came up with another big pebble that she held as if deciding whether or not to throw it. No fire behind it this time, just a quiet stubborn pride and a smile too painful to let loose.

I nodded, started across the lot against a backbeat of bass, thumping like a sick heart inside the bar. I got in my van and backed out, angled for escape, and when I stopped to put it into drive there came a frantic thumping up along the side of the van. Then her splayed hand slapping glass, and there she was in my window, more life in her than I'd thought she had left. I rolled the window down.

"I just saw your license plate."

Florida plate, picture of a manatee in the center. "And?"

"You wouldn't happen to be going back there, would you?" And the hope in her voice, her eyes...they lit up bright as fireworks, put all that damage in the dim background. I would imagine the sad faces of orphans are the same, whenever kind-looking parents tour the home. "Would you?"

"I'm leaving tomorrow morning."

"Can I ride along?" The fingers of both hands were curling over the edge of my door, fierce as eagle claws. "Only as far as Mississippi. I'll go halves on gas."

The last thing I wanted was an argument, her on the one side and my conscience on the other, both of them telling me the very same thing. At least my conscience wouldn't start throwing rocks.

"Mississippi?" I said, and then what must've sounded to both of us like yes. Probably not the best decision I'd ever made.

But the heat does make people crazy, and crazy never runs out of ways to show its face.

I didn't even get her name until the next morning, after I'd followed her directions to a half-size trailer she was renting. It sat on a flat slab of desert browns and scruffy chaparral, a tin can that had been kicked from one edge of town to the other.

Allison. She was Allison Willoughby, and everything she owned looked to fit in two suitcases and a purse as big as a saddlebag. The back of the van, as empty now as it had been full on my way west, swallowed her luggage, and as strangers we bid a welcome goodbye to this weeping lesion of a town. Allison's middle fingers popped up like a pair of switchblades and with a demented ecstasy she jammed both arms out the window, and I believe if we'd known each other better she'd have jammed her bare ass instead.

"Worst month of my life," she told me, before one last bitter lunge out the window: "Fuck you all and the inbred horses you fell off of!"

She laughed then, laughed like a woman freed of unimaginably heavy weights, a woman ready to spread wings and soar. She tumbled back into the seat, radiant with relief. Propping her feet against the dashboard in their cowboy boots, and bare-legged up to faded cutoffs and a purple shirt tied off at her stomach. Last night's blood and oil and grime were washed away, leaving only the black eye, the bruises, the burn. She'd swept her hair down and to one side to hide the worst but it was poor camouflage. Pretty enough, under it all, but the set of her eyes and the tiny lines were like a map of whatever rugged road she'd traveled. One wrong word and her face could go hard enough to dull an axe blade.

"All that hatred in just one month," I said.

"Yeah, well, I didn't sleep much, so it felt like two."

"I'm guessing it wasn't by choice?"

"Real Rhodes Scholar, aren't you?" When she looked at me, her clear eye going to a slit, I felt chastised. "I'm almost afraid to ask what brought you there."

"Just business."

Which amused her. "What business in that godforsaken urinal could've brought you all the way from Florida?"

"You must know the cycle shop there. Coyote's Paw Harley?"

"Naturally." Allison grew a bit more respectful.

"It's the end of a route I drive two or three times a year. I stop at places all across the south, east to west. I make clothes and things, and shops like that are usually my best markets."

She was nodding, a cockeyed smile working its way around the puffier spots on her lips. "A genuine craftsman. Don't see many of those anymore."

This was true. I belonged to an increasingly obsolete breed, and even though the money could get tight at times, the freedom was more than compensation enough. And I liked being master of my own life, lackey to no boss, with a couple of people working for me back in Panama City. Liked to take a stretch of leather and shape it to fit an idea born in my head, or discover the idea sunk into the leather already, speak its language and hear what it had to say for itself. I could look at a rack of vests and jackets, chaps and belts, hats and odd one-off pieces, originals all, see them hanging there and feel that I'd taken something dead and made it live again.

Pitiful consolation, however, for the sad-eyed noble cows.

While steering, I groped around the floor among my strewn belongings, came up with a folder and gave it to her. She flipped through the pages, sketches I'd made over the past few months; new designs, variations on old. I told her that while I could save the van and myself a lot of hard mileage by shipping my wares out by UPS, there was something meaningful in seeing where they ended up. Where they hung, the people that'd be looking them over, wearing them; the ways they were all different, the ways they were all the same. It gave me a better idea what people might like, whenever I could call some new stranger to mind when I took up the sketch pad and pencil.

"Any of these do anything for you?"

Some did, some didn't. She slid one from the stack and held it up, an eyebrow cocked. The paper showed a vest, its origins half-biker, half-bondage. "Seriously?" she asked.

I shrugged. "Some people like a lot of straps."

"Some people *need* a lot of straps," and it sounded like the voice of experience.

I wondered how she'd come to be stuck in Newby for a month, and it took another hundred miles of desert and carrion before the story began to tiptoe out of her. Allison had spent the last couple of years in Las Vegas with a guy named Boyd, a name she pronounced as if it were synonymous with twisted birthmarks and siring by jackals. Boyd suddenly became possessed of the certainty that his destiny lay in Los Angeles, and off they went. Boyd soon lamented that all destiny was subject to mechanical cooperation, as dismayed as she to find them stranded in Newby with a thrown rod. A grinning mechanic eyeballed a four-day estimate on the car, then turned around and had it driveable in three. This she did not find out until the fourth morning.

"Boyd must've received a new message that his destiny no longer included me," she admitted. "And that's just fine with me, but all the same, I hope his destiny now includes syphilis."

I was getting the idea that Allison Willoughby knew how to nurse a grudge and never wean it.

"So my main priority became saving up for a bus ticket home to Mississippi."

"Must've been a lean month, if you couldn't even scrape up enough tip money for a ticket." This brought a glaze of defensive irritation that I thought I recognized: the money had gone someplace else, some higher priority. "Your family in Mississippi couldn't have sent you ticket money?"

"I only said it was home. Who said anything about a family?"

You did. It's written all over your face, I thought, deciding against pressing further. Sometimes, blood or not, a family isn't anything to be proud of; a burden to be shouldered, a last resort for the broken and the lost.

That place where you trade your pride for a few more days of hoping for a miracle.

We were into New Mexico when we pulled off to pass the night. I got a motel room with two beds, thinking surely that would suit everyone's needs, not learning it didn't until after we'd eaten, then sat sipping a couple of contemplative beers while staring off at the moonlit desert in that easy silence that comes when you no longer feel as if you have to prove anything. Little did I know.

"I'll sleep in the van," Allison told me when we got back to the motel.

"There's no reason for that. Look, it's not a handout. I'd've had to get a motel room whether you came along or not."

She planted herself on the parking lot, those bare, booted legs steady as pillars, arms defiant across her chest. "I've slept worse places than that, I'll be plenty comfortable in the van."

"For crissake, you don't owe me anything. I got the receipt and it's a tax deduction, so quit being so damned stubborn and get a decent night's sleep, why don't you."

But stubborn she was, so stubborn that if you threw her from an airplane she'd fall up just to spite you. I argued a minute longer because conscience demanded it, then gave up, and it wasn't until I'd gone inside, then brought her a pillow and blanket from the unused bed, that I caught a completely different look in her eyes. Allison staring beyond me through the open doorway, a basic mistrust of four walls and a door that she wasn't able to conceal quickly enough. Five hundred miles of shimmering road just hadn't quite done the trick: I'd not yet proved myself, overcome whatever she'd endured to prefer the hard van floor to the risk I posed.

"If you change your mind," I told her, "just knock."

But the knock never came, as I knew it wouldn't, and sleep mostly teased. It often does, in a bed slept in by successions of strangers, our only connection the same mattress. Their lives taunted me, kept worrying at my mind and heart.

I got up in the middle of the night to check on Allison, a task neither asked for nor seemingly required, so perhaps it was curiosity more than anything. Beyond the motel squatting at its lip, the desert breathed and hummed, full of life brought out by the moon. I stepped to the windows in the back of the van and peered in.

This was the second night in a row I'd seen her curled up, and while Allison looked far more serene this time, it didn't come without a price. In her makeshift nest of pillow and blanket, surrounded by a protective wall of luggage, she slept with a hand loosely folded around a snub-nosed revolver. Its nickel plating shone with a lethal gleam of moonlight silver. She touched it the way a girl twenty years younger would touch a teddy bear.

I stood watching her for a moment, watching the peace it gave her, and I felt too many things for this late at night. Too many conflicting aches and confusing impulses, but convinced above all that the sooner she was out of my life, the better.

Of course that was logic talking, and logic I'd never been all that eager to listen to.

So when we could argue no longer I went back inside to sleep through as much of the night as would have me.

After my morning shower I offered to go get breakfast in a bag for us while she grabbed her own shower. While Allison agreed to that our eyes held a few beats longer than needed, an unspoken understanding between us that we both knew I was making myself scarce for her benefit. The revolver was nowhere to be seen but I suspected it lurked close at hand, in that giant purse.

I wondered who or what had prompted her to carry it. If it was something she'd owned awhile, or had bought only after finding herself stranded in Newby. The latter would, at least, explain why she hadn't even managed bus fare over the month.

Allison looked a lot fresher when we returned to the road, carrying with her that fine clean smell of a woman with all the taint of the world washed away. Her hair blew wild and free about her face and shoulders, and I imagined what it must feel like between stroking fingers.

"Hey, hey, Tom, guess what I found last night," she said, her voice almost singsong.

"You tell me." But as soon as she went digging through my stuff on the floor I knew what it had to be. The blush started at the soles of my feet, went up from there.

She opened a little flat box and began to pull out books that were just as little, just as flat, and brought them to her lap. As she flipped through them she read the titles aloud: "*Baby Animals. Bobby Meets the Dinosaurs. The Jolly Barnyard. Little Bear Goes to the Moon. Mr Putter and Tabby Pour the Tea. The Ever-Living Tree.* Hmm. I think *The Jolly Barnyard* was also the name of a porn flick that Boyd tried to force me to watch once. These belong to your kids?"

I shrugged uneasily behind the wheel. "Yes and no."

"Either they do or they don't. I can't make it any clearer than that."

"I don't have any kids," I growled, the first time I'd raised my voice to her. "But someday…if I do, if I'm lucky enough…then these books, well…they'll belong to them then. Is that clear enough for you?"

She looked closely at me, but it was more than that. Watching me, looking through me; past the scar that creased the corner of one eye, past the black hair that was showing dabs of gray before I'd even left my mid-thirties. Allison looked and saw all this as if it were new, watched me with that type of wonder on her face that can go so many ways, from slow tears to withering laughter.

"You buy these," she said softly, "and you hang onto them? You just…hang onto them?"

I was wishing she'd go ahead and laugh. Maybe she could tell from my face that I picked them up all across the country during these trips; that I read them, over and over, but no matter how many times I read one it still hurt a little, because there was no one I was reading it to, and I was truly beginning to fear there never would be.

She aligned the books in her hands, with unexpected grace, and returned them to their box. "I think that must be the single sweetest act of faith I've ever heard."

"And probably the most futile," I admitted. "What the hell, I'd make a lousy father anyway."

"Think so? You don't know about lousy fathers."

"Oh, I don't, huh? Any law says you get to have a monopoly on them?"

She rolled her eyes, as if she regretted opening her mouth. "No. No law." Turning the spotlight back on me like an accusation: "What's your problem, you don't have enough faith in yourself to get past the shitty example he set for you?"

"Maybe I'd know the answer to that if he'd stuck around long enough to set an example in the first place." And I didn't want to talk about this. My van, seemed that I retained that right, and just maybe she had more to answer for than I did. "Now suppose in the middle of the night I'd gotten an urge to read *Mr Putter and Tabby Pour the Tea* before I could get back to sleep. Would you have shot me?"

Allison glared then; how she did glare, as if I'd crossed a threshold better left uncrossed, entered a room I should've passed by. "You came out to watch me, is that how you spent your night?"

"Right, leaving tongue-prints down the windows, that's just the highlight of my trip." I shook my head and scowled, making a list of all the things I hated right then. I hated this break in the routine I was used to, hated the town of Newby and myself for stopping there, hated that solitary rut I'd dug for myself back home, and probably hated Allison, too, for dredging this all up fresh and making it look so pathetic.

We were quiet for several minutes, during which I refused to look her way… except out of the corner of my eye, and that didn't count. She stared out the window most of the time, head on hand and elbow on upraised knee, and when I finally saw her face again it didn't look hard anymore. She'd lost herself out in the passing desert, haunted by old ghosts. That's the trouble with ghosts: one place is as good as another when they're of a mind to follow you.

"I wish my father hadn't stuck around," was all she said, and no more for hours, but it was enough, and I knew that she'd never outpace the ghosts no matter how far or how fast she ran.

East, always east, with that highway whine forever in our ears like a mosquito. At last leaving the desert behind somewhere in west Texas, east Texas a different state even if the map said otherwise. It was green here, a land whose lush hills and shaded bowers owed more to the south than the west.

I don't know if it was because of the cross words we'd spoken earlier, or something else, but the more the land blossomed and deepened around us, the more Allison drew herself up inside a dark cloak of mysteries. As though the ghosts were no longer content to walk the backdrop of whatever landscape we traveled, instead shaping it and painting it to suit themselves.

We were getting closer to her home, and when home fires burn cold in your heart, old haunts can stoke up the worst within you.

She broke her silence once we started listening to the blues, tapes that she dug from her bag and handled with reverence, well-played tapes that must have seen a hundred rooms, a thousand bottles. Old music, as primitive and powerful as the elements, those hounded, aching voices made tinny by the funnel of decades. Her favorite was a collection of historic recordings made on the old southern state pen work farms and plantations. Nameless black men singing with fevered hearts, for it was all the freedom they had left.

"Listen," Allison commanded, and I tuned in.

It ain't but the one thing I done wrong,
I stayed in Mississippi just a day too long...

"I have an idea how he might've felt," she said. "How come it's the innocent that get locked up in the worst prisons?"

"You're asking the wrong guy." I held to the wheel until I decided she deserved something more than that. "Maybe it's because the innocent are the first ones to run out of people to fight for them."

"That's justice for you," she said. "A lot of them down here believe in original sin, as I remember. No one's innocent, they preach at you. But the way I see it, it's just something they've convinced themselves of so they won't go crazy. It's a lot easier to stay sane when you think you're getting what you deserve."

"I've heard a few of those sermons myself. Or slept through, at least."

"But then you have to wonder what kind of prisons those good neighbors believe eight-, ten-year-old girls deserve. Especially when their fathers are holding the keys. In their cold hands." I noticed her jaw tightening as she spoke, the words squeezed past clenched teeth. "What do you want to bet they don't spend too much time trying to fit that into their system?"

I wasn't going to argue with her there.

And the more we stopped, the more it seemed people everywhere were intent on proving her right. Gas stations and truck stops and roadside diners, we'd walk in and gazes would flicker our way. You always check out the newcomers, over coffee or a cold drink, with a lazy eye and feigned disinterest. They'd see us and let their minds fill in the rest, grasping for the explanations that were closest at hand. We were one thing but most would see another.

The bruises on Allison's face had, over the past two days, deepened into richer colors, as bruises will do. The purple of royalty, the yellow of sunrise. And on too many of those assessing faces I saw the same reaction, at stop after stop. A welcome to a brutal brotherhood in the eyes of too many men; a grim recognition in those of too many women.

This was not lost on Allison, either. "Maybe I should wear a sign around my neck: he didn't do it."

"Then I'd lose their hard-won respect for me," I deadpanned.

"Look at them. Some loss." She laughed and nudged my shoulder and it was the first time we'd touched, a nice warm circle on my arm glowing with vibrant new life. "Can you read lips? You know what they're saying, don't you?"

"Oh sure," and I didn't really need any special talent. "'The bitch must've had it coming.'"

Maybe we'd achieved a breakthrough in trust, or maybe it was just that the steamier heat made Allison a little crazy too, but she decided she didn't need the van to go to sleep that night. We slept beneath the same roof, lullabyed by an air conditioner that roared and wept cool oily tears onto a soggy carpet.

I didn't ask about the gun, didn't see it. Laid awake in the noisy dark, wondering if her head rested atop a nickel-plated lump in her pillow. I'd hear her shift in sleep, imagining her hand straying to touch its cold comfort, just in case, just in case.

I'm sure she'd trusted her father too, once upon a time.

And the next night?

We'd traveled and we'd talked, we'd opened up what we dared of our lives, and I don't suppose a man and woman can spend every moment of three days together without each at least entertaining the question of what the other must be like to love, if only for a night. The wounded and the wrongly imprisoned are no different, and maybe even need the answers more. Need desperately to believe that the whole world isn't conspiring against them, that there really is a place of justice and grace for them out there after all. That two can find it more easily than one.

If only for a night.

We made love and made of it those things we most needed — a look into the future, a bid to bury the ghosts. A road toward all that was missing from our lives. A week from now would we even remember each other's names? Would we even want to, need to?

We made love and made of it what we could, as good as we knew how, the best parts still locked inside the prisons of our bodies and our hearts. Life builds us that way, and the hell of it is, it so often takes an act of faith or blood or both to unlock the cell door and set us free.

"I won't see you after tomorrow, I guess." Allison seemed to mourn the inevitable as she sat on the bed, ankles crossed and her arms wrapped around both drawn-up legs. The cigarette burns on her bare shoulder looked, in the gloom, like black holes punched clean through to her soul.

"What am I taking you back to, Allison?"

She dodged it, pointing instead to my middle, where a thick scar curled around my left side just over the hipbone. "How'd you get that? It looks like someone tried to cut you in half."

That. My good samaritan badge of honor. "I tried to interfere in a family fight once. To keep somebody from doing something stupid. How was I supposed to know one of them had been laying new flooring…and still had his linoleum knife."

I remembered the blade, dull silver, its wicked curve like a stubby scimitar. Remembered the slippery loop of gut that slid free before I could get my hands over the spillway. But I had to laugh. That'd teach me to pick on carpenters and their sons.

Allison looked away. "Your life seems to have this habit of entwining itself with others that can only hurt you."

"Yeah, but think of the stories I get to tell." I let a moment pass and what she'd said still seemed to demand attention. "Are you trying to tell me you're no different?"

She bowed her head, bruises veiled behind a blonde curtain. When she raised back up, I had my awful answer without her saying a word.

"Tell me what I'm taking you back home to. You owe me that much."

"Why, because you did me the great favor of sleeping with me? Your magic semen is a healing balm, is that the way you see it?"

"No!" I shouted. "Because you haven't kicked in dime one on gas all day, and I wasn't even going to mention it!"

She blinked at me, then we both sputtered with laughter, the kind of laughter that tolerates few secrets, no lies, and when the truth came, there in the night, I wasn't surprised.

"I'm going to kill him. I'm going to put a bullet in him and see if that doesn't unlock this door I've been trying to rattle open for years."

"Your father," I said, and she nodded, as solemn as a judge. "You figure that'll do the trick."

"I've tried everything, Tom, good and bad. This is all that's left, the last thing I know to try. And the reason it feels right is because it's the one thing he most deserves."

While my first impulse was to try talking her out of it, the main problem with that was that it was night out, when ghosts are strongest. There's no talking redemption into someone besieged by darkness inside and out. You can only stay beside them, hoping the light isn't too far away.

Allison opened the small, flat box resting on a table, took out the books it contained, running her hand along covers showing worlds where children could ride dinosaurs, where gentle old men lived new lives blessed by old cats, where sweet-faced animals would never harm a soul.

"When I was a little girl," she told me. "I had a book like this that my aunt gave me. About a horse. I thought if I read the book enough, and said my prayers, then one day I'd wake up and the horse would be waiting for me outside. I must've run downstairs every morning at full gallop for six months before…"

Allison stopped, pulled herself back to now; the awful now.

"It's never like the books say it is, is it? If only, just once…" She couldn't finish, or didn't have the words for it, but still I knew exactly what she meant. Allison held the books to her chest, tightly, while I held her to mine.

And though I knew we all have to grow up and learn the truth of things someday, I wondered why some are forced to learn it so much sooner than the rest, and from the very ones who are supposed to protect them from it.

We rode those last miles through shadows and valleys, the sun burning through green treetop lattices. Miles that felt seeped through with a soul cursed the color of an old barn fallen to decay. Polite little towns that simmered in their own dark secrets watched us pass, and while we weren't their business they watched all the same, for one never knows when another's secret may become public property.

She was going through with it, and nothing I could say made a bit of difference. Her face was set with the anticipation of this day of reckoning, and she rode holding the gun in her lap as if it were the one telling both of us what to do, where to go.

Everything, I suppose, but how to live with it.

Now and then we'd roll past a bus station or a shady inviting curb and I'd wonder why I didn't just put her out to finish the trip alone. Mississippi, after all; my promise was fulfilled. So I'd tell myself that as the voice of reason and harmony only my presence could dissuade her in the end. Then just as readily I'd curse myself, deservedly so, for a liar and a fool.

What I really should've been asking was whether my desire to see her get away afterward was worth being an accessory to murder.

I tried to see the justice of the situation. Very few details had she provided, which made it painfully easy for me to imagine what her father had done. Silent as a ghost, staring from her bedroom doorway until she felt him over her shoulder, felt the force of his compelling smile, his hunger, long before she felt the press of his hands and body. The closer we got the stronger it all rose in my mind; and the

deeper it ached. Men in love, or approaching love, have a burning need to torture themselves with what they know of a woman's past. Must be why love and pain are never that far apart.

We reached the house when shadows were beginning to stretch and good Baptist families were sitting down to dinner. A humble and unassuming place, two stories of peeling paint and loose shutters, behind disinterested trees. Allison had me circle the block once, sitting there assailed by the reek of memory.

"How many years has it been?" I asked after we'd parked.

"Almost thirteen," she breathed. "I ran away a couple months after I turned seventeen. And I've never been back. Not even when Mama died."

"How do you know he's still here, then?"

"I've got a cousin down in Natchez I never lost touch with. Believe me, he's here. By now he should have at least two bottles of Dixie emptied and the TV Guide folded back to tonight's shows."

Well, I thought, and dared not say it, sounds like a man who needs killing.

And as we walked together up the weedy path I was hoping the years hadn't been kind to him. That he'd answer the door and just the sight of a withered, age-wracked man would be enough to restore Allison's sense of justice. That she'd see what he had become and realize he could never compare with the omnipotent son of a bitch who lived only in the past.

Porch steps creaked like screaming souls, and she knocked on the screen door just as bold as Saint Paul could preach.

While we waited, her hand went fishing in her bag.

I heard the scrape of the knob, watched the inside door swing open, heard the chatter of his TV before I saw him standing there trying to make sense of us: two strangers, or maybe one stranger beside his own problematic ghost, returned to flesh after thirteen years. What *does* go through the head of a man like that?

"Hey Daddy," and she was flat and neutral as a hangman.

He stared and blinked. "Well, girl. Always did expect you to find your way back one day." Then he turned his head to one side and spit what may have been a fleck of tobacco. "But I'll give you this much: I always expected you'd be alone and crawling."

"Well that's two more things you got wrong, isn't it? Maybe you'd just better give up on trying to figure me out."

He started to laugh, a liquid rumbling in his chest and the seams of his face pulling back taut. They already drooped in such a way as to give him a look as sour as curdled milk. Willoughby must've been around sixty-five, with the latter-day bearing of a man who'd been as stout as hickory in his prime. He still had the arms, the shoulders, and if he now carried himself with a bit of a stoop he would apologize to no one for it. His hair was a dirty white, thinned well back along his crown, and hadn't seen a comb since morning. When he stepped back from the door to let us in, I saw the tube snaking from beneath his thread-worn shirt, and what it connected with.

A mean old man holding a colostomy bag. I was going to Hell for sure.

Allison barely waited for the door to latch behind us when her hand cleared the purse and the revolver gleamed, the brightest thing in the dingy living room. I shut my eyes until I realized she wasn't going to shoot him first thing.

"Well lord have mercy, what's this?" Willoughby said, staring at the gun pointed at his chest. After an initial wary look, he seemed more amused than anything, as though it were all some game of bluff and bravado, love and hate, jealousy and concession, that only fathers and daughters could understand.

"One bullet for you," she said in a small firm voice, "and four more for each of your friends you whored me out to."

I felt a sudden plunging surge, all manner of new scenes that I never wanted to imagine. A chamber's worth of tortures that could last for years.

"That's five," he said with fresh contempt. "Who's the last one for — your witness here?"

Allison gave it a few seconds' thought, antagonized, not to be outdone. With smug satisfaction she spun at the hip and put a bullet through the center of the old man's television. His face went slack as noxious smoke poured from the hole and fogged to the ceiling.

"Aw hell," he moaned, genuinely remorseful, and sighed. Then he slowly turned and made for the adjacent dining room. An aged oblong table stood there on tired gryphon's feet, and had seen a hundred thousand dinners if it had seen a single one. "Well, I'm gonna sit. You can shoot me in the back if you can't wait for me to get situated."

When he was in his chair, colostomy bag slung from one of the spindles, Willoughby gave me a thorough once-over. "Now where's your manners, girl? Who's your fella?"

"His name's Tom St John," as we joined him at the table. "And he's almost restored my faith that the male of the species isn't entirely made of what's leaking out of you into the little bag you drag around."

Willoughby snorted. "Leaves your face looking like that and still he's Sir Galahad? Now that is a wonder."

"He didn't do this. Tom's never laid so much as an unkind finger on me in all the time we've known each other."

"Well congratulations." The old man winked and thrust his hand across the table for a shake. I let it pass, still dwelling on the bag. "Ain't she something? Now most girls, they'd get a man stirred up to do their killing for 'em, but not this one, no sir. She'll dirty her own hands, won't you princess? That's…still the makings of your plan, isn't it?"

"You shut up, Daddy. You don't think I'll do it?"

He waved her down and kept his eye on me, a shrewd old poker player who couldn't be bluffed. "How 'bout you, Tom St John? Could you put a bullet through your poor old daddy's chest? Right there at his own supper table?"

"I'd have to track him down first." I was trying my best to stand hard, not let Allison see pity and disgust get the most of me. If she saw that, I feared she'd toughen up for the both of us and there'd be no turning her back. "After that, well, whatever happened next I don't think I could be responsible."

"Ran rabbit on you, did he?" Willoughby mused. "Bet he took off on you when you were just a little bitty tyke, didn't he?"

"If he was anything like you," Allison said, "he did Tom the biggest favor of his life."

"Well, now, maybe that could be true, but you still can't stop wondering about him, can you, son?" And the old man smirked at me with his seamed face and his crinkled snake's eyes. "Maybe he just wasn't ready to be a father yet, had a few bushels of wild oats yet spilling out his pants. Got that business taken care of, then who knows, maybe he prospered some since. Started over like young Tom St John never even drew breath at all."

Allison's whisper was like a whipcrack. "Shut up, Daddy."

Willoughby scowled at her. "Now what'd I teach you, girl? You don't go interrupting a couple of gentlemen trying to get to the bottom of a matter of some importance." Another wink for me. "How about you, Tom St John? Any young whelps, bastards or otherwise, wondering where you've got off to this fine evening?"

"I wouldn't be here if there were."

Willoughby reeled back in his chair. "Not a one? You don't say!" He hunkered forward again, and I could just feel him drawing me in, seeking someplace raw and bare to sting. "Not a problem, is there? Lordy, sure hate to think of that following you around for life, and the reason I ask, Tom, looks like gray in your hair already, and it makes a man look some long in the tooth for not even being started in his family ways — "

And I was actually glad when Allison pulled the trigger when she did. Shoved the gun out from her chest and fired, and the old man jumped as, behind him, a big fan of brown splattered across the tired old wallpaper, then ran in rivulets for the baseboard. Willoughby gazed upon the ruin of his dripping colostomy bag and shook his head, and it only took until the smell hit for me to wish she'd at least chosen another target.

"Now that hurt," he said, and some dignity leaked with it.

Two shots so far — had the neighbors heard? No sirens yet, drawn by the first. These old houses were built solid, to hold well their secrets. Certainly this one had held a terrible few. Maybe it could hold this one more.

As we sat in the stench and the after-ring of the gunshot, Willoughby seemed to have gone a shade paler, his bold wrinkles and wattles tightened up as he understood he may have misjudged his daughter. I don't believe he'd taken her seriously until this moment.

"I expect I must be quite the joke to you now," he said, quite humble. "Gotta carry 'round this sack of my own droppings."

"A joke? A joke?" Allison was steadying herself, gun in both hands, lean brown arms outstretched and her cascade of hair going damp with sweat. "Do you see me laughing, Daddy? Did you ever see me laugh? I always thought I'd start laughing again once I could stand on your grave, but I just can't wait any more for you to die on your own."

"God's own time, princess."

She brandished the revolver. "This is all the god you need to worry about now." Allison took a deep breath, gagged on the stink and choked it down. Glanced toward the front door. "Do you still do it? Are there any little neighborhood girls you coax in here?"

"No. It was…just you." Every seam and crinkle loosening and sagging, so limp they nearly slid right off his face. His eyes grew misty, one hand creeping forward atop the table, as though he were groping for some beautiful thing that lived only in his mind, in his dark and twisted heart. Pierced by roses' thorns, where old regrets and older desires nestle deep and turn to cancer. "There was never any other but for you."

Her head started shaking, tiny backs and forths, as Allison slumped in the chair, the gun a nickeled lump at the end of her arm. She still loved him, or a tiny sliver of her still did, some deep ember of love that Willoughby and his friends, for all their grotesque snuffling grunts, had never managed to extinguish.

And I was past knowing whether this was good news or bad.

"Daddy," she breathed, then groaned and turned to me, forcing the gun into my hands. "Just hold it on him," and then she was out of her chair. Convulsions squeezed at her middle as Allison went scrambling down a hallway, disappearing behind a slammed door. I could barely hear her getting explosively sick.

"Girl always did have a tender stomach," Willoughby observed, "even as a little bitty thing. Always getting carsick." Staring at me then, with strange eyes, like a man ready to howl with laughter at a joke that only he has understood all along. "Now as I recall, you were never that way. Good settled stomach on little Tom-Tom."

"What…?"

"Now, no need to play dumb for my sake, son. Allison's busy, can't hear us." Shaking an admiring head. "Yes sir, most men'd let surprise get the best of 'em, walk in ready to blast an old man and who do they see but their own old man, more than thirty years gone. You got some jim-dandy self-control, I'll give you that."

"No, no, no, no," and while I was hearing what he was saying, I couldn't believe it, didn't want to believe it, "that's just impossible, my father's gone forever…"

"And where the hell do you think he's gone to, Tom-Tom?" The old man smiled at me and chuckled as I'd always imagined my own father would; so superior, a bastard who's got the world figured out. "A man can move to Mississippi and call himself Willoughby, as easy as he can call himself St John. Though I don't believe he ever expects to see his kids find one another by pure chance."

I stared into his face, a desperate search for any trace of flesh or bone that I could match with some old picture I'd not seen for more years than I could remember. Or something I could align with what I saw in the mirror…although I'd always taken after my mother, and if Allison did likewise —

No. No, damn it. It just couldn't be.

Willoughby narrowed his rattler's eyes. "Don't know what your intentions are with the girl, but unless you got her fooled as to what a fine man you are…why Tom, you might want to rethink them. Especially if you got thoughts of family going through your head. How do you think it'd affect the poor girl, she finds out her own half-brother's sired her a little mongoloid baby?" He ogled down the hall at a final dim sound of retching. "I don't believe she'd bear up so well, myself."

I felt the house contract around me, like a vast stomach that digested all the hopes and potential out of whoever walked in. All I could think about was running out the door and finding some fine honest shade beneath a tree, where I could lie in cool grass and think all this through, come up with the arguments that would show this man for the conniving liar he was.

But what if…?

"I don't believe a damn word of it," I said.

He shrugged. "Face value, I wouldn't expect so. But if it's proof you're needing, well, son, see that Bible on that shelf over there? Hand it over and we'll get down to some proof business."

I looked over, saw it — an heirloom, maybe. A fat leatherbound Bible with a strap holding it shut, big enough to gag a crocodile.

"Swear on a Bible, you think that'll prove anything to me?"

Willoughby sneered and rolled his yellowed eyes. "What kind of idjit did you grow into, Tom? You're telling me you never heard of a Bible's got a family tree written up in it?"

I looked at it again, sitting on its dusty shelf, waiting to be cracked and its secrets of birth and life and death revealed. I could've left it there and always hoped. But always wondered. Yet what if I saw my name, thirty-six-year-old ink scratched in by Willoughby's hand? He'd know as long as we never looked, I could never truly rest.

I stepped across to the shelf, gun in hand, brought the Bible back and slid it over. Willoughby gave me a simpering grin as I sat, and his fingers worked at the old leather strap.

"I'm calling your bluff."

He nodded, flushed with some kind of twisted paternal pride. "I'd never expect any less from any son of mine."

Willoughby propped the Bible against the table's edge, canted at a preacher's angle. Cracked the cover back and stroked one hand down the pages, then brought it back up, and of all the surprises I never expected this Good Book to yield, a pistol was at the top of the list.

I wasn't even thinking as I scuttled backward in the chair, wood scraping against wood, and fumbled Allison's gun level. But Willoughby's quick-draw days, if ever he'd lived them at all, were behind him. I shot twice across the table into his chest, then clenched the gun in both hands, shaking like a man with chills…

Waiting for a dead man to make another move.

That quick? It was over that quick?

I stood, grabbed the Bible to stare down into its desiccated pages, cut out with a pistol-shaped hollow, and still I flipped from Old Testament to New with my heart squeezing up the back of my throat, in case I still found that family tree.

"Tom? Tom? You…" Hands on walls, Allison braced herself steady in the doorway, an expression on her face as if she'd walked into the wrong room where everyone looked the same, but wasn't.

"He…he wanted his Bible," I whispered. "I didn't know."

"No atheists in foxholes?" She walked slowly over, stepping around the blood and the shit, staring at the man she called her father, slumped in the chair with his gray-whiskered chin drooping to his chest. "No, not him. Never him."

And I'll never truly know what Allison was feeling as she brushed her fingertips over his stilled skull, his face, his hard wide shoulders. She looked relieved and cheated but not quite sure how she should feel about either.

I tossed the revolver across the table to where she stood and it landed with a sharp clatter, to spin slowly, like the bottle in a much more innocent game.

"Two left. He won't feel them anymore." I chewed at the side of my lip. "But… you still might."

She took gun in hand, thinking, thinking fiercely as I turned my back on what had to remain just between the two of them, hoping I wouldn't jump like a scared rabbit when the hammer fell.

Waiting until she told me I could turn around again.

When we left the house, we left with neither ceremony nor accusation, nothing of importance left to say for the time being. It seemed enough to watch the sweltering streets on our way out of town, holding our breath at the sight of a police car, then easing out the biggest sigh of all as we rolled past an old sign bidding us goodbye, come again, you have family here.

Silence dogged us to the highway, but I knew the time for words would come later. A night's worth, or a week's, or even a lifetime's, depending on how we chose to live with this evening. And yet for all we'd shared, there were still those dark regions of the heart where each of us would remain forever alone.

Her father had made sure of that. He'd played each of us like a pro, divide and conquer, his instincts as shrewd as any mean old son of a bitch's could be. As we lit out for the east, then the south, then tomorrow, I told myself that all Willoughby had wanted was to rob us of anything and everything he could.

Maybe he'd known she really would've done it and forced my hand instead to deny her that last redemption. Or maybe he'd known she couldn't, but was ready to die anyway, and by my hand was as good as any. Or maybe he'd have shot us both. Only one thing was sure: he'd taken me from a man who'd hoped to save his life and turned me into his killer. And self-defense doesn't cut much ice with me, not when you walk into a man's house the way we did.

The highway whined, and I imagined Willoughby and the Devil were laughing so hard by now they had to hold each other up.

Allison and I, we couldn't be related. This I told myself over and over again. He was just trying to steal the future, if indeed we had one. He was just trying to get to the gun.

I think.

As we fled the sunset into the deeper night I watched Allison sitting curled and pensive in the seat. Looked for some telltale cast to her face that I'd worn all my life. Knew that if I saw it, I'd just argue it away as a trick of dying light. And then watch for the next. And the next.

I watched as she started to cry, at the end of this long and bloody road, and when she opened up the small flat box, held the small flat books, Allison wept over them like a woman crying over a chest of lost gold.

And if I couldn't yet believe in happily ever afters, well, that was fine for now, because I knew that I was at least ready to turn the page. ■

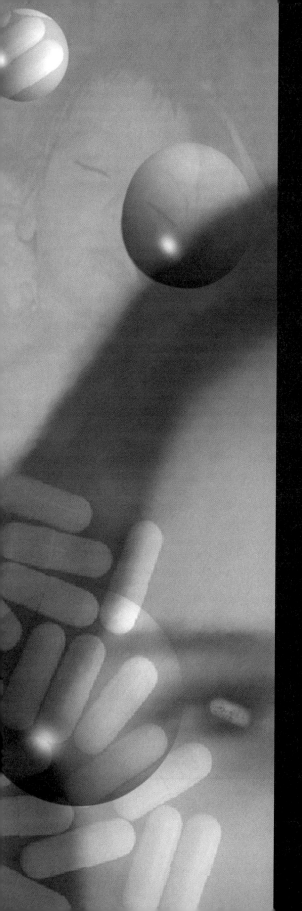

SUSAN SONDE

BREAK-UP

Susan Sonde is the author of two books
– Inland is Parenthetical (Dryad Press)
and In the Longboats With Others (New
Rivers Press) – and a number of stories
which have been published in Southern
Humanities Review, Northwest Review,
Mississippi Review, Quarterly West,
Carolina Quarterly and Ohio Review.
Susan was recently awarded a grant by
the Maryland State Arts Council.

Sunny Garrett sits at the dining room table in her large Victorian home, a state-of-the-art conversion on the inside, and glances out the window at a neighborhood of equally impressive homes, appearing prepossessive on their sizable lawns, and, with a tenacity that has its roots in an urge she doesn't fully comprehend, re-copies her shopping list for the third time. At canned goods she pauses, rises and approaches the cabinet housing the cans, opens and assesses the turntable on which they stand, turning each shelf slowly, checking the ordered stacks. The space where stewed tomatoes ought to be is empty. She knows it, though she has tried to suppress the compulsion to check it yet again.

Cal loves stewed tomatoes. But it has been six weeks since Cal moved out and by now she knows he won't be coming home.

Sunny is making an effort, to forestall the inevitable, to keep the lid on. She does it for the children. But at some deeper level, a more powerful impetus has taken hold. Her thinking is distorted, her behaviors repetitive, and the harder she works to stop them, the more enmeshed she becomes: mornings, after she has poured juice and milk for the children, and filled their bowls with cereal, she prepares Cal's bacon and eggs and sets them out like a talisman to draw him. Initially, the behavior prompted an endless round of questions from the two older children (Tammy is seven, Eric is six) — "Where *is* Daddy, when will he come home?" — but now they ignore it.

The hand that holds the pencil trembles. Sunny lays it down, approaches the spice drawer where she keeps a bottle of Valium and pours out one of the scored pills.

Upstairs, in his crib, two-year-old baby Joey is sleeping. She is grateful for this mid-afternoon break, for as much as she loves to play with him, over the weeks she has grown nervous and distracted. As for the tranquillizer, Cal is a doctor, an ob gyn, who prescribed the pills not long after the move-out.

"Sunny, I know you better than you know yourself," he said. "You'll need them, believe me you will."

She breaks the pill in half, thrusts it way back on the tongue, swallows, and returns the remaining half to the bottle.

She is a proud woman, she thinks, who doesn't need pills, can master the trembling, the occasional bouts of panic. She reasons that she isn't like most women in her position. She has a tighter hold on herself, manifests an outward calm. Her friends marvel at her equanimity, which comes, she says, from dedicating herself to the children.

The pills: perhaps it was just an act of contrition on Cal's part. He has always been considerate, which is what has Sunny so confounded. At some level the move-out makes no sense; it is one of those things she cannot get her hands around. It is the ultimate betrayal, the conclusion to a series of steps: a cooling down on Cal's part that, when she tries to track it, leads to the birth of Joey. And prior to that? She can point only to the establishment of Cal's new practice (the decision to turn his skills to the terminating of unwanted pregnancies is based on the fact that as a sole practitioner delivering babies, his time wasn't his own). Though she doesn't blame Birthrights for the demise of the relationship, the establishment of the clinic has brought its own pressures: there have been death threats over the past two and a half years, the mailing of a fake letter bomb three months ago, and a right-to-life sit-down staged the month before. She does consider the clinic a factor.

It is a busy place and continues to need her. The three days a week she puts in there get her out of the house. She puts up a good front, continues to have a good working relationship with Cal, and her hours allow her to be home in time to greet

Tammy and Eric. The clinic is staffed by two nurses. A full-time secretary doubles as receptionist on Sunny's days off. Cal's considered taking on a partner and occasionally interviews for one. But he is ambivalent about sharing the practice.

As for the move-out, it seems arbitrary — there is no other woman, Cal has told her as much. It is its very capriciousness that troubles her: the relationship she trusted to last a lifetime has ended; the existence she has come to depend on has crumbled, and to compensate for the loss of control she engages in a series of behaviors which give the illusion of control.

She has undergone other changes: her concern for the children verges on being extreme. She is reluctant to let them out of her sight and has suggested to Cal that she home-school them.

"You don't like the public schools? Send them to private school," he says, not comprehending her desperation.

Nor does she want to leave Joey, though his babysitter is competent and gives her no cause to worry.

There is also the issue of Cal's boat, a thirty-five foot, three-masted vessel he christened the Folly-Free. It is high maintenance, requires constant care, and the work he puts into it doesn't seem to make a difference. One day he is going to take on a crew, he says. He intends to take the summer off, sail her through the Gulf Stream to the Bahamas, and go island-hopping with the children.

Now that it is Spring and warm, on his prearranged weekends with them, Cal takes the older children on the boat; these are small excursions spent cruising the Chesapeake Bay and teaching the children to fish.

Sunny has a fear of deep water and gets easily seasick.

Weekends are the worst. Without the children she feels lost. And, because of her aversion to deep water, it is easy to imagine a catastrophe occurring at sea: a storm that sneaks up on the boat, creates monstrous waves that crest over its decks and sweep the children away.

The shopping list is long. She will put off shopping until Tammy and Eric get home. Her neat script ranges down the page. Since the separation (when speaking of it to friends, she jokingly refers to it as the 'abdication'), she is short on ideas when it comes to engaging the children. Despite the apprehension she feels in their absence, their presence makes her anxious.

Going to the supermarket will fill up time. She'll let Tammy and Eric choose a cake mix each, then, to close the gap until dinner, spend the afternoon baking with them.

In his crib, Baby Joey lays on his back, his blanket balled up in his fist. She has just come down from checking on him. It is the fourth time she has been up there. She is afraid he will roll onto his stomach, press his nose and mouth into the mattress and stop breathing. Joey always falls asleep on his back and stays that way. He starts out with his thumb in his mouth. His thumb slides out, leaving traces of spittle. He is not a restless sleeper. She knows her fears are unreasonable. He is an adorable baby. At two, she still thinks of him as a baby and feels the impulse to pick him up, hold him close, draw reassurance from his proximity and the solidness of his body.

Cal has been civil about the break-up. So far, there has been no mention of money, and both of them have avoided any discussion of custody, though it is only a matter of time before the move to finalize will change things. She worries about the outcome, but only in an abstract way, dealing with the future as if it will never come. Meanwhile, Cal continues to pay for everything. The gesture feeds her illusions. She gets her nails done, her hair streaked. Cal has always liked the blonde highlights. It gives her face a certain vibrancy, he says.

She seats herself once more, picks up the pencil and adds bananas to her list. The children love them. She breaks them into fist-size pieces for Joey.

Her hand is steady. Even half a pill works fast, its effect like a drop of mercury sliding to her center. If she needs more, she is not to stint, Cal says, though she never goes beyond one pill.

She checks her watch, puts aside the list and stations herself at the front door where she can see Tammy and Eric get off the bus.

The tulips she planted in the bed Cal dug for her at the front of the house last year are beginning to push through. The unopened buds break through the rain-soaked ground like newborns crowning. It's rained for the better part of two days, stopping mid-morning. The sun crawls from behind clouds and the lawns reflect a dewy brightness.

After the birth of Joey, Sunny wanted a fourth child.

"We've already gone beyond the pale," said Cal. "In my profession anything more than two destroys the image."

Their sexual encounters grew less frequent after Joey's birth. At first she attributed it to the weight she had gained during the pregnancy, but that had dropped off quickly nursing Joey. Then she blamed the nursing itself, concluding that Cal was jealous of her closeness with the baby.

There are moments when she blames *herself* for the break-up, for things left un-said or undone. And tells herself that, if this is the case, there are things she can do to change it.

Tammy and Eric emerge from the bus. The wind crawls under Tammy's plaid wool skirt and billows it out. With lunch boxes and books slowing them down, they run home.

"I beat, I beat," Tammy shouts. She is breathless and throws herself into Sunny's arms.

Eric, slight for his age, comes to a stop halfway up the walk. "It's not fair," he complains, looking balefully at his sister. "She started way ahead of me."

"Fight and there'll be no surprise," Sunny says. Since the move-out she is often short with the children and her voice carries a slight edge. Resentments overlooked while Cal was living at home, now obsess her: when he wasn't on call, he spent his weekends working on the boat; all those nights he took off to grab dinner and a drink, and came home late because of long days spent at the clinic. She feels raw, exposed, the burgeoning of something nameless and big.

In Cal's absence, she feels the need to be vigilant. Strong feelings of any kind frighten her. As a child Sunny experienced bouts of rage that continued unabated through adolescence — episodes of frustration causing her to tear her clothes.

"What surprise?" says Tammy, her high-pitched, excited voice cutting through the air.

Tammy is a head taller than Eric. She stands with her feet planted wide.

"If I tell you," says Sunny, struck by Tammy's resemblance to Cal, "it won't be a surprise."

"Tell *me*, Ma," says Eric, still breathless from running. "I'll keep it a secret, I pro-mise." He reaches for Sunny's hand.

"You silly," she says, forcing a calmness she doesn't feel, and suppresses annoy-ance at the way he pumps it. She takes back her hand, regrets the withdrawal, reaches down and tousles his windblown hair. "How can it be a secret once you know?" she says.

"Because," says Eric, the logic of the thing escaping him, "if I don't tell, it's a secret."

Sunny smiles in spite of herself. She catches Eric up in her arms and nuzzles him, glad for the resurgence of maternal warmth. She holds him tight, causing him to giggle. "You silly, silly," she croons, "secret from whom?" She releases him, holds him at arms length and looks lovingly into his eyes. "You're the ones who are supposed to be surprised. It doesn't work if I tell."

"Keep your jackets on," she says, as they begin to slip out of them. "I'm just getting the baby and then we're going shopping."

"But I'm hungry," says Tammy, "I don't want to go."

"Me not either," echoes Eric.

"No shopping, no surprise." She wants this to be an outing they will all enjoy.

Sunny leaves the two older children standing morosely in the hall. Upstairs, the baby stirs in his crib. Careful not to wake him, she untangles him from his blanket and dresses him in jacket and leggings and lifts him gently. His head flops against her shoulder.

"Shh," she says, addressing the other two and raises a warning finger to her lips. Joey's hot breath fans out against her neck. She opens the hall closet and, with her free hand, takes down her coat, shifts Joey in her arms, and slips it on.

Everything looks fresher, more alive after the rain. The front lawn is still wet and if she squints and looks beyond it, she sees myriad colors reflected off other lawns. In the mailbox, wrapped in clear plastic, lies *The Baltimore Sun*. *The Washington Post* comes first thing in the morning.

Sunny seldom reads *The Post*, she finds the articles from day to day disconcertingly similar and its coverage of violence excessive. *The Sun* is homespun and overblown in its coziness. Cal subscribes to both papers, continues paying for them.

Joey wakes on the way to the store and Sunny yields to Tammy, who has been pestering to tell a series of cat jokes her class has received over the internet. And, though Sunny is Tammy's intended audience, her mind wanders. She should corner Cal, she thinks, pin him down on issues of money, codify the casual arrangement that exists between them. It is just a matter of time before things get major and contentious.

In the supermarket Tammy and Eric push their own wagons. Joey in the cart, strapped in his infant seat, has fallen asleep again and seems uninclined to waken. "You can each choose one," she says, taking them down the aisle to the cake mixes. "That's the surprise."

At home, she puts Joey in his highchair and hands him a breadstick. It is 4:30. She gets out mixing bowls and spoons. The children climb on chairs. She ties aprons around them.

She takes their finished cakes from the oven, lets them cool and frost them.

After dinner she puts Joey in his crib. His thumb goes into his mouth. She lingers over his crib, locks eyes with him.

Downstairs the older children eat cake. She sets out a glass of milk for each. Their discourse is lively; she focuses on the moment, wishes she could freeze it, so that nothing will ever come between her and the children, not Cal, not the issues they have yet to deal with, not the future, which she knows can be cruel.

Her hands tremble. She has never required a night-time dose. She moves to the spice drawer and removes the bottle. She will hold out until the children are in bed, settle down with a glass of warm milk, take half a pill and see this through.

She glances at the children and their glasses half-filled with milk. Crumbs fall from their forks, crumbs litter the floor beneath Eric's feet. She smiles. He is stuffing cake in his mouth as fast as he can swallow it.

She dumps out all the pills, puts back all but eight, sets them on the counter and sets aside two. She counts out two piles of three, segregating six. What is the power of six?

The children empty their plates. "Why don't you clean up," she suggests. They rise, take their dishes to the sink, rinse them as they have been taught, open the dishwasher and set them inside.

She works fast, places each set of three in a napkin, crushes them with the back of a spoon, slips the powdered contents into the remaining milk. Stirs. Tammy and Eric return to the table. Eric finishes his milk, Tammy takes one small sip and puts her glass down.

"Aren't you going to finish?" says Sunny.

"I'm full," says Tammy.

"Full or not, it's a waste, I can't pour it back."

Reluctantly, Tammy picks up her glass and drains it, leaving a coating of milk on her upper lip. "Yuck, it tastes funny," she says.

"That's because you let it stand too long," says Sunny. Her body is trembling. She pours a glass of water and swallows the two pills.

"I feel dizzy," says Tammy. Eric yawns. Tammy folds her arms on the table, cradles her head, and falls asleep. Eric sits on the floor, his back against the dishwasher. His eyes closed, his head against his chest.

Tammy is heavy. Sunny hasn't carried the girl since she's been a toddler. She slings Tammy over her shoulder and struggles up the stairs into the master bedroom, lays the inert body gently on the king size bed.

Lifting Eric from the floor is more difficult. Sunny gets down on her knees, tilts Eric towards her chest, rises on one knee and hoists him over her shoulder. His head flops against her back. She staggers up the stairs with the boy, and places him on the bed beside Tammy, catches her breath and looks down at her sleeping children.

She goes into Joey's room. His thumb is in his mouth. She carries him back and places him beside Eric.

Downstairs, she fills her water glass, takes the glass and the bottle of pills upstairs, sets them down on her nightstand.

She slips a pillow from behind Eric's head, takes a long look at him, places the pillow against his face and leans into it. She does the same with Tammy. There is no fight in the girl.

Joey's mouth opens and his thumb slips out. She puts the pillow over the little boy's face. There is no need to apply pressure. His limbs stiffen right away.

Sunny pours all the remaining pills into her hand. Gets ready to swallow the water in her other hand. Swallowing the pills is an act of will. "Please," she prays, "give me the courage to swallow these." She stands above the children's bodies, the hand containing the pills poised in midair. God or something has betrayed her. She goes downstairs, takes a carving knife from one of the drawers, climbs back up to the children. Swallows two more pills. Raises the knife. Inflicts a superficial wound. There is blood. She ignores it. Lifts, brings the knife only halfway. She enters the bathroom, takes a pair of scissors from the medicine cabinet and aims them at herself. Lets them fall to the floor.

She pulls her shirt out of her jeans, picks up the scissors. Takes the shirt off, cuts and cuts. Holds the scissors to her shoulder length hair, cuts to the hairline. The wavy strands fall to the bathroom fall.

She climbs out of her jeans. Cuts through the heavy denim.

The pills she has swallowed begin to work, and though it isn't enough, she goes back to the bedroom, lays down beside the three little corpses and waits for sleep to come. ∎

Men's health magazine
Shoe polish/new shoes?
New tie
Haircut

June 18
Milk
Newspaper
Sandwich
Chewing gum
Banana
Cat food
Fresh coffee
Wine
Cheese and butties
Toilet deodorant
Kitchen/bathroom cleaner
Bucket
Scourers
Fresh flowers

June 20
Milk
Newspaper
Cat food
Petrol
Drinks cooler
Picnic cutlery
Napkins
Cold meats

ANTONY MANN

SHOPPING

Antony Mann's story 'Taking Care of Frank' from Crimewave 2: Deepest Red won the 1999 CWA/The Macallan Short Story Dagger and will soon be reprinted in The World's Finest Crime and Mystery Stories 1999 (as will 'Symptoms of Loss' by Jerry Sykes from the first Crimewave). Antony's stories have been published in several magazines such as The Third Alternative and London Magazine, and others have been broadcast on Radio 4. He is currently working on a novel.